4—

Praise for BOTTICELLI'S BASTARD

"Stephen Maitland-Lewis' latest book, *Botticelli's Bastard*, is beautifully written and, to its further credit, impossible to categorize. Part thriller, part intriguing mystery, this book is compulsive reading. Above all, it is a first class novel."

Sir Ronald Harwood, Playwright and Oscar® winning and Oscar® nominated writer of THE PIANIST, THE DRESSER, and THE DIVING BELL AND THE BUTTERFLY. Former President of PEN International and current President of The Royal Literary Fund

"*Botticelli's Bastard* is a fascinating, complex and completely compelling novel. It has everything I love, history, art, suspense, intelligence and creativity. I was captivated!"

M. J. Rose, International Bestselling Author

"Art restorers bring life to paintings, Giovanni Fabrizzi, the hero of *Botticelli's Bastard* brings paintings to life — literally. What ensues is a dazzling tale set in today's art world where a painting reveals its history, from its origin in Florence to its fate during WWII and beyond. Determined to do the painting and its rightful owner justice, Fabrizzi risks his reputation, his sanity and more importantly his relationship with his wife to establish the truth. Part thriller, part psychological novel, Maitland-Lewis' new book takes the reader through the back alleys of the art world, where greed, passion, and connoisseurship are masterfully set against the tragic background of history."

J. Patrice Marandel, The Robert H. Ahmanson Chief Curator of European Art, Los Angeles County Museum of Art

"If Edgar Allan Poe and Oscar Wilde collaborated on an uplifting novel it would have been *Botticelli's Bastard*. Maitland-Lewis beat them to the punch. A marvelous, soulful tale."

Stephen Jay Schwartz, L.A. Times Bestselling Author of BOULEVARD and BEAT

"My interest in collecting important art came together with my love of thrillers. Stephen Maitland-Lewis' *Botticelli's Bastard* is a great read."

Arnold Kopelson, Oscar® and Golden Globe® acclaimed producer of PLATOON and numerous award-winning films including THE FUGITIVE

Praise for BOTTICELLI'S BASTARD

"Who has not, when confronted by an interesting or unknown object, frustratingly wondered, 'if only it could speak'? In the history of art, with often so little known about a work's authorship, original commission or subsequent provenance, the imploration is even more acute and, alas, the silence more palpable. Maitland-Lewis's fantasy, Botticelli's Bastard, takes this concept to its heart. From its astonishing beginning to its appropriate conclusion, the author takes the reader on an emotional journey from the baseness of humanity to its generosity, from deception to forgiveness, from desperation to redemption. In addition, we join the central character on whirlwind trips from London to Italy and elsewhere on the continent to New York and back. Botticelli's Bastard is of the moment — dealing as it does with art and its desirability, its various owners and, ultimately, its just place in the world."

Scott Schaefer, Curator emeritus, J. Paul Getty Museum, Los Angeles

"In this riveting work of historical fiction, Stephen Maitland-Lewis brings a remarkable portrait to life. The centuries of history culminate in a vivid, moving, and highly accurate account of Nazi art plundering and postwar restitution efforts, replete with ethical implications. This story shows how a single painting can intersect with the lives of so many people, and also provides fascinating insight into the contemporary art world."

Jonathan Petropoulos, Professor of European History, Claremont McKenna College; author (The Faustian Bargain) and former Research Director for Art and Cultural Property on the Presidential Advisory Commission on Holocaust Assets in the United States

"Maitland-Lewis has surprised us once again with a thoroughly engrossing tale of a mysterious five hundred year-old painting, the bizarre and colorful characters that owned it through the ages and its profoundly romantic 'restoration' — in every sense of the word. A terrific read for lovers of art and lovers of life."

Michael Findlay, author of THE VALUE OF ART

Praise for BOTTICELLI'S BASTARD

"In this art world mystery story, a cosmopolitan painting's conservator has a better relationship with a rediscovered Renaissance masterpiece than he does with his beautiful wife, his son and friends. As Giovanni Fabrizzi pursues the picture's pedigree in London and on the Continent, he learns a great deal about collectors, his family secrets, and himself. An enjoyable and enthralling read!"

Walter Liedtke, Curator of European Paintings, Metropolitan Museum of Art, New York

"Botticelli's Bastard is a terrific read! Like all great fiction, this book introduces the reader to people, places and unique circumstances, unknown and hard to believe at first, but we are taken in and swept away by this extraordinary story. Along the way we learn about art, art history, fathers and sons, husbands and wives, the power of persistence and belief, and finally, the Nazi theft of art during the Second World War. Ambitious ground to cover for sure, but the author does so with passion and panache. With the summer reading season upon us, this is the book you should take with you on vacation. An ancillary benefit to the book is that the reader will never look at a portrait – any portrait – in the same way again!"

James A. Cobb, Jr., author of FLOOD OF LIES, Adjunct Professor of Law, Tulane University

"Unputdownable, fascinating, I devoured *Botticelli's Bastard* in a single sitting and only wish it could have lasted longer. This incredible (quite literally!) story delivers on every level... full of riveting historical color, the plot has as many twists and turns as a corkscrew and I can't wait to see the movie."

Gully Wells, author of THE HOUSE IN FRANCE

"*Botticelli's Bastard* is a wonderful story. A portrait leads an art restorer on a journey to unmask the truth of a stolen painting and restore honor and love to those involved. A read for all seasons. An entertaining, educational book with an inspirational ending. Loved it. And — If you like this book there is *Ambition, Emeralds Never Fade* and *Hero On Three Continents* to enjoy."

James A. Misko, author of FOR WHAT HE COULD BECOME

Praise for BOTTICELLI'S BASTARD

"One man's longing for distraction becomes a life-changing journey to find redemption for many, as he struggles to strike a balance between integrity and desire. Well-played and imaginative, *Botticelli's Bastard* is the story of learning to trust in the heart of truth in order to liberate oneself from the prison of the past.

"Not often do we see a historical fiction that navigates us through themes of thirsted-for resolve, the complexities of exhuming shameful secrets, and coping with the guilt, strain, and doubt that accompany tragedy, while remaining strangely charming from its first page until its satisfying dénouement. An out-of-the-ordinary novel that is a pleasure to read, Stephen Maitland-Lewis has achieved a reader's delight; simply open the book and he will take over from there."

Jack Deadmen, author of
NOBODY SPECIAL: THE DEATH OF JOHNNY SALINGER

"In this one book, Stephen Maitland-Lewis has intrigued me with an original mystery, entertained me with good humor and educated me in the world of art, all while taking me on a tour of Great Britain, France and Italy with a side trip to New York. Most appealing is the lead character who is the most moral of men living with a most unusual secret."

Saul Turteltaub, television writer and producer

"When I was introduced to the protagonist in Stephen Maitland-Lewis's novel, Botticelli's Bastard, I realized that destiny is not necessarily carved in stone. With every journey, we can either lose ourselves completely or return with a greater knowledge and awareness. Page after page, I was immersed in the mystery of the Botticelli painting but also I was simultaneously drawn into a world of emotion and drama through the moral dilemma of the painting's restorer. Botticelli's Bastard — Pure Elegance!"

Mario Canali, Major Italian contemporary artist and pioneer in Digital Art.

Praise for BOTTICELLI'S BASTARD

"Maitland-Lewis has crafted a canvas of his own as he masterfully weaves an intriguing story about an heirloom. It's an enjoyable, informative, and an entertaining read from beginning to end. And, after having read it, you will never look at a painting of a portrait the same way again."

Rabbi Jerry Ram Cutler, Movie critic, Beverly Hills Courier

"Maitland-Lewis' *Botticelli's Bastard* is an exciting novel that will likely make most collectors pay more attention to an item's provenance. This is a MUST read for anyone who has ever collected anything… especially fine art."

David Niven Jr., Former Vice President of both Paramount Pictures and Columbia Pictures and an art collector

BOTTICELLI'S
BASTARD

ALSO BY STEPHEN MAITLAND-LEWIS

Hero on Three Continents

Emeralds Never Fade

Ambition

With all best wishes,

Stephen Maitland-Lewis

BOTTICELLI'S BASTARD

S TEPHEN M AITLAND-L EWIS

Glyd–Evans Press
Portland Oregon

Glyd–Evans Press
P.O. Box 14946
Portland Oregon 97293-0946 U.S.A.
info@gepress.com

BOTTICELLI'S BASTARD

by Stephen Maitland-Lewis

ISBN
978-0-9832596-8-8 Hardbound
978-0-9832596-9-5 Softbound
978-0-9915084-0-2 E-book

Library of Congress Control Number: 2014931314

Edited by Brad Schreiber and William Campbell
Cover artwork by Alan Gutierrez

Also available in electronic form for most e-readers
For more information visit www.gepress.com

1   3   5   7   9   10   8   6   4   2

This novel is dedicated, with affection, respect and gratitude, to my own Mr. Chips - Peter Waterfield - the headmaster of my English preparatory school.

He imbued me with a love of history and literature and was the finest and most inspiring schoolmaster any young boy could ever have had.

*The most beautiful thing we
can experience is the mysterious.
It is the source of all true art and science.*

Albert Einstein

1

Seated at the vanity in their bedroom, Arabella Fabrizzi faced the mirror as she selected jewelry to complement her evening gown and upswept dark strands. Consumed with herself, she failed to notice her husband's troubled expression.

Behind her, Giovanni stared into the mirror, first at her loveliness and then at his sagging face, that of a man thirty years her elder. His wife was the epitome of elegance, yet he felt his insides wither. She was still attractive to him, physically, as she had been a year ago. Many had teased him about taking a child bride, mostly other men, no doubt envious.

The color drained from his face, washing away his normally dark, Mediterranean complexion, leaving him more the color of his graying hair and wispy beard.

He watched in horror as Arabella cinched the clasp of a delicate bracelet with thin strands of gold and silver intertwined, circling a total of nine rubies.

"I rather like the way it looks." She raised her wrist to admire the jewelry. "I certainly hope you do."

He did not reply.

She turned to him. "What is it? What's wrong?"

Giovanni stared helplessly at her. He was speechless and she was puzzled, each waiting for the other to say something.

"You're upset," she said. Then she noticed Giovanni looking down at her arm.

"This?" She held her wrist high to display the bracelet.

He turned away.

"You gave it to me. You said I could wear it."

"You're right," he mumbled, avoiding her gaze. "I said that. I just didn't know it would affect me like this."

"I don't know why you're holding on to it." Her resentment grew stronger. "I mean, I know it makes you think of her, and then you get morose, and then you have no..." She began to remove the bracelet. "No passion. For anything."

"No, wear it." Giovanni stopped her and tried to clasp the bracelet but his aging fingers could not manage.

"No!" She pulled free and dropped the bracelet into a jewelry box on the vanity. "I can't get you out of this flat, or your studio, so I go to these social events on my own. The least I was hoping for is that I could without you sulking, but I suppose that's too much to ask."

Up from her seat, Arabella went to the closet and sifted through her coats, looking for one heavy enough to keep out the chilly London night.

Giovanni felt helpless. "I know. I just cannot get rid of her things. Not all of them. I'm sorry."

"I don't want to go on like this." She made an effort to contain her aggravation. "I think we need to see a therapist about this."

She threw on a coat, grabbed her keys to the Jaguar, and started downstairs. "You're either married to me or to your memories, Gio. Not both."

~

The next morning after breakfast together, during which nothing of substance was discussed, Giovanni kissed Arabella on the cheek, carried his dishes to the sink, and promised to be home by six o'clock.

As he did each morning, Giovanni traveled by train to Green Park's underground station where he joined scores of commuters pouring from the exit. Outside the station, he flung back his scarf and buttoned his overcoat, ready to endure the early drizzle. His fellow travelers hustled past, rushing about like sheep and scattering as each sought out their individual offices. How he hated his new daily routine.

It was not his occupation, at which Giovanni excelled. The restoration of fine art was a craft passed down by his father, which Giovanni was equally pleased to pass on to his son, who oversaw the family's operations in Florence. That he was among a family of talented conservators should be reason for pride, and it was. The part that gave Giovanni daily grief was the new location of his office. If his father were still alive, he would probably be dismayed as well.

For decades, Fabrizzi & Sons conducted business in Soho Square, occupying the top floor of a building that had served it well since Giovanni's father, Federico, had come to England and established the London branch of the world-renowned art restorers.

Federico Fabrizzi soon established good relations with the National Gallery, the two major auction houses, Christie's and Sotheby's, and the curators of many of the major collections. It was not unusual for Federico and one of his assistants to disappear for weeks, traveling across the country to visit many of the great estates, where they would take up temporary residence and perform their craft.

In time, Federico became a regular at Buckingham Palace and Windsor Castle, leading to further prestige when the firm was granted the Royal Warrant, allowing the addition to its letterhead *By Royal Appointment to His Majesty King George V.* Similar honors followed from George VI and Queen Elizabeth.

Eventually, Federico entrusted the London studio to Giovanni, who was proud to follow in this father's footsteps. Father and son continued working side by side, but as the years passed, Federico split more of his time between London and Florence. Giovanni assumed that his father, in his later years, yearned for his homeland of Italy. After his father died, Giovanni entrusted his son to manage the Florence studio while he remained in London, where increasing pressure from clients demanded him to find a new location.

Moving from Soho Square was not only a physical drain but an emotional nightmare. Giovanni felt it had been forced on him and that it was ultimately unnecessary. But the art business had changed. It had new blood, though that didn't make it better. Young turks in St. James's concluded that Soho Square was no longer a convenient place to have their artwork restored. They claimed that parking was difficult. The building, they insisted, was impossible to adequately secure against break-ins. There was a constant risk of fire on account of the old wiring, and the potential for water damage due to the ancient pipes. Some of them had the audacity to present Giovanni with an ultimatum—*Either move to safer premises or we are likely to take our business elsewhere.*

What a bloody nerve. The House of Fabrizzi had been in Soho for decades and never as much as a paintbrush had been stolen. When Giovanni told his neighbors in the building that he was seeking a new location, all were saddened by the news. Mr. Genaro, a restaurateur whose family had served the Fabrizzis lunch for decades, was inconsolable. Regardless, and against Giovanni's futile protests, the auction houses prevailed. They demanded a modern studio and even suggested a site that suited their preferences.

So Fabrizzi & Sons was forced to take residence at the corner of King Street and St. James's. The new construction still smelled like the glue that held together all the granite, glass, and chrome. Ah, but it had, as the realtor pointed out with an air of superiority, *all the latest amenities.* Climate control, security cameras capturing every angle inside and out, bulletproof windows, and alarms with direct lines to Scotland Yard, Savile Row Police Station, Brinks Security, and likely, Giovanni surmised, to the Prime Minister himself. It was all too much. He hated it. It had no soul.

A mere two miles away, Soho Square was such a different world. Even the Soho hookers and pimps, nightclub bouncers, strippers and drug dealers treated him with more warmth than the scarce few who might recognize him arriving for another day of work at the impenetrable St. James's facilities.

He thought of Beth, the hooker who worked the corner of Frith and Old Compton Streets. She had fallen in love with one of Mr. Genaro's waiters. She had a nest egg built up over the years, so he quit the restaurant, she quit the corner, and they bought a coffee shop in the north of England. The last Giovanni heard, they owned three hotels and had a villa in Sardinia.

Another of Mr. Genaro's waiters had a son who qualified as a barrister and later became a high court judge. There was another, the son of the chef, who became a cabinet minister. Prestige didn't keep them away from the Soho neighborhood, and their visits weren't accompanied by displays of class difference or attempts to impose their superiority. They remained the same people just like everybody else. People who enjoy the simple pleasure of knowing a bit about each other's lives.

Then there was Harry, who had a stall at the Berwick Street Market. He always picked out the ripest fruit for Giovanni. And the French patisserie around the corner where he went every morning for a croissant; the newsagent on Wardour Street who stocked the Italian newspapers; the hefty bouncers who kept an eye on Giovanni when he got in or out of a cab, laden with paintings. The old neighborhood was a melting pot of big-time entertainment executives, the denizens of late night clubs, ballet dancers, and restaurant staff. In contrast, the St. James's crowd was strictly business. They all dressed alike, talked alike, and few rarely explored the world outside their offices. Most of Giovanni's fellow tenants were dour old men who couldn't crack a smile if they tried. Thinking about it, perhaps he had become a perfect fit for his new neighborhood.

As he did every day, from his wallet Giovanni pulled out a

business card, on the back of which he'd written the long list of codes to gain access to the building and get into his studio. He had given up all hope of trying to memorize them.

At the building's entrance, there was a panel of buzzers for each business that shared the premises. Giovanni wanted to put up the old brass sign that was proudly displayed outside Soho Square for so many years, alongside King George V's Royal Warrant, but the landlord had refused.

Giovanni slipped his key into the lock and studied the business card with access codes. After punching in the required numbers, he waited for the green light and then turned the key. A buzzer sounded and the door unlatched. Past the threshold, he proceeded into the lobby as the heavy door swung closed and sealed out the world, along with any audible hint that it still existed. The white marble floor stretched out before him, flanked by barren gray walls. The sterile facility was devoid of art and furniture.

At the elevator, again Giovanni had to study his card with access codes. Apparently, the fortress's front entrance wasn't enough to thwart intruders. Perhaps the developers should have added a moat.

After mistyping the code and retrying without sounding any alarms, which as Giovanni had understood, would occur after three failed attempts, he boarded the elevator and ascended to the fifth floor. He was the only tenant on the floor. In fact, there was only one tenant for each of the seven floors. He had met most of them, but none were interested in pursuing a conversation of any length.

At the door to his studio, another key and code were required.

The light turned green, he turned the key, and he pushed his way in.

No alarms yet, but Giovanni was greeted by the high shriek of warning that alarms would sound in sixty seconds if the proper codes were not entered. He moved quickly to the panel past the doorway, studied his list of codes, and silenced the annoying squeal.

The glass-topped desk and chrome lamp gave the reception area a sleek and modern look. His secretary and bookkeeper, Mrs. Anderson, was not present as she only worked Fridays, so the room was dim and the computer on her desk was turned off.

Bookcases surrounding the room were teeming with art books and endless archives relating to the many restoration commissions that Fabrizzi & Sons had completed over decades. In the center of one wall was a barred gate from floor to ceiling, beyond which was his work area. Another key and code opened the gate and again another alarm had to be disabled. Giovanni waved at the motion sensors and security cameras with the same contempt that he had greeted those in every corridor since the building's entrance.

His workshop was fifty feet square with bulletproof windows that overlooked St. James's Street. Instead of the homely wooden floors of Soho Square, with the cracks that Giovanni found charming, the marble floor was like glass, the walls were bright white, and small spotlights shone down from the dark void above. Of all Giovanni despised about his new quarters, he had to admit the lighting was an improvement, as it aided his restoration work. Two large easels were stationed in the center of the room, and a large oak table along one wall was stocked with brushes, paints, oils, and other tools of his trade. An armoire on the opposite wall held more equipment.

Giovanni took off his coat and scarf and hung them on the coat stand, which stood alongside the Fabrizzi & Sons sign that he was not allowed to display outside the building's entrance. Next to that were the Royal Warrants and framed letters of appreciation from grateful clients, a number of whom included several monarchs, curators of the world's major museums, and some of the most important collectors and dealers such as Paul Mellon, Baron Thyssen-Bornemisza, Lord Duveen, and others. He went to the armoire and turned on the stereo. He liked to work with music in the background and chose one of his favorites, Vivaldi, to put his mind in a more relaxed state.

Deeper in the room were two steel doors to the fireproof strong rooms. Each had a separate key and access code. In one of the strong rooms, Giovanni kept works in the process of restoration. In the other he stored those waiting to be restored and paintings of his own that he had collected over the years. As he did each morning, Giovanni unlocked both strong rooms.

He went to the stereo and adjusted the volume, then into the kitchen and made a cup of espresso. After a few sips, he returned to the first strong room of work in progress and brought out the Pieter Brueghel that he had started months ago, and still it was not complete. It takes as long as it takes, he would tell the client and justify his procrastination, when really, deep down he knew the restoration was dragging out far too long. The turmoil of life delays such things, he would conclude, only further justifying his inability to finish the job.

With great care as always, he set the Brueghel on the easel, then fussed with the adjustments until it was secure and positioned at the correct height. He fetched his stool, rolled his cart of tools closer, and sat facing the painting.

Sweeping melodies of Vivaldi poured from the stereo as Giovanni worked on the Brueghel, concentrating his tiny brush on one little square after another, bringing the color of each back to life. The process of improvement was tedious, but it energized Giovanni to engage in the gradual transformation, leading to the ultimate triumph when he would present the fully restored work to the museum, collector, or dealer and watch their smile stretch wide.

Lost in his work, all sense of time vanished, and Giovanni became detached from reality. Enough so that it took him a minute to realize the telephone was ringing. He kept working, thinking that Flavio would get the phone as usual. But reality came crashing back—his assistant Flavio was in Florence, helping restore a large canvas. Giovanni knew that. He was lost indeed, to have forgotten that he was alone in the studio that day.

He put down his tools, then went to the stereo and muted the volume. The phone rang again as Giovanni reached for it.

"Fabrizzi & Sons. May I help you?"

"Giovanni, dear boy." It was Martin Bryar, an English gentleman who had been a client for over a decade. "I have a request, and it is a bit different from the usual."

"Anything to help," Giovanni said.

"Well, I don't require your excellent restoration skills this time. I know you have a considerable collection of art of your own. I have a nephew who is getting married, and I thought about buying him a painting for his new home."

"I see." Giovanni smiled. "You aren't asking me to sell my Titians or anything like that, I hope."

Bryar laughed. "No, Giovanni. I know you have a nice stockpile of paintings in your strong rooms. If there is something you can part with at a fair price, I would be very obliged. Dinner whenever you and Arabella can manage, too."

The mention of her name brought the sadness of their last encounter back to Giovanni. He shook it off.

"Martin, you don't have to take us out. God knows, you've brought me enough work over the years."

"But we haven't seen you two in quite a while. Is everything well?"

Giovanni could not find the courage to say anything about the widening gulf between him and his new wife, nor could he admit to the confrontation that had recently occurred, despite his need to address it in some way.

"All is well," Giovanni said. "You know, Martin, come to think of it, there are some items my father had stored in our Florence studio. I never did find out why he hadn't stored them here in London. Anyway, they were shipped here after he passed away. I could look through those."

"Oh, Gio." Martin Bryar became concerned. "I don't want anything that might have sentimental value to you."

"Don't worry about that. The shipment was a considerable collection, surprising really. Dozens of paintings, and most I haven't even looked through yet. There's probably one that will suit you and your nephew."

11

"There's a good man," Martin said. "Have a look at what you have, think about what you'd like for them, and I'll come by at your convenience. You let me know. And dinner for the four of us. On me, I insist. All right?"

Giovanni was struck by the second offer for dinner in the very same call. Martin was more than a client—he had become a friend, and here it was being demonstrated. His interest in Giovanni was sincere. But it only reminded Giovanni of how he had withdrawn from so many friends since his marriage to Arabella.

"I look forward to seeing you," Giovanni said, and he meant it. "I'll call soon."

Off the phone, Giovanni sifted through a toolbox for a hammer and screwdriver. The crates that had belonged to his father were in the second strong room and most of them remained unopened. Not all were mysteries though. Many were labeled outside of each crate, which Giovanni had studied when the crates first arrived before the move to St. James's. They were valuable and he would not be parting with any of those. However, deeper in the room were other crates that arrived at the same time, all without markings to indicate the artist or subject. One of them should do.

The first crate he opened revealed a landscape. It was decent work, competent, and it was signed, but not by a recognizable talent that would garner much attention from a dealer or collector. The next two crates produced similar results, one of the paintings depicting a bridge over a river. Nothing of particular value, leading Giovanni to wonder why his father had collected them. Any of the three might please Martin Bryar, but having a greater selection to choose from would be best, so Giovanni continued sorting through the remaining unmarked crates.

A crate leaning up against the wall was probably too large, but another crate hidden behind it looked a more appropriate size. Giovanni reached behind the larger crate and strained to slide the smaller one along the wall and into view. Then he laid it flat and used the screwdriver to pry open a small gap, bringing up the nail heads enough to get the hammer claw underneath. He worked the nails one after another, each squealing as they were pulled from the wood.

Giovanni reached into the crate and slid the painting out, then removed the wrapping to discover a panel rather than canvas. He propped it upright atop the crate but the room's light cast a glare across the face. He lifted it from the crate and shifted the angle so he could better study it.

Clearly, the painting was old, evidenced by cracking of the paint in one corner. Giovanni judged the style to be Italian but it lacked an artist's signature, so he couldn't be sure. The subject of the portrait was an Italian, he was confident of that. A nobleman, probably early Renaissance. The subject's haughty expression exuded supremacy, disdainfully proud of himself while looking down his nose at the inferiority of others, certain to find fault in anyone who dared to approach. Giovanni found it amusing that any artist would portray their subject, even if it were true, with such an air of arrogance.

Beyond the pretentious subject, there was something impressive about the painting. Even though it was not signed, it had a fine style. Giovanni could not understand why the artist had not identified himself. Of course, an unsigned painting of any quality was worth less on the market. Perhaps this portrait, he thought, or one of the landscapes would please Martin and his nephew.

Giovanni set the painting atop one of the crates and stepped back. The work looked less impressive from a distance. He started toward the bridge and river landscape to have another look at that one.

Stepping away, he was stopped in his tracks by a guttural sound, like a man groaning. Giovanni whipped around.

"Who's there?" he demanded.

Not a soul was in view.

Giovanni seized the hammer and screwdriver, his only defense, and rushed out of the strong room. He scanned all directions but there was no one. He searched the reception area and then the kitchen, but still he found no one else present.

He must be going mad. It was impossible for anyone to break in to this fortress, he concluded.

Calmer, after convincing himself it was just the day's strain, he went back to his work area. He approached the toolbox to put away the hammer and screwdriver, then rubbed the high bridge of his nose, massaging out the tension that had twisted his brain into a tight knot.

Again he heard the groaning sound, but it was quieter.

It was a human sound, Giovanni was sure. And it was not his imagination.

He stood motionless, surrounded by the art. He slowed his breathing and listened.

Another groan. It came from the second strong room.

He crept closer, past the doorway, and scanned every corner

of the strong room. There was no one, only the crates and the few paintings that he had pulled from them.

Speaking Italian, an unseen voice said, "Get me out of this room. Please. I need light and air."

Giovanni bolted out of the strong room and then swung around. He stepped back, another and another step, staring at the open door to the strong room, until he backed into a wall and could go no farther.

He advanced on the strong room door and slapped it shut, then dug into his pocket and pulled out keys to lock the door. Once secure, he hurried from his studio to the elevator and out of the building without activating any of the alarms.

～

Moving at a brisk pace along the sidewalk, Giovanni embraced the cold air, but out on the street without a coat drew attention from passing pedestrians, all of whom dressed appropriately for the chilly day and developing drizzle.

The voice was right, whatever its source—he needed air. Giovanni certainly did. The cool weather was calming, and though he soon realized his lack of warmer clothing, he would not immediately return to the building. Not yet. It was all too strange.

Giovanni's thoughts were stuck on the language—Italian. His father spoke Italian, English, and some French, as did Giovanni himself. Perhaps that was it—Giovanni himself—was urging for a needed breath of fresh air. It was possible, given the strain he was under, and the fresh air was helping to clear his mind. But doing so only opened the door to thoughts of the recently deceased.

This must be what they call a *psychic experience,* he thought. Nothing like it had ever happened to Giovanni before. He did not believe in ghosts, at least, he didn't want to. At that point he had to question his sanity, but then again, he had plenty of reasons to lack perfect mental health. He had lost his dear father, and then his first wife, Serafina. Any man would go mad. Her death had affected him deeply. He still could not part with her clothes, wanting to occasionally smell them and recall the warmth of her embrace, of course, only when Arabella was not present, and there was no risk that she might suddenly appear.

After six months of wondering what to do with it, Giovanni had willingly given Serafina's ruby bracelet to Arabella, but he had no idea how it would affect him. Seeing her wearing the bracelet brought it all back—like being forced to relive the agonizing loss of his beloved Serafina. He could not bear it.

He knew his inability to release Serafina was threatening his marriage, even before the confrontation over the bracelet. Each day he was on the verge, inching closer to some horrible precipice, past which he would fall into territory that he could not recognize, and from which it might be impossible to recover.

Giovanni realized—he had not secured the Brueghel. If the client knew, they'd have his head. He must return immediately to the studio.

2

Giovanni unlocked the door to his studio and opened it slowly, afraid an intruder might leap out. There was no one in the reception area. He crept in and checked the kitchen next, saving his worst fear for last. There was no one in the kitchen, either.

He gathered his courage, ready to dash for the toolbox and get the hammer, the screwdriver, anything, in the event an attack was imminent. There was no one in his work area, and the Brueghel was still on the easel. He breathed a sigh of relief.

But his senses remained heightened—someone could be lurking in the shadows. Again he armed himself with the hammer and screwdriver, the only weapons available, however ridiculous, and searched every corner of his studio. There was no one.

Back in his work area, he stared at the closed door to the second strong room, beyond which his madness began. Then he realized his tense grasp of the makeshift weapons, making his arms tremble.

He felt like a fool.

It was just one of those things, he told himself, whatever it was those things were, or could be. He dropped the tools in their box and went to the window overlooking St. James's Street. The world outside looked okay. Normal as it should be. Any problem had to be inside—of him.

On a desk near the window was a photograph of Giovanni with Serafina and their son, Maurizio, back when he was a cherubic, early teenager.

Giovanni picked up the photograph and studied it, almost mystified by it. Serafina was more than beautiful—generous, caring, and the most understanding person he had ever known. Each day he woke to the truth—she was gone, well before her years. If only it were just a bad dream. But no, the cancer had run its horrifying course within a short six months, and her beauty was washed away to a sallow complexion. Toward the end, her eyes silently begged to be relieved of the misery.

Maurizio came to London once during the time, trying to be as much help as he could, but when he was alone with his father, he crumbled, the tears unimpeded, and Giovanni found himself reassuring both his dying wife and his bereft son, yet feeling there was no one on earth to comfort him. Consoling friends would take him out to dinner, some of whom insisted on visiting Serafina, but as her stamina waned, both the doctors and Serafina decided it took too much energy to engage visitors.

Giovanni fixed his gaze on the photograph. They were all smiling, happy, living a good life. It seemed so impossible, so distant, like a far-off cloud that might actually be a puff of smoke or nothing at all, just a trick of light.

Gently, as if her image were alive and delicate, he set the photograph down and went into the bathroom. Over the sink he doused his face with cold water, again and again. To be in mourning was a natural thing, he convinced himself. But now he felt that he was losing a grip on what was real, and it was intolerable.

He took a hand towel and patted himself dry, then saw himself in the mirror. His bulging eyes were those of a madman.

He returned to the photograph and stared at the angelic image of his only son. He sat at the desk, reached for the telephone, and dialed the Fabrizzi studio in Florence.

Flavio, Giovanni's assistant, answered the call. Giovanni asked to speak with Maurizio and Flavio responded by asking how things were lately. Giovanni ignored the cordial small talk and again asked to speak with his son. Flavio went to fetch him.

There was a long pause. Giovanni fully expected that Flavio would return to the line only to claim that Maurizio was too busy for calls, even one from his father. Which could actually mean, particularly calls from his father.

Giovanni was surprised to hear his son's voice, pleasant enough but also hurried, indicating that he was busy. Giovanni did not modulate his voice as smoothly as usual. He was relieved and went on to tell Maurizio how much he wanted to talk to him, and to know how he was doing, and how the progress was going with the large canvas that he and Flavio were restoring.

"It's going well, Papa," Maurizio assured him. "We'll be done on time, don't worry."

It saddened Giovanni to imagine that his son only thought of his father as a boss, calling to check on the progress of a deadline.

"That's not why I called," Giovanni said.

There was another long pause.

"Oh? Then what is it?" Maurizio asked.

There was no simple way to tell him, in the middle of a busy workday, that his father feared he was going mad and that his life was coming apart, like an old crust of bread between one's fingers. But something had to be said.

"I just needed to hear your voice, Mau." Giovanni had no idea how to speak to his son about his feelings. "I haven't seen you in months, you know."

"I know. Are you well? How's your work on the Brueghel?"

"I'm not working," Giovanni hesitated to reply. He reached for the family photograph and tilted it face down on the desk. "Things are not going well, Mau."

"Is it mother?" Maurizio asked.

"Her absence is difficult to..." Giovanni couldn't finish. Thinking of it was never pleasant, but voicing his pain only made it come alive.

"But Arabella..." Maurizio let her name linger on the line, as if implying his stepmother should be the balm for his father's sadness and that nothing else was needed.

"It's just hard," Giovanni said. "I know you miss her too."

"Of course I miss her, Papa."

"Usually I'm all right, but the last couple of days, things have been bad."

There was another long pause. Giovanni gauged that his son was just as uncomfortable with their conversation.

"I wish there was something I could do to help," Maurizio said. He sounded small and pitiful, despite being in the prime of his life.

"I think there is something," Giovanni said. "You could come and stay with me. With us. For just a few days."

"Well, of course. But I should probably finish this project first. I can't leave it all to Flavio."

"Maurizio." Giovanni spoke with firm clarity. "It would mean a lot to me if you would come soon. I need to see you. It's not something Arabella can help me with, if you know what I mean."

"Papa, can you tell me what it is exactly? Are you having trouble sleeping? Or is it just your mood? Is it something a therapist could help with?"

Giovanni winced at the word *therapist*. He dreaded the idea—confide his darkest secrets in someone who quietly sat listening, asking how he felt, who then charged him an enormous sum of money. It was not that therapy wasn't useful. It just saddened him that he and Maurizio could not talk about Serafina's death in any substantial way.

"I know you have a commission to finish," Giovanni said. "When you get that done, please consider coming for a few days."

"All right, but I think you should seriously consider the therapy idea."

"We'll see how it goes. If it comes to that, I'll give it some thought."

"Take care of yourself, Papa."

Giovanni hung up the phone and stared out the window at the gray sky. He was incapable of any further work that day.

He carried the Brueghel to the first strong room, locked the door, and set the alarms of both rooms. After turning off the lights and activating the remaining alarms, he locked the office and started toward the elevator. Rather than going straight home, he decided to pay a visit to his old Soho neighborhood.

~

At his flat, Giovanni turned the key and stepped in. It was well after six o'clock as he had promised. Most every light was off, except for the kitchen. He guessed that Arabella would be there waiting for him, and she would not be happy.

He hung up his coat and went to the liquor cabinet. He poured a scotch, not his usual drink, but it appealed to him at the moment. Standing before the cabinet, he relished the smoothness of it.

He poured another two fingers and then turned on the stereo, put in a CD of Beethoven's Eroica Symphony, and turned it up loud. He sat down on the sofa, in the dark, and let the music sweep over him. Eyes closed, he sipped his scotch.

The room filled with light. With eyes adjusted to the dark, Giovanni had to squint, and then he saw Arabella across the room, hands on her hips, glaring at him.

"Where on earth have you been?" she asked. "Look at the time. I called you at your studio and on your mobile phone, and you never answered."

Giovanni raised the glass to his lips and savored a long, slow sip of his scotch. Better than the conversation that was to come.

"I had a very bad day," he said. "I left the studio early and went to dine in Soho."

"Why didn't you tell me?"

He shrugged, as telling the truth would have been worse. Being with her only reminded him of how she was not Serafina. His marriage to Arabella felt unreal.

"I miss Soho," he said. "I miss a lot of things that I don't have anymore."

Arabella moved toward the stereo, preparing to put a halt to Beethoven.

"Please, don't," he said.

She reached for the controls. "I cannot hear you." She lowered the volume but left it playing, then sat down on the sofa near him, but not next to him.

"Gio, I feel you pulling away from me. We need to talk about this."

"I don't think it's a good time." Giovanni studied his drink as he swirled it around in the glass. "I want you to know that I love you, and I'm trying not to think about Serafina. It's not something that arrives and departs on schedule, like a train."

Her tone shifted to desperation. "We've only been married six months." She scooted along the sofa cushion, closer to him. "When we were together, after she passed, you were so passionate and kind. It hasn't been like that, even close to that, for months. My God, Gio, I don't want to beg for your attention the rest of our lives."

He looked at her and lingered on her words *the rest of our lives.* Her eyes were welling with tears. He set his drink down and took her hand in his.

"Nothing lasts forever," he said.

Arabella became puzzled.

"Don't worry," he said. "Things will work out."

She pulled free and shifted away. "I'm going to bed." She rose from the sofa. Looking down at him, she softly said, "Gio, will you come to bed with me?"

"In a while." He got up from the sofa and restored Beethoven to a commanding volume.

~

The next morning, Giovanni arrived at his studio ready to continue the restoration of the Brueghel. He went to the first strong room and brought out the painting, set it up on the easel, and situated his tools closer.

As he worked, his focus wandered. The painting before him didn't help, which portrayed a Flemish village rejoicing in a carnival. The irony didn't escape him, that his own feelings were the polar opposite of those depicted on the canvas.

He would normally play classical music and get lost in his work, but that day, he had not put on any music. He worked diligently for what seemed like an hour, but he couldn't concentrate. Thoughts of Arabella taunted him, and more so, he could not stop replaying the memory of hearing a voice in the second strong room the day before.

He couldn't get it out of his mind. It perturbed him, but he vowed not to be obsessed by it. But it wasn't a natural occurrence, and nothing like it had ever happened to him before. He needed to find a way to either dismiss it or explain it.

With resolve, he set down his brush and let the joyous celebration of the Brueghel sit. He took out his keys, unlocked the second strong room door, and flipped on the light switch.

He cautiously ventured into the strong room. Most likely, yesterday's events were his imagination, he concluded, and after a casual inspection, he would find nothing amiss and be done with it. Then he could devote all of his thoughts to a crumbling family life.

Giovanni moved past the crates of art until he could see the paintings that he had unpacked the day before. All were still as he left them, the landscapes and the Italian nobleman. The cocky fellow still looked as entitled as ever, probably a real arrogant snob in his day. Giovanni slipped past and checked behind other crates deeper in the room, looking for anything unusual. There was nothing that could explain what had happened the previous day.

"Please, I beg you, get me out of this room."

The Italian voice.

Giovanni couldn't move. He didn't know what to do other than keep listening, though his noisy thoughts made it difficult to hear anything outside of his head. Could he be talking to himself, in his thoughts? But he heard the voice clearly, as if a person were standing before him. It couldn't be.

The Italian voice said, "Over here."

Giovanni scanned the room, then looked over his shoulder at the doorway to the strong room. Nothing had changed, and no one else was present. He turned back to study the paintings he had placed atop crates in the room. He ignored the landscapes and stepped closer to the portrait of the nobleman. Something was strange about it—the eyes. They were unmoving, as one would expect of any painting, but somehow it seemed the eyes of the subject were actually looking at Giovanni. He could *feel it.*

"At last you acknowledge me. Thank heavens."

25

The mouth didn't move, the brows didn't twitch, but that thing just talked. Didn't it? Giovanni heard the voice clearly, having moved near, directly facing the panel.

"This must be a dream," Giovanni mumbled to himself.

"A nightmare I would say," the voice uttered. "You try living in that wretched crate for decades."

"It's impossible," Giovanni said, though it made him feel ridiculous. Talking to oneself can be embarrassing if another catches you, but this...

"Yes, of course, you've never spoken with a painted image before. There's always a first time. Now, let's get past all of that. What is your name?"

Silent, Giovanni reached for the panel and brought it closer, trying to make out some clue that would explain what was happening.

"Are you suddenly deaf!" the Italian hollered.

Giovanni shifted the panel back, keeping the nobleman at arm's length.

"No, I can hear you," Giovanni said. "Which I'm thinking is unfortunate, maybe. For the sake of my sanity, that is."

"Do you have a name?" the Italian asked.

"Uh, Giovanni."

"This is quite tedious. Surely your father gave you more."

"More...?" Giovanni was somewhat dazed, then he realized the answer. "Oh, more name, you mean. Yes. Fabrizzi, Giovanni Fabrizzi."

"Fabrizzi?" The Italian's interest was piqued. "The son of Federico, perhaps. Or another relation?"

All of this must be in his head, Giovanni thought. How else could a painted image, with which he just so happened to be engaging in conversation, know such details.

"Federico is my father." Giovanni flipped the panel over to study the back, then tilted it down, side to side and up, checking the edges for any clues. Surely there was a small speaker and microphone, and this was all just a sick practical joke.

"*Madonna mia*, be careful! Crashing to the floor is not a pleasant event."

"Oh. Sorry." Giovanni stopped juggling the panel and set it upright on a crate and leaning against another, sensing that it might be rude to set it flat and force the subject to stare at the ceiling. "Is that better?" he asked, though it made him feel silly. It's just a painting.

"Better would be air, light, a view," the Italian said. "What is this dreadful room without windows?"

"It's to keep you safe. And others."

"I would prefer the risk of crashing to the floor. Please, remove me from this wretched space."

3

Giovanni removed the Brueghel from the easel and carried it to the first strong room. He locked the door and set the alarm, then wondered why he had. He wasn't going anywhere. No matter. It wasn't a time to analyze his unthinking acts.

From the second strong room, he brought out the nobleman's portrait and placed it on the easel. The panel remained silent, as did Giovanni. He stepped back to admire the painting in the better light of his work area. The artist was accomplished, again leading Giovanni to wonder why it was unsigned.

The painting was relatively small, about eighteen by twenty-six inches tall. The panel remained silent, and Giovanni began to question if it would speak again. Perhaps the strange phenomenon was limited to the strong room.

His chest felt tight, and his head hurt. He needed to relax, and music was the best remedy. He went to the stereo and put in a disc, then poured himself a glass of wine, another effective remedy, even though it was midmorning and he rarely drank so early. The day's events justified a drink at any hour.

He stood before the painting, enjoying his wine and the music as he studied the panel further. Still it was silent. Perhaps his madness was temporary and had passed. Perhaps none of it really happened at all.

The Italian voice cried out, "Would you please, *please,* put an end to that mournful, gray, miserable bleating of Ludwig van Beethoven."

"You don't like—"

"Heavens no! Surely you have something from my native Italy. Oh the torture I must endure, if imprisoned in a crate were not enough. *Have it stop!*"

Giovanni hurried to the stereo and reduced the volume. "Is there something else you'd prefer?" he asked.

"Have you any Vivaldi?"

Giovanni nodded.

"Then for God's sake, end that depressing German music!"

Giovanni set his wine down, nearly spilling it as he fumbled to open a CD case and swap discs in the player.

"Ah, much better." The Italian hummed a few bars. "What are the round objects?" he asked. "They are the music?"

Giovanni did not understand. Then he realized, still in his grasp was the Beethoven CD from the player.

He held it up for the Italian to see. "A compact disc. Yes, it holds the music."

"Hmm."

"I guess a lot has changed since your time." Giovanni put the CD down and picked up his glass of wine.

"Hmm," the Italian murmured. "My time. Yes, so much time."

"Who are you?" Giovanni asked.

The Italian gasped. "You do not know?"

Giovanni searched the panel for an expression, perhaps eyes wide, but there was no change in the painted surface. "Sorry," he said. "I've been around famous works of art all my life, and I've read plenty of history, and I can't say that your face is familiar."

With great pride, the Italian announced, "I am Count Marco Lorenzo Pietro de Medici."

Giovanni nodded. "I see. Well then, I know of your family, certainly, but still, I can't say that you have any particular place in history. I'm afraid, Marco, you're just another nameless face to pose for one of countless portraits painted throughout the centuries."

A silence passed.

"First," the Italian said, sounding as though pushing the words past clenched teeth, "you will address me as *Count*. Second, your claim is *preposterous!* I will tell you of the events I have witnessed, the individuals of stature who—"

"We'll get to that, Count, but first I want to know about my father. You mentioned his name."

The Count took a moment to compose himself. "He is a good man, and I do not say that only because he is your father. He cared well for me while I was in his possession. And might I ask, how is it that I am no longer?"

"His things came to me. You know, after he passed. But I guess you didn't know that." Silly as it was, Giovanni paused to watch if the Count would nod or shake his head. The image remained static. "Anyway, after he died, your portrait and other works he had stored in Florence were shipped to me."

"Then it is now in your hands to reveal the truth."

"What truth?" Giovanni asked.

"Look at me," the Count said. "Do you not notice anything special?"

"Other than you're a talking painting?"

"Yes, other than that," the Count said, annoyed.

"You seem like a handsome gentleman, as befits a Count." Giovanni actually thought differently, but for the moment, good manners seemed a better choice than the truth.

"Yes, but what about the painting itself?"

Giovanni stepped back, sipped his wine, and studied the artwork anew. "The condition of the paint is quite good. It would only need a light cleaning, if exhibited."

"Ah-ha!" the Count called out. "And where would you hang such a painting?"

"I don't know. To be honest, I was thinking of selling you to a client who wants to give his nephew a wedding present."

"Are you utterly mad?"

"I am beginning to wonder about that."

"Signor Fabrizzi. I can only surmise that your appreciation for fine art matches that of your father. Do you not notice anything particular about the style of this work?"

"It's..."

"Yes? Yes?"

"It almost looks Italian Renaissance."

"You restore art, yet you cannot recognize the artist?"

"Perhaps you're not aware of it, being the subject of the painting rather than viewing it, but there is no signature."

"Of course I know that. I have known that for five hundred years."

Giovanni didn't want to offend the Count further, but the fact of the matter was unavoidable. "I'm sorry to say, Count, but your portrait isn't the work of anyone significant if they didn't bother to sign the panel."

"Your impertinence is astounding." The Count grew louder. "You are looking upon a portrait painted by no less than the great *Sandro Botticelli!*"

Giovanni covered his mouth to stifle his laughter.

"You doubt my word?"

Giovanni sipped his wine as best he could while chuckling. "You'll have to forgive me, Count, but here I am, drinking at eleven in the morning, and I'm talking to an unsigned portrait that I'm supposed to believe is by the great Botticelli."

"Well, at the very least, you recognize his greatness."

"Of course. But to think my father sent me an unsigned Botticelli that talks? Jesus Christ, it's ridiculous." Giovanni couldn't stop laughing.

The Count cleared his throat. And again. "Signor Fabrizzi. May I respectfully remind you that I am a Medici. My family has provided the Italian church with several popes and many cardinals. I would ask that you do not use His name in such a manner. If you persist in blaspheming our Sovereign Lord, our friendship will prove to be short-lived."

Giovanni stopped laughing. "Pardon me, Count. But you can understand, it's hard to believe."

"Yes, I can understand that. Just as others will have difficulty believing that you and I are able to converse."

"It's tough to imagine anyone believing that," Giovanni said. "I can hardly believe it myself, but here I am."

"You still do not believe that I exist."

"I have my doubts."

"Then you doubt your own sanity."

The words struck Giovanni hard—however strange, this experience couldn't be a delusion. If he were going insane and all of this was a product of his imagination, his fantasy would not remind him of that possibility. And the Count had done just that. But still, it was beyond all boundaries of reality. Could he believe in ghosts? He had little choice. That it might be his imagination was no longer valid.

"You are real," Giovanni said, almost with reverence.

"Well, I am confined to two dimensions within a frame, but I can see and hear. Unfortunately, my only view is the direction I face. Would you be so kind as to give me another? Please, turn me toward the window. I want to see the sky."

Giovanni swung the easel around.

A silent moment passed. The Count's lack of enthusiasm for the gray London sky was not surprising.

"There is an image on the desk," the Count said. "Of you and others. Your family?"

Giovanni glanced at the desk and then back to the Count. "A photograph." He went to the desk, picked up the framed photo, and brought it closer for the Count to see.

"The signora is lovely," he said.

"My wife, Serafina. I lost her almost two years ago. The boy is my son, Maurizio, but he's grown now. He works in Florence as a restorer."

"Yes," the Count said. "I had heard Federico speak fondly of wanting to see you and his grandson again. Before I went into that wretched crate."

Giovanni put the photograph back on the desk.

"I am sorry for your loss," the Count said. "You still wear her ring? I would point to your finger, but you understand…"

"Arabella," Giovanni said. "I remarried."

"Hmm. Yet there is no image of her on the desk."

Giovanni pulled out his wallet and found a snapshot of her, which he held up for the Count to see.

"She is quite striking," the Count said. "You have married, if I may say so, a considerably younger woman, Signor Fabrizzi."

"Arabella is my mainstay. She was so good to me when I was in the depths of mourning."

"I must say, you still appear to be in mourning."

Giovanni was taken aback. "Why would you say that?"

"You do not smile when you show me Arabella. She is a beautiful woman, no? A man of your age is very fortunate to have a woman, oh, I am guessing at least thirty years his junior. Is that correct?"

Giovanni bristled. "I am not interested in discussing my age or the age of my wife with you, Count de Medici."

"Do not be offended," the Count said. "I am merely reacting to what I see and hear after years of no stimuli. My keen observations are due to my situation. When I am taken out of storage, I have only fleeting hours, sometimes moments, to absorb what is before me. You, Signor Fabrizzi, do not have the perspective of five hundred years of life. Many aspects of the world have changed, but the relationships between men and women have not changed so much."

"What are you getting at?" Giovanni asked.

"I am merely reporting what I see. After all, you are not a young man. You convey a weariness about you."

"I've told you. I lost my first wife. That's not easy to get over. And my new wife is being difficult at the moment."

"What is it that troubles your marriage, Signor Fabrizzi?"

Giovanni gazed out the window at the traffic along St. James's Street. "It's not something I really care to discuss."

"This is the first conversation I've had in a considerable amount of time, so please, let's try to make it interesting and enjoyable."

Giovanni whirled around to face the Count. "What do you want me to say?"

"Can you still perform?"

"What do you mean?"

"Can you please her?" the Count asked. "Need I be specific?"

"I'm not going to answer that."

"My dear Signor Fabrizzi, you are talking with someone who secretly oversaw Giacomo Casanova in action with Madame de Pompadour at Le Petit Trianon. You can confide in me. Who am I going to gossip with, for heaven's sake? Sandro Botticelli?"

"I don't care who you saw or what they were doing. You're getting too personal. And stop claiming you were painted by Botticelli. The style is similar, I admit, but he would have signed the panel."

"You do not know that," the Count said. "Perhaps he had not yet completed it. I do not know how to convince you."

"Then stop trying," Giovanni countered.

"Hmm," the Count murmured. "Perhaps I could tell you about Botticelli. Then you will know I am telling the truth."

"And just what can you tell me that I don't already know?"

"His real name was Alessandro di Mariano Filipepi. Sandro Botticelli was a nickname given by his elder brother. Meaning, *The Little Barrel*."

"Any art student knows that."

"He was first trained as a goldsmith, and later became an apprentice to Filippo Lippi."

"Then Pollaiolo. You're not telling me anything special."

"It is rumored that a number of Lippi's paintings may have actually been painted by his apprentice, Botticelli."

"It's of little consequence. Botticelli made his mark nonetheless. Take his masterworks, *Primavera* and *The Birth of Venus*, for example."

"Lippi would be proud, certainly," the Count said. "Or deathly envious."

"Okay, that I wouldn't know either way, even though I did my thesis on Lippi. But on the other hand, your suggestion could be pure speculation."

"Are you aware the masterpieces of Botticelli to which you have referred were commissioned by my beloved uncle Lorenzo?"

"Is that so? Then you should know the *Adoration of the Magi* contained the likenesses of your other uncle, Cosimo, and his son and grandson."

"You have impressed me," the Count said. "Indeed. Uncle Cosimo took himself far too seriously. You know, don't you, that Pope

Sixtus commissioned Botticelli to paint the frescoes on the walls of the Sistine Chapel."

"Count, all you've told me could be gleaned from a book. It does nothing to convince me that Botticelli painted you."

"And how might I read such books?" the Count pointed out. "Or have read them, at any time during the past five hundred years."

Giovanni couldn't argue the point and remained silent.

"These books you speak of," the Count said. "Do any expose that Botticelli was homosexual?"

"We use the word *gay* these days," Giovanni said.

"Gay? That is to be cheerful and lighthearted. The acts involved may certainly lead to similar euphoria, though I believe homosexual has a more specific meaning. Botticelli was homosexual, as I understand the term, and in fact, he was accused of sexual relations with a young man. Fortunately, the charges were dropped, as the punishment for such acts—"

"I'm well aware of the era's brutalities, and it's not anything I'm interested in hearing about, nor what Botticelli may or may not have done with others. Please, enough of this gossip."

"I was merely attempting to strengthen my claim. That I would know such intimate details must surely convince you that I speak the truth."

"Not really." Giovanni went to the kitchen. He decided against more wine and rinsed out his glass. When he returned to the Count, Giovanni brought out his stool and sat down facing the easel, studying the panel as though he might begin restoring it.

"You do realize," the Count said with trepidation, "before you start working on me, that I am of tempera, not oil."

"Of course I know that. I also know you're on panel, not canvas. I'm not an idiot."

"Hmm," the Count murmured. "I simply wanted to make sure before you hover over me with your brushes and scalpels. What do you know about tempera?"

It irked Giovanni to be treated like an ignorant schoolboy. "Count, I have been working with tempera all my life." He pointed to the armoire across the room. "I have over two hundred powdered pigments, and in the refrigerator in the kitchen are dozens of eggs for the yolks. The pigments are from minerals and wood, plants, and clay. I have a full range. You don't need to question my abilities."

"Of course. I ask you, Signor Fabrizzi, do not give me away to a private party. They will never know my true origin if you do. You will be depriving the world of a major work. As a lover of art, how could you?"

Giovanni took the panel from the easel.

"What are you doing?" the Count asked, worried. "Don't put me back in that horrible room. I am Italian. I need sunlight."

"You won't get much either way. You're in London now."

"England? Ugh, such dreadful food. Thank heavens I lack a stomach to turn. Nevertheless, Signor Fabrizzi, please reconsider your actions. I beg you, do not return me to the dark."

Giovanni opened the door to the second strong room. "I need time to think. I'm just leaving you in here for safety." He set the panel down and picked up the crate in which it was shipped.

"Don't be cruel," the Count said. "You have no idea of the loneliness I've endured."

"Don't worry, Count, we'll talk again. In the meantime, I can't leave you out."

When Giovanni lifted the crate, an envelope slipped out and fell to the floor. He bent down to retrieve it.

"What is it?" the Count asked.

Giovanni opened the envelope and began reading the contents, a single sheet. Then he became stern. "Did you know about this?" he asked the Count.

"Know about what? What is it?"

Giovanni fixed his stare on the Count's image. "You didn't know this letter was in the crate when you were shipped."

"I swear, I know nothing about it. What is it? Tell me."

"It's a letter from my uncle. To my father."

"What does the letter say?" the Count asked.

Giovanni ignored him, folded the letter, and returned it to the envelope. He noticed a sticky substance on the back. He picked up the portrait of the Count and studied the reverse side.

"What are you doing?" the Count asked, worried.

On the back of the panel was a spot similarly sticky. Previously, the envelope had been affixed to the panel's backside.

"It must have fallen off and settled in the bottom of the crate."

"The letter?" the Count asked. "What does it say?"

Giovanni set the painting down and studied the crate. It had the typical markings such as gallery or other names stenciled on the side, and it had multiple shipping labels, all of which except the most recent were crossed out. It had last come from Florence, which he expected, but he was curious where it had come from before that. He found an earlier crossed-out label addressed to his father and the Florence studio, sent from an address in Switzerland.

"Well?" the Count asked. "What is the letter about?"

"It's not something I'm prepared to discuss with you, Count." Giovanni took one last look at the Count's portrait. "I promise you, I will take you out again soon."

"Please," the Count said.

Giovanni carefully slid the portrait back into the crate and leaned it against the wall. Letter in hand, he stepped out of the strong room and locked the door.

At his desk, Giovanni sat down and opened the envelope, delicately this time. Again he read the letter, treating it like a relic, as though the finest painting in any museum.

Dear Federico,

I have long regretted that we haven't spoken with each other in so many years. I don't know how two brothers could come to such a sad state of affairs. In looking through my art collection, I found some works that you might want or might want to sell.

I want this gift to be a peace offering. I don't need for you to reciprocate with any kind of gift. All I want is that we can be brothers again, that I might see your family. I am alone. My wife died two years ago and you are all I have.

We have lived too long and have seen too many hard and terrible times to let the past separate us. Please be in touch.

Your loving brother, Maximiliano.

4

It took fifteen minutes for Giovanni to attract the attention of a waiter in the crowded restaurant so that he could settle the lunch bill.

Arabella asked, "We're not in a rush, are we?" She gave him a teasing look with her dark eyes.

He smiled, feeling caught.

"No, my dear, but I am anxious to see what you think of this painting, whether you like it or think I should sell it."

Their waiter finally delivered the bill and was off to another table. Giovanni placed money in the tray, helped Arabella with her coat, and escorted her out. Their arms entwined, they moved along the congested, lunchtime sidewalks, destined for his studio.

He punched in the required codes and they stepped inside.

Arabella set her purse and coat on a chair. "I need to use the bathroom."

During her absence, Giovanni opened the second strong room and went to the back. He slid the painting of the Count out of the crate and spoke in a whisper.

"Count?"

No reply.

"Count, are you there?"

"Yes, I am here," he replied. "Where else would I be? And why are you whispering?"

"My wife is here. I'm going to show you to her. Will she hear your voice?"

"I do not know," the Count replied. "I never know. I did not know if you would, or others I have conversed with. You are one of very few, after all these years."

Giovanni started out of the strong room but stopped in the doorway. "Please don't say anything upsetting to my wife. Things are tense enough between us, and I don't know how she will react."

"I am not stupid, Signor Fabrizzi. You are afraid that your wife will think you are insane if she cannot hear my voice and you can."

Giovanni was still uneasy with the notion that his mental state might be impaired. And it didn't help having the reminder come from an inanimate object.

"Perhaps we shouldn't talk until after she's gone," Giovanni suggested.

The Count did not reply. Giovanni could only hope it meant the Count intended to remain silent.

Giovanni came out of the strong room and went to the easel near the window. He set the painting on it and waited for Arabella to reappear. When she did, Giovanni expectantly watched her come closer.

She glanced at the portrait. "So this is the painting from your father, eh?"

"Yes. Take a look. Tell me what you think of it. Honestly."

She crossed her arms and studied the work. She moved closer, then to one side, taking it in from various angles.

Giovanni silently stood watching her.

"It has a Renaissance feel to it," she said.

"Yes," Giovanni agreed.

"How old is it?"

"I have no idea."

"It's a handsome subject."

"Mmm-hmmm," the Count murmured, satisfied by Arabella's compliment.

Giovanni watched her for any reaction to the odd response. She continued to gaze at the portrait. Perhaps she thought it was Giovanni agreeing with her.

"It's very nicely done, whoever did it," she said. "But I wouldn't think twice about selling it. I certainly wouldn't choose it for our flat."

The Count bellowed, "Because you have absolutely no sense of taste, nor any inkling of art history."

Giovanni stiffened and cleared his throat.

Arabella continued to gaze at the portrait, then glanced at Giovanni. "What?"

"What?" he asked.

She turned her full attention to Giovanni. "What is it?" she asked.

"What do you mean?"

"You look strange," she said.

The Count said, "And you look like someone who wouldn't

know a Botticelli if it smacked you on the ass!"

Giovanni took a swift breath, fearing how Arabella would react. But she didn't have any reaction. She could not hear the Count.

Giovanni released his breath in a long sigh. "I suppose you're right."

"Why are you so fond of it?" she asked.

"I don't know. It... it speaks to me. If you know what I mean."

"Well, it says very little to me."

"Because you are not worth talking to!" the Count hollered.

Arabella gathered her coat and purse, then started toward the door. "If you want to sell it, you go ahead. I'm going back home."

Giovanni kissed her on the cheek, the lightest peck. He opened the door and watched her walk to the elevator, then shut the door and returned to his studio.

The Count said, "I am sorry to speak against your wife, Signor Fabrizzi, but I have never been so insulted. How anyone can overlook the timeless quality of my portrait is incomprehensible. However, she is correct that I am not fit to hang in your home. The Uffizi is the only place for me. Anything less is a disgrace to the memory of the artist. Furthermore—"

"Will you stop!" Giovanni shouted.

There was silence, during which Giovanni paced back and forth, running his fingers through his thinning, gray hair.

"Is there a problem?" the Count asked.

"You know I was nervous about showing you to her," Giovanni said. "You said it yourself, if I told her that you spoke—actually spoke—to me, she'd think I was mad. And next she would contact an attorney and file for divorce. I have enough problems without giving her the legal foundation to leave me and take half of what I own."

"Do you actually believe she would leave you?" the Count asked.

Giovanni sat at his desk and hung his head. "I don't know. I don't know anything anymore."

"I have an idea," the Count said. "You should have a small dinner party here in your studio. I would like to see Arabella and your friends talking with one another. It will be a grand and enjoyable event, and it will bring you and your wife closer together. And most importantly, it will entertain me. I miss watching the interactions of people. Trust me, you do not know this dreadful fate, to live hundreds of years in the dark."

"Perhaps you're right," Giovanni said. "I'll talk to Arabella about it."

"You can hang me on the wall," the Count said, "and see what others have to say about me."

As always, the Count's expression was frozen in time, forever unchanging. Even so, Giovanni could imagine the Count's beaming smile, overly satisfied with himself.

~

That evening when he arrived home, Giovanni proposed the Count's idea of a dinner party. Arabella was surprised, but in the best possible way, as the suggestion to host a party in the unique setting of the studio delighted her.

The Count had been right—the idea of organizing a party added a needed spark to Giovanni's relationship with Arabella. In the days that followed, she threw herself into preparations for the social event, selecting the menu, arranging for the caterers to deliver the tables and chairs, and purchasing small books of great artists as both gifts and place markers for the guests.

Arabella expressed her pleasure with Giovanni's improved mood, coming out of his dark abyss, and his desire to spend time with her as together they planned the event and sorted out the many details. She was more a part of his life than ever. They discussed who they should invite, not only for pleasant company but those who might lead to further business for Giovanni.

Giovanni suggested they invite an Italian art dealer who was in London. He might help Giovanni gain more commissions from Italian museums and private collectors. Arabella agreed and mentioned that she knew the first secretary at the French Embassy, via a girlfriend, and that he too, with strong connections to the art world in France, would be a wise choice as a dinner guest. The table would be a mixture of old friends, business contacts, and others who could open the path to new clients. Giovanni and Arabella had a common goal and were working as a team, which brought them closer together.

The day of the party, Arabella spent all morning busy on the telephone, attending to details with the caterers and making sure the small kitchen of the studio could be sufficiently adapted to accommodate the servers. Everything had to be just right and set up well before the event began.

In the late afternoon, Giovanni went by himself to his studio. He brought the portrait of the Count out of the second strong room and asked for his opinion on where he should be hung.

"I want to oversee the entire table," the Count replied. "Hang me in the middle of that wall and not too high, as I want to hear their conversations."

Giovanni did as the Count asked. He had to reposition the portrait a few times until the Count was satisfied, then he stepped back to gauge its place overlooking the center of the dinner table.

"Thank you, Signor Fabrizzi," the Count said. "I appreciate your doing this for me."

"In a strange way, it is more for me than it is for you. I needed a project other than restoring the Brueghel, something that could involve Arabella. She's taken to this idea with great enthusiasm, which was surprising. I thought she would say no."

"Women are the ultimate mystery of life," the Count said. "I was intimate with many in my time. I can assure you, their subtlety and complexity is a puzzle and a challenge to every man. But that is part of their charm, their allure, is it not?"

"I suppose you're right."

"I want to help you," the Count said. "I know how sadness has impaired your marriage. If I can watch and listen to Arabella tonight, I might be able to suggest the best means to rekindle your love for each other."

"I admit," Giovanni mumbled, eyes downcast to avoid the Count's unchanging gaze. "I have to fight what's inside of me. I know it sounds absurd, but sometimes, one has to fight to be happy. One has to ball up one's fists, dig in one's feet and say, over and over, *I will not give in to misery.*"

"Whenever I felt sadness," the Count said, "I relied upon ample glasses of wine to elevate my mood."

"Things are more advanced now," Giovanni said. "We have drugs to lift us out of depression."

"Drugs?"

"You know. Pills."

"Hmm," the Count murmured.

"An elixir, I guess people from your time would call it. Just made solid and a tablet small enough to swallow easily."

"And these remedies are effective?"

"Not always."

"If I may ask, Signor Fabrizzi, are you consuming these elixirs to lift your spirits?"

"No. I am trying to do this without drugs. I think I can."

Giovanni looked at his watch. He needed to get back to his flat.

"I must dress for the party," he said.

"I am most excited," the Count said. "And please remember. Seat Arabella directly beneath me so I may come to know her better."

Giovanni took a cab home. Together he and Arabella went over all the details, reviewed the guest list, and ensured that everything was in order. Satisfied with the arrangements, and anxious to get back to the studio before the caterers arrived, they began changing into formal attire.

Giovanni finished dressing first and sat on the bed watching Arabella. Still in her underwear, she sat facing the mirror at her vanity. He admired her beauty and thought about how much he loved and needed her. She had saved his sanity when Serafina was dying, and their becoming intimate only months later was not opportunism. It felt like destiny. Giovanni watched her paw through a jewelry box, trying to decide which to wear. He could only think of how fortunate he was to have her in his life. After Serafina, he had been alone. Without Arabella, he would have gone mad from the grief, the loneliness, and the absence of love.

As Arabella sifted through jewelry, Giovanni stood and moved closer, then paused to stand behind her. When their gazes met in the mirror, she had a look of concern. Giovanni smiled and brought his hands to her smooth, graceful shoulders.

"I'm not sure what to wear," she said.

"I like very much what you're wearing now," he said.

She smirked, then smiled to make up for it. She opened another jewelry box and poked around in it, as Giovanni began to gently stroke the soft skin of her shoulders.

"Anything you wear will be beautiful," he said.

She stopped sifting through jewelry, becoming more aware of his soft touch across her shoulders. Giovanni reached past her and opened one of her jewelry boxes, black leather with gold inlay bordering the edges, that he had purchased years ago in Italy and had given to Arabella after their wedding.

He lifted the brass latch and opened it. Arabella remained still as Giovanni reached into the jewelry box and brought out a necklace that he had always been fond of.

"This is not a good idea," Arabella said warily.

"No, my dear. I want you to wear it. I feel good about you wearing it." He spread apart the thin strands of hammered gold and draped the ruby cluster above her cleavage. "You will look magnificent."

"It's hers," Arabella said.

"No. It's yours now." He began to work the clasp behind her neck.

"Gio, this is a bad idea. You're going to get upset. Let's not do this now."

"I assure you, I am ready for you to wear this, to wear all of the jewelry I bought for her. Really, I am."

Before he could clasp the necklace, she reached for the strands and pulled it away.

She met his gaze in the mirror. "I don't want to wear her jewelry. I'll find something of my own."

~

After dinner, Giovanni and Arabella stood at the doorway, saying good-bye to their guests. Arabella had invited one guest to remain, to have a glass of after-dinner liqueur with them.

François was Arabella's friend from the French Embassy, with strong connections to the art world. Giovanni was anxious to speak with him further, as the topics of dinner conversation, in the presence of other guests, was mainly general subjects of the day and only lightly touched on the business of fine art. Dinner among mixed company was not the time or place to explore specifics that Giovanni wanted to propose, and he was delighted that Arabella had invited François to remain for a drink, so that he could delve deeper.

François was a dashing young man, as might be expected of someone holding the position of first secretary at the embassy. But Giovanni sensed more than that. His estimation of François, beyond his persona of worldliness and sophistication, was the sort of fellow who spent more time before the mirror grooming and admiring himself than the ladies would spend applying their makeup. His effort to present a maintained appearance was obvious, and he seemed to enjoy the admiration from others that it generated. Throughout dinner, Arabella certainly admired him more than once.

Giovanni may have gauged his guest as somewhat vain, but he also sensed opportunity. The slick fellow could help develop leads among French collectors and dealers, leading to new commissions for Fabrizzi & Sons.

Seated at the table, Arabella and François sipped their wine and engaged in conversation while Giovanni went to the kitchen to check on the caterers, who were making some ruckus as they cleaned up and packed their dishes, flatware, and serving platters. They asked about the dining table and chairs, and Giovanni requested that they take it last, so he and his remaining guest could finish their drinks. Then he rejoined Arabella and François.

"Well, that certainly went well." Giovanni sat down next to Arabella.

François raised his glass. "It was quite delightful. I am pleased to make your acquaintance, Giovanni, after hearing so much about you from Arabella."

"How long have you and Arabella known each other?"

Their gazes met and they were silent.

Arabella began, "I think Louisa and I went by the French Embassy, what was it, about a year ago?"

"That sounds about right," François replied.

After ample glasses of alcohol, Giovanni felt relaxed, and the evening's success added to his satisfaction. He brought his arm around Arabella's waist and pulled her closer.

"And a handsome fellow like you," he said to François, then asked Arabella, "Does he have a special woman in his life?"

François chuckled. "A secretary at the embassy may have important responsibilities, but I cannot pretend the salary is impressive. I may require a job with better pay before considering the possibility of settling down."

"I might be able to help you there." Giovanni sensed his opportunity. "In terms of increasing your income, that is."

"Really?" François flashed his exceedingly white smile.

"Arabella tells me that in your position, you have contact with a number of French art collectors and dealers who either live here in London or travel here regularly. Is that so?"

"It is true, Giovanni."

"Well then, if you should, by any chance, recommend my services to a collector or dealer who is not already a client of mine, I would be happy to compensate you."

François appeared genuinely pleased and looked at Arabella. She smiled and nodded, assuring François that Giovanni would indeed be generous, were François to refer any new clients.

"I will definitely keep you in mind," François said.

Two of the caterers struggled to hold the door and get their equipment cart past the opening.

Arabella suggested, "Gio, you should help them."

He rose to assist.

"And," she continued. "Get them down the elevator and to the street. With all your building's security, you never know. We don't need an incident."

"Good thinking." Giovanni held the door while the caterers pushed their cart through, then accompanied them on the elevator ride down to the lobby. He ensured that no alarms would sound and then got them out to the street where they loaded their van.

"And the table, sir," one of the caterers said.

"Yes, of course." Giovanni led the way as they returned upstairs to the studio. He was first to enter.

Arabella and François were standing near the table.

François shifted away from her and moved to one end of the table. "Let me help." He waved off Giovanni's approach. "You've already done enough this evening."

Giovanni welcomed the offer and allowed François to assist the caterers. However, Giovanni felt a tinge of resentment. It almost seemed that François was suggesting that Giovanni was old and feeble, while François, a man in his prime, was better suited to the task.

François held the door open so the caterers could carry the table downstairs.

Giovanni reconsidered his thoughts. Any resentment toward François was silly and he didn't want something so trivial to ruin the fine evening they had all enjoyed.

He patted François on the shoulder.

"Thank you, François. You're a good man."

5

The next morning, Giovanni returned to his studio. The previous night's party had been a success and one telltale sign remained—a few empty wine bottles in a box near the door. In his haste to put away the Count's portrait the night before, he had overlooked that. He would take care of it soon enough, but first he wanted to know what the Count had to say.

Giovanni opened the second strong room, brought out the portrait, and set it on the easel.

"Where is the Brueghel?" the Count asked. "Are you no longer restoring that abomination?"

"You don't like Brueghel?" Giovanni was taken aback. "How can you possibly say that?"

"I speak my mind, and Brueghel's work is simply dreadful. And you may include Goya and Caravaggio. Their work is heavy-handed and unceasingly bleak."

"So who do you like?"

"Rembrandt, Raphael, and Velasquez," the Count replied without hesitation.

"What about modern painters?" Giovanni asked.

"My portrait has not hung in the company of many modern works. I was able to admire Turner and Degas, though I suppose your term *modern* may or may not include such artists. Of course, I have been denied opportunities, due to that wretched crate, of viewing the work of more recent artists. Regardless, I doubt any could surpass Rembrandt."

Giovanni pulled a stool closer and sat down. "Count, I want to know about last night. What did you think of Arabella?"

"Your wife is lovely," the Count said, then continued in a rush of words, "You know, women are infinitely fascinating. Take my wife, for example..."

"I'm asking about my wife, Count, not any wife you—"

The Count charged ahead. "It was my uncle, Lorenzo de Medici, who arranged for me to marry Maria Pitti, the daughter of Luca Pitti, the Florentine banker who had built the Pitti Palace. It was not a happy marriage. I understand the difficulty a marriage presents. There is much that may go awry. For example, my wife could not bear children, and she was quite promiscuous. A scandal arose in Florence when her affair with Fancelli was exposed. Fancelli, you will remember, worked with Brunelleschi and had designed the Palace."

"Sure, but what about Arabella? I hung your portrait like you asked, so you could—"

"To keep matters quiet," the Count continued, "the family sent us to Venice, in the hope that a change of scenery would restore calm to our turbulent marriage. But it wasn't long before Maria embarked on another affair and this time with Andrea Gritti. *Enough!* I returned to Florence, taking with me the very painting that you now look upon. So if you ignore those turbulent years in Venice, when my portrait was hung by a window that was left open more often than not, overlooking the Grand Canal, I do not consider that I was properly hung until I returned to the Pitti Palace in Florence."

"Andrea Gritti. Wasn't he the Doge?" Giovanni asked.

"That is the one. He had a distinguished military career and was elected Doge in 1523. What chance, Signor Fabrizzi, would I have stood had I stayed in Venice with a wife who was the Doge's mistress? It was quite humiliating. I knew Gritti a modest degree. Any degree was quite enough, Signor Fabrizzi, I assure you. He was a fierce man with a bad temper. The swine Titian painted his portrait."

"You don't like Titian either?" Giovanni was dismayed that anyone could dismiss the great master so easily. "Did you know him?"

"It was Titian who introduced my wife to Gritti and encouraged their relationship."

"Why would he do that?"

"Oh, I am sure it was simple spite and Florence-Venice rivalry." The Count was bitter.

Giovanni hoped to steer the topic away from past wounds. "Did you enjoy living at the Pitti Palace? It must have been very grand."

"Indeed it was," the Count replied. "It was a magnificent building, and the location superb, on the south side of the Arno, near the Ponte Vecchio. We all lived there in typical family disharmony. I had my own quarters, a luxurious apartment with a perfect view of the Ponte Vecchio, where I kept to myself. I felt some shame and embarrassment, you understand, without an heir and having a wife who would bed every man who came within her sights. So I began an affair with a first cousin, Maria de Medici. The family did not approve. She was only fourteen."

"*Fourteen?*" Giovanni choked on the word. "You, your cousin? Fourteen? If you did that today, you'd be put in jail."

"I would have preferred that to the actual outcome."

"Don't tell me—it gets worse."

"It begins to," the Count said. "Maria's brother, Francesco, challenged me to a duel. He won. I died at far too early an age. My portrait, that which you look upon now, was taken off the wall in the Grand Salon. How I would know this, being dead, I cannot say, but somehow I did not cease to be, perhaps because I cared so dearly for the fate of my portrait, as dearly as I cared for my life, which by then was extinguished. But not the portrait, though it too would be removed from sight, banished forever to the cavernous cellars at the Pitti Palace. I could not bear for that to happen any more than I could bear to lose my life. My prayers were answered by another young cousin, Catherine de Medici. How I loved that sweet girl. If not for her, I would still be in that damned cellar. It was after she became the Countess of Auvergne, on her aunt's death. The poor girl had been orphaned when she was barely one month old and had been brought up by her aunt. Her father was Lorenzo de Medici II, another cousin, of course. When she was fourteen, she married the Duke of Orleans in Marseilles. At that wedding, it is said that Catherine wore high heels. The first time in recorded history that any woman wore high heels."

"I'm not interested in the history of footwear." Giovanni was getting irritated. "You wanted to listen to our guests last night, and Arabella. You haven't told me—"

"Catherine moved to France," the Count continued. "After all, her father-in-law was the King. It was during preparations for the move that she saved me. Her ladies-in-waiting were helping her decide what she should take, and one of the ladies glanced upon me and urged Catherine to bring my portrait with her to France. When Catherine asked who painted it, another of the ladies told her it was Botticelli. As her grandfather Lorenzo was Botticelli's patron, Catherine could not leave my portrait behind. And so I left Florence, saved from a certain life of dust and solitude, and instead taken amidst great style and luxury to France. First at Fontainebleau, then Chambord, Versailles of course, and then I was taken to Le Petit Trianon."

The Count paused, allowing Giovanni a chance to respond.

Giovanni rose from his stool, crossed his arms, and said nothing.

"Signor Fabrizzi, you seem to have something on your mind."

"I asked you to tell me what you thought of Arabella. In fact, it was your idea that we host a dinner party so you could listen to her and others having conversation."

"Well, yes, I—"

"I asked for your opinion of my wife and all you do is talk about yourself. Your life history is fascinating, I'm sure, but I want to know about Arabella."

The Count was not quick to respond. "I have already told you that I found your wife lovely. Beyond that, I cannot say the party conversation was of great interest to me."

"Really?" Giovanni was disappointed. "Why not?"

"In my time, Signor Fabrizzi, there was more a sense of revelry. Dinner guests would tell bawdy stories, rumors about court intrigue, and other tales far more captivating. I am sure your guests are fine people, but all they talk about is how difficult it is to get from place to place in London, about their precious and wonderful children, and I must say, very little about art."

Giovanni hung his head. "It's a sad fact about the world today. People will sooner talk about the latest movie, which of course everyone will forgot about next month, than discuss the awe inspired by a work of art centuries old."

"I believe this age has less passion," the Count said. "Or perhaps it is England. My people in Italy might be quite different. I would venture to say that Italian women today are filled with more vitality than any of your female guests last night."

"Arabella?"

"As I said, she is lovely."

"But what else?" Giovanni asked. "What do you make of her?"

The Count hesitated. "Signor Fabrizzi, women are more complex than men. Their motivations are not always clear. At times one must read between the lines, as they say."

"I don't want to read between the lines." Giovanni was getting aggravated by the Count's repeated dodging of the question.

The Count responded, "I do not know what else you are hoping that I might say."

Giovanni stepped closer to the portrait. "I want to know why there is this ever-expanding gulf between Arabella and me. You seem to be the expert on women. You tell me."

"Expertise is not required to see the problem." The Count's arrogance had reached new heights. "One must simply keep eyes wide open."

"What the hell is that supposed to mean?" Giovanni was getting close to losing his temper.

"It means," the Count calmly explained, "that if your wife seems distant, and you are not making love to her regularly, and she invites a young, attractive man to your dinner party, that perhaps, just possibly, your eyes are closed. Are you blind?"

"What are you suggesting?"

"How can you be so naïve?" the Count asked. "Have men become absurdly ignorant in the last few centuries?"

"I won't stand here and be insulted. Especially by an inanimate object."

"Oh no, of course not. You shouldn't have to put up with the truth."

"Stop avoiding the question. Tell me!"

"Your wife is having an affair with her young French friend."

Giovanni recoiled a step, speechless.

"No man wants to be a cuckold, Signor Fabrizzi, but that is the truth."

Giovanni narrowed his eyes. "You vile, cruel man. Or whatever you are. You are so bitter, stuck in that painting, that your only entertainment is to fabricate malicious gossip and watch others suffer as a result. I may well give you away for free to my client."

"Signor Fabrizzi, please."

"Shut up!" Giovanni took the portrait from the easel and started toward the second strong room.

"I am a witness," the Count said. "You must listen. When you joined the servants."

Giovanni stopped. "The caterers?"

"You stepped out to help them," the Count explained, "and you left your wife alone with him. I take no pleasure in telling you this. They were in each other's arms."

"Liar!" Giovanni continued into the strong room.

"I have their words. He wanted to lay with her last night, but she was reluctant. He said, *Don't you want me anymore?* And she said, *Oh, François, you know I do.*"

Giovanni seized the crate where the Count would be spending some time. "You are sick and cruel, making up outrageous lies for your own twisted sense of pleasure. Go in your box and stay there." Giovanni slid the portrait into the crate, wanting to shove it hard, but it was a work of art after all. His code of conduct would never allow anger to damage a piece, even when the work was vehemently despised and worthless.

The Count's muffled voice penetrated the wood. "You ask her. Go ahead. *Don't you want me anymore? Oh, François, you know I do.* Ask her!"

Giovanni locked the strong room, but the Count's voice lingered in his skull.

He pounded his fist against the metal door.

"Goddamned liar!"

He picked up the box of empty wine bottles and took them to the service elevator.

~

Giovanni tried to concentrate as he sliced mushrooms for the pasta he was preparing. The small kitchen of his flat was steamy and warm from the boiling noodles and simmering sauce, bubbling at an agreeably low rate. With each slice of mushroom, as the blade dropped, his mind would flop from the Count to Arabella and back again, as it had all afternoon since his confrontation.

That she was gone when he arrived home didn't help. But when she called, the sound of her voice reassured Giovanni. He did not mention anything about the day's events in his studio, but he did ask why she was not home. Two of her girlfriends had arranged an impromptu dinner for a third who was feeling ill, and Arabella wanted to join them, to help out, to commiserate. She asked if Giovanni could manage dinner on his own, or go out, and to expect her later than usual.

So there he was, home alone, making himself dinner. Normally, Giovanni wouldn't have thought twice about such a turn of events. But as he sliced mushrooms and made a neat pile to dice into smaller sections, he couldn't stop thinking about the Count's vicious words. What if it were true? Giovanni would be devastated. But it couldn't be true. The Count was pretentious, pompous, and self-serving. All he wanted to do was talk about his own adventures, probably all lies, and his cruel fantasy about Arabella was just another sensational tale. It had to be.

After all, Giovanni thought, it was Arabella who had been so loving to him when he felt dead himself, barely able to get out of bed, for weeks after Serafina's funeral. Arabella had been cheery, had come to his flat with food, and had invited him out to concerts. She had taken him to art openings that he would have normally attended, but after his tragic loss, he dreaded. His depression had not completely immobilized him, but it seriously prevented him from entering social situations in which well-meaning friends would generally make him feel worse. He would try nonetheless, with Arabella at his side. There were occasions when friends, their faces pinched with concern, would ask how he was doing. It was out of the best intentions but he found the weight of their questions unbearable. He did not want to hurt them, or to reject their heartfelt inquiries. Thankfully, Arabella was always a loving interloper, steering the conversation to a livelier or simply completely different topic, for which he was eternally grateful.

He would never forget the night they came back from an evening out, a little tipsy from too many drinks, laughing about a petty argument two friends had over the look of a handbag. It was then that he realized—it was the first time he had laughed since losing Serafina.

I owe my life to you, he told Arabella in that moment, and he kissed her, not an innocent peck on the cheek, rather his lips to hers and without any reservations. His eyes slipped closed as he indulged in the wondrous sensation, and for a moment, he was lost in time, until he realized what he had done and withdrew, fearing how she might react. Arabella gasped lightly, surprised but not scolding, and she did not voice disapproval. Gazing at him, she tugged at his shoulder, pulled his lips to hers, and returned the caress, deeper, more passionately. He did not remember exactly how, but their lips never parted as he guided her to his bedroom.

Giovanni looked down at the mushrooms he was chopping. Or what was left of them, minced to a gooey mess and juice that was running off the cutting board. He wiped the blade and set it down, then turned off the stove. He sat at his kitchen table and dropped his head in his hands.

The irony did not comfort him. He suspected the very woman who had saved him from darkness. And worse, his suspicion was based solely on the voice of a painting. How absurd, he thought. And the further irony, how the painting had come to him, from his father, who received it as a peace offering from Giovanni's uncle, banished from the family for some murky reason.

This was ridiculous, Giovanni thought, to let his suspicions so unnerve him. It was not only pathetic, it was damaging. His stomach ached. The last thing he wanted was his favorite pasta of vermicelli, mushrooms, duck sausage, and Roma tomatoes. He wanted the acidic burn of his innards to cease.

There was a nagging fear that the Count might have been telling the truth. The distance that had grown between Giovanni and Arabella was undeniable. Although they never had a ferocious fight of any kind, he knew that his physical affections had been dampened of late. The issue of Serafina's jewelry had merely brought that into focus.

He thought about François. He certainly was handsome. But Giovanni had seen nothing between them during dinner that suggested a sexual relationship. Arabella said François might bring more business to the House of Fabrizzi, via his worldwide French contacts. She was making a sincere effort to aid her husband, not betray him.

Then why did he feel ill, suspicious, and at the very center of it all, icily afraid? He did not want to confront Arabella with this. What good would come of it? She would resent his not trusting her and it would surely strain their relationship, complicating it even further.

And yet, he could not imagine living another twenty-four hours with the gnawing unknown that was burrowing through his intestines. He wanted to interpret the Count's words as vindictive. And his words may well have been in that moment. But what if it were true? Giovanni was most disturbed by the Count's precision in recounting the tale of Arabella. He had not simply claimed that she was unfaithful. He had repeated their conversation. *Don't you want me anymore? Oh, François, you know I do.*

If it were true, a painting could contain the soul of its subject, overhear conversation, and speak to Giovanni, then why this out-come? Of all the people in its history, the portrait chose to upend Giovanni's life by suggesting he organize a dinner party and then inform him that his wife is having an affair. Could such cruelty be the Count's only reason to exist?

Giovanni admitted to himself that the Count's words could be true. It was a possibility, but still an unknown. Giovanni would have to do something. He could not ignore his doubts, but he had no idea of how to approach the topic with Arabella. Telling her that a painting spoke to him would be reason alone for her to leave. Yet, if she was guilty of adultery, he would not want to remain with her anyway.

Perhaps the Count didn't exist, and Giovanni was going mad. Was it all himself, he wondered. His subconscious could have picked up on the signs of her betrayal, and rising out of the depths to protect him, invented the Count as means to expose a truth that was in plain sight but Giovanni refused to face, at least, consciously. Enough of that, he thought. Ideas like that were more outrageous than a talking painting, and trying to analyze himself only made his head hurt. Besides, calling it madness wouldn't change anything. However he arrived at doubting her fidelity, there was no going back.

"What are you doing in the dark?"

Arabella's voice startled him. Her silhouette was in the doorway of the kitchen.

"I don't know," he muttered.

"For God's sake, Gio." She reached for the light switch.

"Don't."

She flipped the switch on and he squeezed his eyes shut.

"Gio, I've had it with your moods. I'm tired, do you understand? I'm tired of hoping you come out of these morose dives into misery." She went to the stove and saw the unfinished dinner left out to rot. "I don't want to live this way!" she shouted. "I don't want your doomed attitude dragging us both down. And I don't want the memory of Serafina always hanging over us."

He vaulted upright. "I have not been thinking of her. It's not that, it's—"

"Yes it is!" She jabbed him in the chest. "It's always her."

Giovanni was shocked. She had never before called him a liar, nor so much as hinted that he might be.

She continued. "Gio, this has to stop, or... I don't know. I can't go on like this."

"Is that so?" Giovanni imitated a boyish voice, the best he could imagine that François might sound. *"Don't you want me anymore?"*

Her eyes pinched, confused.

"Wait," Giovanni said. "Let me guess your answer." He seized her shoulders to make her look at him. He raised the pitch of his voice to that of feminine mockery. *"Oh, François, you know I do."*

She staggered back and her face went blank.

Giovanni let her slip from his grasp, and he became equally baffled. Her reaction was an admission of guilt.

"Then it's true," he said, though still he could not bring himself to believe it.

Her eyes welled with tears, and her lips began to quiver.

"Tell me!" he hollered.

"How..." Her voice cracked. "How could you possibly..."

"It doesn't matter, and you wouldn't believe me anyway."

"But you were..."

"Don't lie to me! Tell me the truth, now."

She began to sob. "You don't understand. If you would just hear me, see me, you would know I needed to be the only woman in your life. Maybe you would have shown me more affection. Maybe you would have touched me more. Maybe..."

Giovanni sat down at the table.

He was right. The Count was right. He had never felt so awful to be right. He wished that he had never opened that crate. Never talked to the Count. Never...

She wiped at her tears and tried to compose herself.

He calmly said, "I'd appreciate it if you would sleep in the guest bedroom tonight. Then in the morning, we'll talk about where you will be moving."

As he stared down at the table, her footsteps shuffled away. After she was gone, he got up, turned off the kitchen light, and sat down at the table, in the dark. Sleeping would be impossible, or even to lie awake in the bed that he had shared with Serafina, the bed he had shared with Arabella, and the bed that awaited him, alone.

6

Days after Arabella had moved out, Giovanni felt the rawness of her absence. He would not invite her to return, but at the same time he felt lost, unanchored, having to continue life without her.

He did not go to his studio, even though he wanted to flee the loneliness of the flat. Going to his studio meant inevitably facing the Count, and Giovanni was still angry about his revelation of Arabella's affair. Instead Giovanni wandered about the flat, sleeping late most days, some days lying in bed until noon. After a long bath, he would put on some tranquil piano music, Schumann or Bach, and make himself something to eat, then pick up a book to read or watch television, but these distractions never lasted very long. His attention would wander back to the mess his life had become, until forcing himself to ignore it and again search for something else to occupy his time.

He did not have the strength to call on his friends and inform them of what had happened. It wasn't only a matter of pride. Just as he did not care to discuss how his mourning for Serafina had damaged his marriage to Arabella, he did not want to discuss his reason for asking her to leave.

However, three days of unfocused meandering and feeling sorry for himself, not to mention zero interaction with other human beings, wasn't helping him cope, either. He concluded that remaining in his flat was no way to work through his suffering. So he went to his studio.

There he stood before the strong room doors, unable to decide which one to open first. He should bring out the Brueghel and get back to work on it. He should also confront the Count, but there was no telling what he might say next. Giovanni opened neither door. Instead he sat at his desk, picked up the phone, and dialed his son in Florence.

After they exchanged greetings and inquired about each other's well-being, there was a pause.

"Papa," Maurizio said, "the work here is going all right. But I still need Flavio. I hope that's okay with you."

"I'm not calling about Flavio. You use him as long as you need."

"Grazie. Well then, why are you calling?"

Giovanni dug his fingertips into the flesh of his forehead. He inhaled deeply and then came out with it.

"Mau, I asked Arabella to leave. I found out she was having an affair."

"God, I'm so sorry. You mean, she's already gone?"

Giovanni attempted to say *yes*, but all he made was a soft hissing sound. He cleared his throat. "Mau, I'm not doing very well. I haven't been able to work. I'm feeling kind of lost, you know?"

"Oh, Papa, I'm so sorry."

"I'm sure you're busy, but it would mean a great deal to me if you would visit. Even if it's just for a couple days." Giovanni closed his eyes and prayed that his son would agree to visit. When there was no reply, Giovanni added, "Whenever you can manage."

"I'll come this weekend," Maurizio said. "Don't worry. I'll ask Flavio to work extra so we don't fall behind schedule. Let me call the airlines, and I'll let you know my arrival time."

"Thank you, Mau."

"I love you, Papa. Don't worry. Talk to you soon."

"Love you too, Mau. Ciao."

Giovanni hung up the phone. It pleased him that he would see his son again, but it wasn't enough to lift him out of the hole created by Arabella's absence. He expected his depression to lighten if Maurizio agreed to visit, but after the call, though a positive outcome, it failed to make Giovanni feel any better.

He opened the second strong room, brought out the Count's portrait, and set it on the easel. Minutes passed without conversation between them. It was as if they both realized how explosive the situation had become and that the wrong word or phrase could result in something terrible, even irreparable.

Giovanni broke the silence. "Count, I need to speak with you."

He waited for a reply. There was none.

"Count, I'm talking to you. Do you hear me?"

When no reply came for the second time, Giovanni felt dizzy. The voice was gone, just when he needed it most. The injustice of it made him furious, but then he began to question all that had happened since the first day the Count had spoken to him.

"So you're abandoning me, are you?" Giovanni said. "Well, then I will abandon you!" He grabbed the panel off the easel, tempted to smash it against the wall and throw it in the garbage.

"Signor Fabrizzi!" the Count called out. "Please. I hear you. Put me back."

Giovanni held the portrait at arm's length and searched the panel for a change of expression, hoping to see fear on the smug bastard's face. As always, the Count's haughty stare was never-ending. Giovanni returned the painting to the easel.

"I will surmise," the Count said, "from your absence these few days, that my news of your wife was not well-received."

"I asked her to leave," Giovanni said. "Are you happy now?"

"Such an outcome is not a source of pleasure, no. Please forgive me, as I did not mean to cause you harm. I wanted to see your wife and your friends interact, simple as that. I had no idea this unfortunate revelation would be the result. You must believe me."

"Why did you have to tell me?" Giovanni asked.

"It was only right that you should know the truth. You may be angry with me, Signor Fabrizzi, but I must tell you, if the circumstance arose again, my actions would be no different. It is a matter of honor. I would expect the same from you, were our positions reversed."

Giovanni considered the possibility and concluded that, despite his woes, trapped in a painting would be worse. And if he were, he could not honestly say that matters of honor and truthfulness would be his foremost concerns.

"May I ask if she will be coming back?" the Count inquired.

"I don't think so," Giovanni replied. "I spoke to her last night and she didn't ask to come back. She's made her decision to leave me."

"I sympathize. A marriage in which spouses do not cohabit is awkward. I know firsthand."

"It's different now, Count. When people no longer get along, we can get divorced. But it takes a good attorney to keep from getting screwed. I've made an appointment to see mine tomorrow morning. If this is what she wants, so be it. Of course, it's going to be lonely without anyone, but that will pass."

"I am insulted and hurt, Signor Fabrizzi. How can you speak of loneliness? Do we not have a stimulating conversation on a regular basis?"

Giovanni almost laughed but kept his silence. No need to further the insult, but conversation with an inanimate object did not compare to a relationship with another living, breathing human being. Particularly the warmth that intimacy provided.

"I suppose it helps," Giovanni admitted. "Our talks are something." Rather than sit on the stool facing the portrait, Giovanni poured himself a glass a wine and slumped in the chair at his desk. "I've spent days at home. It's empty, I'm alone. The telephone never rings. No one comes. It all feels wrong. We used to dine out all the time with friends. We went to art shows. To the theater. Together."

"Signor Fabrizzi. As sad as you may be about your life, I urge you to be happy with what you have. The suffering of others has exceeded yours, I assure you. Take for example, one of my most unfortunate owners, Marcel Radisson."

"Someone I should know?" Giovanni asked.

"Surely you know of the Hudson's Bay Company, the oldest company in North America."

"I've heard of it."

"And what of events leading to its formation?" the Count asked, though not expecting an answer as he fully expected to provide it. "The story begins when two French fur traders, Pierre-Esprit Radisson and Médard des Groseilliers, learned of better fur country farther north. Seeking to finance their expeditions, they approached investors in Boston, and after their solicitations attracted attention, they were eventually brought to England where many were eager to exploit opportunities in the New World. With the money raised, Radisson and Groseilliers commissioned sailing vessels and embarked on their expedition to the Hudson Bay. When they returned to London with a cargo of premium furs, it was not difficult to raise more money. Soon after, King Charles granted a Royal Charter and the Hudson's Bay Company was established. Many of the expeditions were financed by English bankers Moorgate & Eringham, one of whom was Lord Moorgate, a friend of Marcel Radisson, Pierre-Esprit's nephew. At the time I belonged to Lord Moorgate, you see."

"I was wondering when you'd work yourself into the story," Giovanni said.

"My place in the story allows me to tell it," the Count said. "Being the nephew of one of the founders of the company, Marcel was offered the opportunity to manage an outpost at Fort Nelson. As a farewell present, and in quite a theatrical gesture, Lord Moorgate gave me to Radisson. I was horrified.

"Take this painting with you, Marcel," Moorgate said. *"Hang it*

with pride in your new office at Fort Nelson. Let it bring you prestige,
just as it has to our bank, and may it always remind you of Europe."

"I was put on board a ship and we set sail. The weather was atrocious, so bad that we had to turn back more than once. Eventually the weather cleared and we crossed the Atlantic, to a stark fortress near the Arctic Circle, visited by primitive fur traders who resembled barbarians. During the summer and spring, the traders paddled their canoes upriver to the fort where they sold their pelts in exchange for food, hunting equipment, and other supplies. During the winter months, everything was frozen.

"As for the young Marcel Radisson, he had the administrative skills of a moron. Even so, or due to the nepotism that awarded him the position, he managed to hold the post for a time, but then changes in English rule brought complications. First King Charles died, and his successor, his younger brother James, was deposed after a short reign of only four years. England's new rulers, William and Mary, were not so favorable to the French as James had been. We will never know the truth, but given that James fled to France, one can surmise that he may have incited much of the trouble that followed. After all, what king wouldn't be bitter about losing his throne? In any event, France and England went to war, in great part due to disputes over the territory in which the Hudson's Bay Company was operating. The French, under the command of Pierre Le Moyne d'Iberville, raided many of the company's forts and caused much grief for the English."

"So what happened to the younger Radisson?" Giovanni asked.

"When the French overtook Fort Nelson, they found him sitting at his desk. I was on the wall behind him. He was trembling like a leaf, and d'Iberville was quite rough with him. However, because Radisson was a Frenchman, he was given a choice rather than share the fate of his dead colleagues, all of whom swore allegiance to the King of England.

"*Join your countrymen in defeating the English,*" d'Iberville said. "*In which case your post is secure. Refuse and I doubt the Frenchmen I intend to deploy here will be so kind.*"

The Count explained, "Radisson convinced d'Iberville that he would cooperate, when in actuality, he had no intention of doing so, as I soon discovered. In the dark of night, he took me from the wall and we boarded a ship destined for England. He was a coward, pure and simple. Fearing execution, he sought to escape by any means available.

"I was pleased to escape that god-forsaken wasteland. However, I was quite anxious about my future. The young Radisson was very fond of me, but upon our return to England, he was impoverished. The sale of animal pelts barely kept him alive, and in time, his supply was depleted. Sooner or later, if circumstances did not change for the better, he would've had to sell me to support himself.

"Fortunately, before Radisson was completely destitute, he called on his friend and my former owner, the banker Lord Moorgate. He seemed much friendlier than before, a little plumper and less aggressive. He was happy to receive Monsieur Radisson and even kind enough to invite him to share in a glass of sherry.

"*The British have outsmarted d'Iberville.*" Moorgate said. "*They have forced the French out and regained control of the fort. Our invest-ment is safe and we have already seen a handsome return on it. Your courage and loyalty to us have not gone unnoticed. We are all very proud of you."*

"And so," the Count continued, "because of loyalty and luck, perhaps in equal measure, Radisson was saved from a life of poverty. If only Moorgate had known the truth of Radisson's cowardice, perhaps he would have withheld the cash award, in gratitude for service to the company, that solved Radisson's hardship. The irony was appalling, yet it would only become more outlandish. Lady Moorgate, the daughter of an English duke whose name escapes me, was an acquaintance of Anne, daughter of the deposed King James. At a dinner party hosted by Lady Moorgate, to which Radisson was also invited, Anne was in attendance and they were introduced. I cannot say their relationship was sexual as I never witnessed acts between them, though in either case it would not last. Anne's sister Mary, the reigning Queen, was outraged that Anne shared company with a Catholic Frenchman, intimate or otherwise. Earning the Queen's disdain was not a wise course of action, so again Radisson chose to flee, this time to his native France, where for all he knew, a firing squad or guillotine was waiting for him due to his abrupt exit from Fort Nelson."

"He was executed?" Giovanni asked.

"Quite the contrary," the Count said. "Through a highly improbable set of events that I failed to witness, Radisson somehow managed to come into the service of the former King James, exiled in France. Apparently it was his fluent French and Spanish. Oh, and he played the harp. I understand that had some bearing as well. Or more likely, though I cannot say with certainty, perhaps it was Anne who sought favors of her father."

"Now hold on," Giovanni said. "You said Radisson was one of your *unfortunate* owners. Working for a king, former or otherwise, doesn't sound unfortunate to me."

"The story is not yet complete," the Count said. "Indeed, Radisson was quite pleased with his outcome, at the time. Serving King James meant everything to Radisson, and to live that lifestyle, well, he was in heaven. Later, given his linguistic skills, he was the natural choice when King Louis of France wanted an interpreter in Versailles and asked his guest and good friend, King James, to recommend a suitable candidate. So Monsieur Radisson and I moved into the Palace of Versailles. It was very grand, as you can imagine."

"I imagine it was, but how is any of this—"

"Bear with me, Signor Fabrizzi." The Count continued, "Sometime after settling in Versailles, Radisson began a relationship with la Duchesse de Chavigny. She was quite beautiful. At last, I had the opportunity to see Monsieur Radisson with a woman. It was the first time that I had, and many more instances followed. He was inept at the beginning, but la Duchesse was a woman of great experience, and she helped him along. I had a most convenient view from the wall, you understand, and I was in no position to look away. Oh, but she was so loud. She frightened the pigeons away. It was said that King Louis had also enjoyed a few nights of pleasure with la Duchesse prior to her meeting Radisson. After several months of their new affair, she approached the King and suggested that Monsieur Radisson should be ennobled. I believe money changed hands. It was a common means to enter nobility. Imagine, only a few years earlier, Radisson was nearly a vagrant, and now at Versailles, he was sleeping with a former paramour of the king's who was busy promoting his advancement at court. And sure enough, the King agreed. So young Marcel became le Marquis Radisson, and the King's Grand Chamberlain allocated him far more luxurious quarters. I had a wonderful view of the lake. It was spectacular."

Giovanni was perplexed. "It sounds like his life just got better and better."

"For a time that was the case," the Count said. "Radisson, who easily could have been executed in Canada, had the most amazing reversal of fortune one could ask for, in addition to a mistress who promoted his career while he sat about and accomplished nothing. To relieve the boredom, there were frequent balls, and of course, nonstop sexual activity. The infidelity was constant. I must say, your wife would have been quite at home."

"Just tell the story." Giovanni didn't care to be reminded of his wife's affair.

"Gambling was also a great preoccupation," the Count explained. "Many of the apartments resembled casinos. And it was gambling that brought down le Marquis Radisson. He became addicted to baccarat, I'm afraid."

"He couldn't pay his losses," Giovanni suggested.

"La Duchesse helped him on several occasions. Other times he would give a promissory note to cover the debt in the hope that by the time the note fell due, he would have had better luck. It saved him a few times but I always expected that one day his luck would run out. After a time, la Duchesse grew tired of Radisson, and who could blame her? Wanting to divest herself of the lay-about Marquis, she cleverly introduced him to Elizabeth LaCasse, the wealthy daughter of a tax collector. In little time they were married, though it did not please Elizabeth's mother, Madame LaCasse, when she learned that Radisson was constantly in debt and often asked her daughter to cover his losses. Elizabeth's mother was Italian, a former actress from Venice who was unhappily married to Elizabeth's father. As a result, she divided her life between Venice and Versailles. However, as I witnessed on more than one occasion when mother and daughter argued, Madame LaCasse felt the large meals at court were pompous and all the fancy balls were boring. She couldn't enjoy the plays, she complained, because the theaters were too hot and overcrowded. However lavish and wonderful it all seemed from the outside world, she wanted out of Versailles. But she could not leave her daughter behind, particularly in the unsupervised company of a son-in-law for whom she had contempt."

"And did they discuss this with Radisson?" Giovanni asked.

"Of course not. Signor Fabrizzi, the story is about how women subtly control activities, sometimes without our even being aware of it."

"Apparently, in my case."

"As in Radisson's as well," the Count said. "Madame LaCasse was a resourceful woman. In the palace, she learned that King Louis's envoy to the Republic of Venice was due to retire. The King had selected le Duc de Grimaud to succeed him, though not for any obvious reasons, such as his capability to hold the post. Rumor has it, King Louis had taken a fancy to Grimaud's wife and wanted him out of the way. So the King appointed him as the new envoy to the Republic of Venice. Madame LaCasse saw this as an opportunity to return to her beloved homeland. She took a stroll one afternoon, knowing Grimaud would also be taking some fresh air, as it was generally known that he walked the rose garden every afternoon. She approached the poor unsuspecting man, and before nightfall, they were in bed together and her son-in-law's gambling debts were paid. What's more, she extracted a promise from Grimaud that he would ask King Louis to allow le Marquis Radisson to accompany them to Venice, where he would become counselor at the embassy."

"Well there he goes again," Giovanni said. "Just when he's down and out, he ends up on top. The guy's life is anything but unfortunate."

"Signor Fabrizzi, if I may remind you, I have not yet completed the tale. Please, allow me to finish."

Giovanni nodded and remained silent.

The Count continued, "Grimaud offered Radisson the position in Venice and he agreed, though reluctantly, as he had become quite comfortable in Versailles. Of course, his wife Elizabeth was thrilled. Given that her mother had a magnificent residence on the Grand Canal and was well known in the Republic, Elizabeth knew that she would be far happier in Venice, rather than Versailles, where most of the aristocracy looked down on her."

"So you went to Venice."

"I would have preferred Firenze, but never mind that. Elizabeth insisted that Radisson show appreciation to her mother. After all, she had introduced him to Grimaud, who had paid his debts, and better still, offered him a prestigious post and the new opportunities it provided. And so Radisson, that incompetent man who had more luck than brains, gave me, a great and historic work of art, to Madame LaCasse. Can you believe that? He takes me across the Atlantic Ocean twice and then gives me up because he is a wastrel and an unrepentant gambler. I had been with him for decades. A week later, Madame LaCasse and I set off to Venice and her daughter and Radisson followed a month later. His gambling resumed and, after the most remarkable of lives and more benevolent turns of fortune than any man deserves, he dissipated and died, making nothing of his life's opportunities. He passed away at a relatively early age, despite the efforts women had exerted on his behalf."

"Okay, so his end is not so fortunate. Is there a point?"

"I was rather hoping, Signor Fabrizzi, if you were to compare the misfortune of others to your own, surely you would see that your life is not so terrible. And by realizing that, perhaps it would lift your spirits."

"That was supposed to *cheer me up?* Maybe it worked in your time, to show how rotten someone else's life is, and somehow that makes people feel better about themselves. That's not the way these days."

"Is it not?" the Count asked. "I counter that people today are not so different. Do they not indulge in the misery of others? And in doing so, feel better about their own situation?"

Giovanni considered the newscast he had watched on television earlier that morning. He had never thought of the news, specializing in all that was awful outside the comfort our living rooms, as a means of cheering up anyone. But given the popularity of such programs, the Count's suggestion wasn't so outrageous.

"It's an interesting story, Count, but to think I should be happy with what I have, after all that's happened, is a lousy moral of the story."

"Your problem, Signor Fabrizzi, is that you have no historical understanding of the relationships between men and women. And if I may also say, you don't appreciate the greatness of the artwork before you, the fact that my voice can reach you, and that my portrait was created by one of the greatest painters of all time, Botticelli. I deserve to be hung in the Uffizi."

"I've already heard that story," Giovanni said. "It's a good tale, too, though I still doubt it has any basis in reality."

7

At Heathrow Airport on Friday evening, Giovanni proceeded to the passenger arrival area. He stood waiting with others as an endless stream of travelers poured from the concourse. For twenty minutes he searched for his son's face within a flow of people that seemed enough to fill fifty planes that had landed all at once.

At last Maurizio emerged from the crowd. He was the perfect image of his father's youth. Thick dark hair, Mediterranean complexion, and inviting smile. It would be years before he shared Giovanni's gray.

"Papa! So good to see you."

"And you as well, Mau."

They exchanged a warm embrace as other travelers flowed past, then Giovanni pointed toward the baggage claim.

"I don't have more." Maurizio rattled the overnight bag slung over his shoulder. "After all, I'm only here for the weekend."

Giovanni nodded and instead they moved directly to the street exit. Outside, a string of taxis were waiting.

"To Scott's on Mount Street," Giovanni told the driver.

"Very posh, Papa." Maurizio climbed into the backseat. "Not on account of my visit, I hope."

Giovanni settled next to his son and the taxi rolled into traffic. "Of course it is, Mau, and how happy I am to see you again. It has been months."

"I guess it has," Maurizio said. "Actually, since the..." He didn't finish.

Giovanni knew the rest. *Since the wedding.* His wedding to Arabella.

"It's okay, Mau," Giovanni said. "I'm not going to get upset."

"Do you want to talk about it?" Maurizio asked.

"Not yet. First let me have a look at you." Giovanni studied his son as the taxi moved through traffic. He smiled. "Next we shall eat. I am famished, and I can't imagine your airline snack was much."

~

Throughout dinner, Giovanni did not touch the subject of Arabella and her infidelity. Not so much because he was avoiding the topic, rather because he was interested in Maurizio and all that was happening in his son's life. More than anything, he was simply pleased to have him near. A weekend was such a short time, and there was so much catching up to do.

"And how is your girlfriend?" Giovanni asked. "I'm sorry, but I've forgotten her name."

"The one I brought to the wedding? Don't worry about her name. That didn't work out anyway."

"Oh, I'm sorry to hear that. Is there anyone new?"

Maurizio smiled and reached for his wallet. He produced a snapshot and handed it to his father.

"Wow," Giovanni said. "She's a catch. Well done, son."

"You'd like her, Papa. She's an intellectual, an art student. You know how it goes when you talk with someone about art, and the next thing you know, you're talking over their head. Not her. You'd be surprised."

"You really think so?" Giovanni handed the photo back. "Well then, I look forward to meeting her."

Maurizio put his wallet away and an uncomfortable silence passed as father and son continued eating.

"Papa," Maurizio said. "Don't you want to tell me what happened?"

"I already have," Giovanni said. "She was having an affair and I asked her to leave. Simple as that."

"Was it someone you know?"

Giovanni savored another bite of his Dover Sole and then sipped his wine. "There isn't much more to say."

There was a great deal more to reveal, but Giovanni didn't feel it was the right time. He would show the painting to Maurizio first, and perhaps that would soften the blow. There was no telling how his son would react to Giovanni's new friend, the Count.

～

Saturday morning, Giovanni went to the kitchen with the plan of making breakfast for his son, as a surprise. But Maurizio was already up and it appeared he had a similar idea, hoping to surprise his father. He had heated a skillet and was just about to crack a pair of eggs when Giovanni halted in the doorway, dumbstruck though pleasantly so. They exchanged glances, stood silent for a moment as if both were caught, and then they shared in a round of laughter.

"I'll set the table." Giovanni arranged plates and poured coffee while Maurizio continued at the stove. When the eggs were ready, they sat down and enjoyed the simple time they could share together.

"I want you to come to my studio this morning," Giovanni said. "Before the rest."

"You have big plans for today?" Maurizio asked.

"Indeed. We have a gallery opening, then later, I'm taking you to the theater. But first I want to show you a painting. It's from your grandfather's collection."

"Something valuable?"

"That's questionable. You see, it's unsigned. But word is..."

"Whose word?" Maurizio asked.

"That's just the thing." Giovanni wasn't ready to tell his son about the Count. "I'll explain, in time. First you have a look, then we'll discuss it."

Maurizio agreed and they finished breakfast.

～

Outside the St. James's Street building, Giovanni went through the ritual of access codes as Maurizio trailed behind him. Once inside the studio, Giovanni opened the second strong room and stepped in. He paused to consider if he should inform the Count that they had a visitor, but he decided against it. He would bring out the Count's portrait and see what would happen.

He set the painting on the easel and stepped back. "There it is."

Maurizio took a moment to study the panel. "It's an interesting piece. Looks Renaissance. No signature, you say?"

"None," Giovanni replied. "What do you think of it?"

Maurizio examined the cracking paint. "Shouldn't be a difficult restoration."

"But what do you think of it? I mean, compared to other paintings."

"It's okay." Maurizio glanced at Giovanni. "We've both seen better, Papa. And without a signature, I can't imagine it's worth much."

Giovanni waited for the Count to protest, as he had when Arabella wasn't impressed by his portrait. The Count remained silent.

"What's so important about it?" Maurizio asked.

"I just wanted you to see it, that's all. We should go now. We have a gallery opening to attend."

"Yeah." Maurizio chuckled. "Surely we'll see something better than this."

Giovanni took the portrait from the easel, expecting the Count to groan, or worse, start hollering that his portrait was crafted by the one-and-only Botticelli. But the Count never made a sound. Giovanni returned the painting to the strong room and locked the door.

~

The gallery opening was just the medicine Giovanni needed. To again socialize with others was a joy, even though he bumped into acquaintances at the show who asked about Arabella and how she was doing. He didn't reveal that he was separated and told everyone that she was fine, then pushed the conversation in other directions. When he and his son left the gallery, on their way to the theater, Maurizio insisted that his father should talk about what had happened with Arabella.

"In mixed company," Maurizio said, "I can understand you don't want to talk about it. But, Papa, I'm your son. It concerns the family."

"Please, Mau, don't ruin our wonderful day together. We'll talk about it, just not now." Giovanni rattled his son's shoulder and smiled, upbeat and playful, though actually, he was becoming annoyed by the repeated probing for more details. Fortunately, his mood improved as the evening progressed. The play was excellent, during which Maurizio was unable to continue asking about his father's marital problems. Despite his son's nosey questions, Giovanni thoroughly enjoyed the day and evening spent with him. Such quality time with his family was well overdue, and he vowed in the future not to let there be so great a lapse between visits with Maurizio.

Sunday morning before his flight back to Florence, Maurizio wanted to visit friends in London that he hadn't seen for some time. He and his father had spent an entire day together, and Maurizio proposed that it wasn't too much to ask. Giovanni agreed that it would be fine except for Maurizio's suggestion that his friends give him a ride back to the airport. Giovanni insisted that he would take his son. He still wanted to tell Maurizio about the Count, but it wasn't the right time. The airport would be his last chance. Maurizio promised to return in time for them to make his flight.

Giovanni spent Sunday morning alone in his flat. It was a welcome chance to relax. The previous day had been a whirlwind of activity, but it was a refreshing change from his recent daily routine. However, all of the day before and into the evening, Giovanni couldn't stop thinking about one nagging mystery—why the Count had remained silent as Maurizio examined his portrait. It brought back Giovanni's earlier fear that the Count's voice might suddenly cease, and he would never have an explanation as to why, nor why he had heard the voice in the first place.

He decided to visit his studio before Maurizio returned. There was enough time.

～

Giovanni unlocked the strong room and brought out the Count's portrait. After setting it on the easel, he pulled his stool closer and sat down.

"Count? Are you there?"

"I am," the Count replied.

"Why were you quiet yesterday?"

"Given the outcome the first time I was confronted with one of your visitors, I concluded silence would be a better course."

Giovanni nodded. "Fair enough. So what did you think of—"

The Count continued, "However, now in our secluded company, I shall clearly voice my dissent. I have never been so insulted."

Giovanni wanted to laugh, but he knew that would be rude. "I suppose that answers my question. The one you didn't let me finish."

"Your son?" the Count asked. "I imagine he is a fine young man, however offensive he may be toward me."

Giovanni laughed. He couldn't hold it back. "Count, you really have an ego problem. If someone doesn't care for the style of your portrait, it's nothing personal. It's like if others didn't care for your style of clothing. It doesn't mean they don't like you."

"Hmm," the Count murmured. "Ego, you say?"

"I think so," Giovanni replied. "It has occurred to me more than once during our conversations. You talk a great deal about yourself."

"It is difficult for me, Signor Fabrizzi, to discuss that to which I am not a witness. I am sorry that my stories include me, however, it cannot be otherwise. Is this fact so difficult to comprehend? I am at a loss to grasp your trouble with the idea."

"Your point is completely understandable," Giovanni said. "It's just the way you always seem to become an important part of every story."

"Hmm. I must focus on others, you suggest."

"It might help." Giovanni thought for a moment. "Tell a story to which you're a witness, but let me care about the people, not what happened to your precious portrait. You know what I mean?"

"Your request is fair. Very well, then consider the tale of Catherine. I will skip the saga that led to my portrait becoming the property of a Russian Prince and Princess. She died first. 1861, I believe it was. The Prince died a few years later. In any event, I was passed down to one of their children, Natasha. As a descendent of nobility, she had made a choice in life that was rare for the era. She married a commoner. Not to mean that he was poor, as he had profited handsomely from the steel industry, supplying materials for steam locomotives and such. They had a daughter named Catherine. She wasn't a noble, of course, as her father was not. But as a successful businessman, he was displeased when she married Alexi in 1885. He was quite effete, but most upsetting to her father was the young man's bleak financial future. He was a dancer with the Bolshoi Ballet. He claimed to derive inspiration from viewing me. Of course he did."

"Count," Giovanni said. "This is what I'm talking about. Tell me about the people, not you."

"I cannot completely remove myself from the story. Alexi and Catherine were given me as a wedding present, by her mother Natasha."

"Stop there. To say they were given *me*, or even *I was given*, or *I was* this or that, comes across as arrogant, you know?" Giovanni didn't want to insult the Count, but something had to be said. And he quickly considered—it should be said as tactfully as possible. "I'm not saying you're arrogant, just the way you tell the story *sounds* arrogant. Do you understand?"

"I see," the Count said, and then he was silent for a moment. "I will consider your advice. Alexi and Catherine were given *my portrait* as a wedding present, which was hung in an apartment close to the Bolshoi."

"Better."

The Count continued, "Certainly the apartment was not the splendor of my previous homes, but it was comfortable, and more importantly, it was warm. The winters in St. Petersburg were brutal. Alexi was continually paranoid of contracting a cold or influenza so there was always a stack of wood burning in the fireplace. He would roll up the large Persian rug and practice his pirouettes in front of the fire."

"Was he any good?" Giovanni asked.

"He was a reliable performer, though not by any means the star of the company. When the Bolshoi's theater in St. Petersburg was demolished to make room for a new conservatoire, the ballet company moved to Moscow. So we moved as well. I did not care for Moscow, nor did Catherine. Her father was so incensed that she had disobeyed him by leaving St. Petersburg that he discontinued her allowance. Alexi had no money to speak of, so they were obliged to live solely on his earnings from the Bolshoi. They managed for a number of years, and then one morning, in a rush to get to the theater, Alexi ran across Shabolovska Street and was knocked down by a streetcar. This form of transportation was new in Moscow and people were not yet accustomed to looking carefully before crossing the road. They frequently misjudged the car's speed. He was badly hurt, and his dancing career was over."

"Gracious, the poor man. What became of him?"

"The Bolshoi felt sorry for him. After nearly a year in the hospital, he was offered a job in one of the administrative departments. His heart was broken, and tragically, he chose to kill himself, leaving poor Catherine a widow with a five-year-old son. She moved back to St. Petersburg and lived with her father, who reinstated her monthly allowance, though the meager sum was hardly a generous amount. She wasn't completely destitute, but it was a struggle, as she was untrained for any form of employment. As her son Sergei grew older, he began to show talent as an artist, especially drawing. The boy's grandfather was so impressed that he arranged for a meeting with a professor at the Imperial Academy of Arts."

"And the result?" Giovanni asked.

"Never to be certain, as events of the time interrupted their future. In Russia, the Industrial Revolution had taken place so rapidly that it triggered an undercurrent, which led to great social unrest, and ultimately, an uprising against the Tsar, Nicholas II. Workers went on strike at a factory in St. Petersburg, and within days, thousands of textile workers had walked off the job. Catherine's father stayed home that day, afraid he would be lynched in the street. Those on strike were demanding food and there was fighting in the streets. The Tsar ordered the people back to work and then commanded his troops to shoot any demonstrators. This led to many deaths. His promises of reform kept him in power for a time. However, most people would forever resent his use of force against his own subjects. Further complications arose during World War I, when the government printed millions of ruble notes to finance war operations, and in doing so, they devastated the Russian economy with runaway inflation. The Tsar struggled to maintain power but it was hopeless. The revolutionaries, fueled by deteriorating conditions, as well as the Tsar's brutal acts some years earlier, turned against their government. Even the military sided with them. The Tsar had no choice but to abdicate."

"So what happened to Catherine and Sergei?"

"Catherine told Sergei that he should leave for Paris. Many of their friends had already fled St. Petersburg. Catherine felt that her son, as a developing artist, would have better opportunities in France. He agreed without a moment's hesitation. His mother helped him pack, gave him money, and then, to my surprise, she gave him the portrait of me as a gift, to take with him to Paris."

"Better than Russia at the time. But probably not to a fancy palace like before."

"The change of location was pleasing, indeed, even with modest accommodations. However, I was not pleased with the change of ownership. To tell you the truth, Sergei was not a nice young man. He was a thief. One day I saw him steal money from his grandfather's pocket while the poor man napped on the sofa. On another occasion, he stole a pair of earrings that his grandmother had left out. An innocent servant was accused of the crime and Sergei never came forward to clear the matter."

"The little creep."

"He was one of my less than ideal owners."

Giovanni glanced at his watch. "Oh, shit." He stood quickly. "I'm late. I have to get Mau to the airport."

~

Giovanni's taxi stopped along the curb in front of his flat, and he slid across the seat to open the rear door. Sure enough, Maurizio was waiting outside.

"Where did you go?" he asked. "I've been here for twenty minutes."

"Sorry," Giovanni said. "I got caught up in a conversation. Let's go."

Maurizio tossed his overnight bag on the seat and hopped in. The taxi launched into traffic.

"A conversation with who?" Maurizio asked.

Giovanni still wasn't ready to tell his son about the Count. Especially not in earshot of a taxi driver. But he was running out of time. He had until Maurizio boarded the plane, otherwise explain it later over the telephone.

"We'll talk at the airport," Giovanni said. "How were your friends? Did you have a good time?"

Maurizio recounted his morning and the fun he had, during which Giovanni showed great interest and probed for more, successfully postponing the topic of the Count until they arrived at the airport. Giovanni could only hope there would be enough time, and he was in luck. Maurizio's flight was delayed.

Giovanni chose a secluded end of the waiting area and they sat down. In the rush to pick up Maurizio and get to the airport, Giovanni hadn't any chance to dwell on the cold reality—his son's weekend visit was ending. It had passed so quickly.

"We've had a wonderful time," Giovanni said.

"Yes, we have. I'm sorry I couldn't spend more time with you." Downcast, Maurizio fiddled with the tag on his overnight bag.

"It's all right, Mau. It was good to have you visit."

Maurizio's face pinched with concern. "Papa, you haven't really talked much about Arabella. I'm worried about you being alone."

"I'm not exactly alone."

"You said it yourself at the gallery opening yesterday. You ran into countless friends you haven't seen in months."

"True," Giovanni admitted. "But there is someone I have relied on for conversation during all of this."

"Who is that?" Maurizio asked.

For two days Giovanni had sifted through his thoughts, comparing the possible ways in which he could tell his son about the Count. He had wanted to tell Arabella, but the tension between them was already high. Explaining that a painting talked to him would have only made matters worse. But he had to tell someone, and the one person Giovanni felt closest to in the world, his son, was sitting next to him. Maurizio would soon board his plane back to Italy, and Giovanni would not see him again for months.

"Mau, let me ask you something. Do you remember the portrait I showed you in my studio yesterday?"

"Yeah. What about it?"

Giovanni smiled nervously. He thought back to previous arguments with the Count and then to how Arabella looked at him when he suggested the painting spoke to him, though surely she didn't take him literally. In any event, it was the closest he could come to telling her the truth of the matter.

"That painting has a special meaning for me," Giovanni explained. "I feel I know the subject, even though I'm not sure who painted it."

Maurizio waited for his father to continue.

Giovanni scratched his head, trying to find the right words.

"Mau, I need you to try to understand. The painting of the Count, it has affected me strongly."

"Of course, because it was Grandpapa's."

"It's more than that." Giovanni was given a slight reprieve as a woman's voice over a loudspeaker announced the arrival of a flight. He waited until the end of the announcement, and then he thought about the Count's voice and how it had so controlled his life of late. "That painting, Mau, it speaks to me. I don't know how it's possible." He lowered his voice and grabbed his son's arm, as if the embrace would help convince Maurizio of his sanity. "At first I thought I was losing my mind, just as anyone would. But there is an incredible history behind the painting, and the painting has told me about it."

"Told you?" Maurizio shifted back and narrowed his eyes. "What do you mean? Like someone talking?"

"We've had a number of conversations, actually. It's amazing."

Maurizio squeezed his eyes shut, as if a great pain had suddenly lodged in his skull. "Oh, Papa, I'm so sorry. It's the pressure you're under. Look, I'll help you find someone you can talk to, a therapist. There's no shame in it. You really need it with this separation. And you've got to keep working. The Brueghel. You have a deadline, don't forget."

Maurizio stood, gathered his bag, and checked his boarding pass.

"You still have time before your flight," Giovanni said. "Where are you going?"

"I'm just getting ready." Maurizio appeared distracted, straining to read signs at the other end of the waiting area.

Giovanni stood. "I'm not crazy." He was a bit too loud and a few people glanced his way. He stared back at the strangers. The only one who did not look away was a young girl, whose wide-eyed, innocent gaze was not the best of manners. Her mother pulled the child closer and whispered in her ear.

"Mau, listen to me," Giovanni said. "The Count is real. I don't understand it myself, but he's the one who told me that Arabella was having an affair. When I confronted her, she admitted it. How else could I have known?"

"You're under great strain," Maurizio said. "You could think you're hearing a voice, the voice we sometimes hear in our heads when we're upset. You must have sensed Arabella was pulling away from you. That's the logical conclusion."

"Then how could I know so much of the painting's history?" Giovanni asked. "It has told me about its owners, their names and details of their lives, dating back to the sixteenth century, in France, in Italy, America, and England. How could I imagine that?"

"I don't know," Maurizio said. "Maybe it's from books you read long ago, when you were young. You must understand, Papa, what strain can do to a person."

"I'm not under that much strain," Giovanni said. "Yes, it has been difficult, but this is real. Why on earth would I imagine the portrait was painted by Botticelli?" Giovanni chuckled at the notion. "Botticelli. Ridiculous, isn't it? To think my father had a Botticelli and didn't know it. Well, if it really is."

"I agree," Maurizio said. "It is ridiculous. Can't you see that, Papa? Please, don't continue this."

"Mau, I need your support, your understanding. Don't shut me out like this just because it's too incredible for you to believe."

Silent, Maurizio considered the words for a long moment, gazing at his father and forming a look of regret. "I'm sorry, Papa. You're right, I should be more supportive. I'll tell you what. Maybe you should have the panel tested. A full scientific evaluation. You'll at least get an idea of when it was really painted. That might give you some peace of mind."

Giovanni could read between the lines—his son's suggestion was more in the hope that testing would prove the panel was a fake, giving him the leverage to convince his father that it was all his imagination.

"That's a good idea," Giovanni said. "And what if it dates to the sixteenth century?"

Maurizio sighed. "Papa, let's talk tomorrow. I want you to keep working, and I want you to talk to me, and others, about what's going on with you."

"I don't need a therapist."

"Think about it. And maybe I can finish early with Flavio."

"I don't want you discussing this with Flavio or anyone else. This is between us."

"We'll talk about it more on the phone."

Maurizio reached out to hug his father and they embraced. Giovanni did not want to let go. Then the woman's voice over the loudspeaker announced a departure.

"My flight is boarding." Maurizio pulled away from his father and picked up his overnight bag. He prepared his passport and boarding pass.

"Thank you for coming, Mau."

He looked up, sadness in his gaze. "I'm sorry I've been so busy."

The guilt in his son's voice made Giovanni feel even worse.

"I'll call tomorrow," Maurizio said. "Take care of yourself, Papa."

Giovanni nodded and watched his son fade into the crowd of travelers filing through the security checkpoint.

8

After seeing his son off at Heathrow, Giovanni had trouble sleeping that night. By three in the morning, he resorted to a sleeping pill, but still he did not completely fall asleep until well past four o'clock.

When he woke up a few hours later, still drowsy, he didn't feel rested, which was no great surprise. Giovanni was not prone to insomnia, but the absence of Arabella's warmth next to him through the night could not be ignored.

He showered and dressed, then made breakfast. As he sat sipping his coffee, he thought about his life and how each day it was only becoming worse. He doubted Arabella would even talk to him anymore. She certainly wouldn't if she knew about the Count. Telling Maurizio hadn't been a wise choice either. His son likely thought Giovanni was senile, and from that moment forward he would treat him as an overly imaginative child who could easily bring harm to himself.

His life was better before all of the recent upheaval. One of the things he missed most about his former life was the sights and personalities of Soho. The thought alone brought him pleasure, like a favorite food, and it was one aspect of his life that he could control—he would visit Soho. It wasn't any desire to see his old building. There was little benefit in that. But at that moment, he was in no mood to face the Count, and further work on the Brueghel could wait. Both were perfect reasons to avoid the impersonal streets of St. James's.

He took the tube and transferred to Piccadilly Circus, then walked toward Soho and the familiar streets that had been a part of his daily life for many years. Giovanni wanted to see people he knew, have someone offer a warm greeting, or run into a past acquaintance with whom he could enjoy a genuine, heartfelt conversation.

As Giovanni wandered the streets of Soho, he recognized the futility of revisiting the past. Just as he could go to his flat, which no longer felt like home, the district where he had once worked was not the same. Even if he did bump into an old friend who insisted Giovanni tell all about his recent life, there was little he would be willing to say. There was no pride in his second marriage falling apart, nor his son's concern about Giovanni's mental health. There was little motivation to work, and other than during his son's brief visit, he had not socialized with anyone for weeks. He felt cut off, adrift from the pleasant busyness of his prior existence, and he had no idea of how to get it back.

At half past ten, Giovanni decided it was a good time for a coffee, as the morning rush would be over. He reached Golden Square and was drawn to a familiar spot, the Nordic Bakery. Over the years, he had enjoyed many delightful breakfasts there, watching the morning hustle roll past. He ventured inside.

The dark blue walls, pinewood, and high ceiling were still the same, and he was delighted to be greeted by the bubbly blonde, Annie, whom he had always enjoyed *chatting up*. When he stepped up to the counter, her eyes widened in surprise and she reached out to take his hands in hers.

Not wanting to get too specific about his recent life, Giovanni immediately told her how much he missed Soho, the Nordic Bakery, and her.

She smiled. "Giovanni, you're an Italian charmer, you are."

He beamed, enjoying his decision to visit Soho, as it was the perfect remedy for his troubled state of mind. He ordered a double espresso and his favorite, a soft rye roll stuffed with salmon tartare, chives, and red onions. He paid and added a healthy tip that Annie tried to refuse.

"You have to earn that tip," Giovanni said. "Before I go, Annie, you must join me at my table and tell me all about your life."

She had another customer waiting but agreed to join Giovanni when she brought his order.

He found a table and sat down. While waiting, he exchanged brief but pleasant greetings with a few people who stopped in to buy takeout. He lingered, luxuriating in the feeling of an oppressive burden temporarily lifted from his shoulders.

Annie spoke briefly to a fellow waitress, then brought Giovanni's order to his table and sat down with him. He asked her to update him on her life, and with relish, it spilled out of her, all the little trappings of her existence. Her kitten Jonquil, the young man she was dating, the rock band they had just seen. Giovanni did not know anything about rock music, but he drank in Annie's enthusiasm, as her exuberance for such seemingly small things clearly brought her great happiness. Twice Giovanni deflected her inquiries about his life, and he did so with such interest in her affairs that again she would launch into another tangent, talking nonstop.

Annie glanced over her shoulder. Her coworker had the store under control, handling the one customer at the counter. Back to Giovanni, she said, "Now tell me, what is going on with you? Eh? You're being rather quiet, aren't you?"

Giovanni smiled and considered taking a risk. He could ask her about the Count, without, of course, telling her who the Count was, just to see what she might say.

"I know you have to get back to work," he said, "but may I ask your opinion about a friend of mine? I like him very much, but he is upsetting me."

"Of course," she said. "I'd be glad to help. Is this someone in the art world?"

Clever young woman, he thought. "Yes, Annie. You might say he is an expert on art as well as history. I love his stories, utterly fascinating. But he is, how shall I say? Abrupt. He does not mince words. If he does not like something, he says so without hesitation. And when he does not like other friends of mine, he does not spare my feelings in telling me."

"Is he cruel?" Annie wrinkled her nose. "One thing I simply cannot tolerate is cruelty."

"I wouldn't say cruel," Giovanni replied. "It's just that he doesn't censor himself. Still, I value his friendship. The problem now, dear Annie, is that he and I have an argument over an unsigned painting."

"Oh, that's a shame. You mean, you disagree on the price?"

"Not that. He insists the painting is by a famous painter, and I say it is not."

"Well, in your field, how does one normally go about resolving these arguments?"

"There are special laboratories that analyze the pigments, X-ray the artwork, and other scientific procedures that determine the work's age. If the time period is correct, then art historians are hired to judge the work's authenticity. The entire process can be very expensive."

"I don't know much about art," she said. "Would the painting be worth a lot if it is done by this famous artist?"

"Oh, yes." Giovanni chuckled. "I would not have to work for a long while, if it is. But I doubt it."

Annie twiddled strands of her blond hair. "Still, Gio, what if it's the real thing? I would go mad, not knowing for sure. It's like, well, like being a semi-finalist in a contest and never finding out if you've won." Annie looked back at the counter. It was getting close to the lunch hour and three customers were waiting. She got up from the table.

Giovanni rose with her. "Annie, you make a very good point. I must think seriously about what you've said."

"And think seriously about coming by more often, will you?" She gave him a peck on the cheek and then hurried off to help the waiting customers.

~

Filled with food and lighter cheer, Giovanni walked back to St. James's and to his studio. He came off the elevator, unlocked the door, and punched in the last of the security codes.

He sat at his desk and thought about all that had happened since the painting had first startled him with its disembodied voice. His life had been jolted so abruptly that all he had taken for granted was now unpredictable, uncomfortable, unrecognizable.

Giovanni realized that the Count had become a reliable source of distraction from his woes. But at the same time, the conversations they had, in a very real sense, took him away from the normal realm. Even talking to Annie, he regulated his words so that she would not think he had lost his mind. Giovanni's behavior had changed dramatically since he had opened that crate. He felt haunted. Then Giovanni had a new thought, as the murky noon sun struggled through the window in front of him. He wondered if his father had heard the Count's voice. If so, it must have startled him too. But if true, his father had never shared the secret with him, as Giovanni had with his son.

He wanted the answers to these questions and more. He went to the strong room, brought out the painting, and set it on the easel.

"Hello and good afternoon, Count. Are you there?"

"I am not likely to be anywhere else, am I?"

Giovanni smiled. He was beginning to enjoy the Count's sardonic responses.

"I told my son about you."

"Then surely he felt remorse for his insults directed at me."

"Not really," Giovanni said. "If I had to guess, he's more worried about me. He probably thinks I'm entering a period of dementia."

"Do you think you are imagining my voice, Signor Fabrizzi?"

"No," Giovanni stated flatly. "But my son does."

"Then he questions the information I have shared with you."

"He thinks I read it in a book and just don't remember."

"Hmm," the Count murmured. "Some are apt to choose the first supposed explanation, however improbable."

"He's right though," Giovanni said. "It's all improbable. I don't have an answer to explain it."

"I do," the Count shot back. "My spirit is alive, simple as that, and no amount of your trying to explain it, scientifically and rationally, will ever suffice."

"Can't you understand?" Giovanni said. "I feel like I have a secret life that I have to hide from others. Where is your humanity?"

"My humanity," the Count replied, "is trapped inside of a painted panel that has been generally ignored for hundreds of years. And worse, you nor anyone else will recognize that I have been painted by one of the greatest artists who ever lived."

"Not Botticelli again." Giovanni shook his head. "Please, let's not go into that. You didn't finish telling me about Sergei, Catherine's son. He took you to Paris. What happened?"

"I have no intention of discussing more of my past until you have me examined and see that I was painted by Botticelli."

Giovanni sighed. "Come on, don't be that way. I've had a lovely day visiting my old neighborhood, and I don't need you spoiling it."

The Count remained silent.

Giovanni continued, "If experts in my field don't agree that you were painted by Botticelli, I'm going to look very foolish."

"The potential gains," the Count said, "which I am certain will result, outweigh your imagined disgrace, were you right and I were wrong. Verifying my authenticity will make you a wealthy man."

Giovanni recalled Annie's analogy—it was like being in a contest and never learning the results. Even her logic was difficult to argue against.

"I'll consider it," Giovanni said. "Now tell me what happened to Sergei."

"I am not asking you to consider the possibility," the Count said. "I want your promise that you will have my portrait examined."

"All right," Giovanni relented. "I will make this agreement with you, and I always honor my word. If you will just for today tell me about your time in France, I will agree to send you to a laboratory for analysis."

"Do you swear?"

"Yes. I swear."

"As a gentleman and restorer?"

"Yes, Count."

"I agree to your terms," the Count said. "But I must warn you, Signor Fabrizzi, my time in France was a disturbing period."

"Did something bad happen to Sergei?" Giovanni rolled his desk chair closer to the easel and sat down.

"It was appalling," the Count replied. "When we arrived in Paris, Sergei was given the name of a lady who lived just off the Avenue George V. She was an American. A professional widow. She made a career of marrying rich elderly men, soon to expire, and inheriting their fortunes. However, her apartment was rundown and suffered from countless leaks that she had neglected to repair."

"You stayed in her apartment."

"Thank God, no. With all those leaks from the apartment above, I would have been in great danger. The lady had two servants' rooms on the top floor. They were small but had a pleasant enough view. She allowed Sergei to stay in these rooms rent-free, provided he walked her hideous little dog three times a day and serve as her butler whenever she entertained, which was often. He was also required to do some shopping and cooking. It was at Avenue George V that Sergei realized he was a homosexual. The American lady surrounded herself with many such men, regularly inviting them to her frequent parties. There was a former Mexican male prostitute, a Portuguese jeweler, an Italian florist, an American antique dealer, several hairdressers, and an assortment of designers, actors, and poets. A particular fellow, another Russian whose name was Antinko Fetisov, seduced Sergei. I believe Antinko was attracted to Sergei's exotic appearance, with his long hair and angular features. I myself have never seen a man with so small a waist. In any case, their relationship developed and Antinko invited Sergei to move into his opulent apartment on Rue Jacob in Saint Germain des Prés. So that became my next home. Antinko also offered Sergei a monthly stipend to work full-time as a dress designer."

"Sounds like he did all right for himself," Giovanni said. "But was he still a thief? Earlier, you said Sergei stole money from his grandfather while the poor man slept."

The Count hesitated. "The acts I witnessed in Paris did not include further thievery. Perhaps he had reformed. Perhaps his change of interests was a factor. Sergei was very fond of clothing design, among other passions. He soon established a reputation for designing attractive Cossack-style blouses with ample embroidery and with emeralds and sapphires for buttons. He designed flamboyant pajamas and elegant headdresses for evening wear as well as small, chic handbags. He was also well known for his accented waistlines."

"I get it." Giovanni assumed that he had detected a pattern to the Count's stories. "Your owners. At first they are successful and rise to the top, so the fall is that much harder."

"I would not say that is true in all cases. The story of Sergei ends when we parted. You see, Antinko did not have a great eye for fine art, and he told Sergei to sell me because he did not like my portrait. Can you imagine that? More concerned with pleasing his lover, Sergei took me to one of his favorite clients, Henri Meyerstein, and proposed that he should become the new owner of my portrait. For a price, of course."

"But you were a gift from his mother," Giovanni said. "Then he sells you? That little creep. But maybe I don't get it. You said it was appalling. It's not that terrible."

"Sergei did not have a terrible end," the Count said. "In fact, I later learned that he had become enormously successful, famous even. It was his acts of decadence, many of which I was forced to witness, that were appalling beyond description. I was hung in their bedroom, you understand."

"Oh." Giovanni realized, "You mean, you watched them..."

"Yes," the Count replied. "Pry no further, please. Certain details are best to remain unsaid."

Giovanni nodded. "Agreed. What about your new owner? Monsieur..."

"Monsieur Meyerstein, and his family. Oh how I loved them, and their home as well, an apartment on Avenue Foch, which was richly decorated with other artwork. I was in very good company, you could say. They were much better owners, perhaps, I might even say, superior to all of my previous owners. Not only kind, Monsieur Meyerstein was a striking man. Tall, dashing, and very elegant. He would walk out of the house every day with a top hat, cape, and a silver-handled cane."

"And his wife?"

"She was great reason for my love of their household. You see, Carmella was from Florence. Elegant and beautiful. When she laughed it was like a Tchaikovsky symphony. The Meyersteins were great patrons of the arts, music, ballet, and theater. I still recall how Monsieur Meyerstein, when he first saw me, went to the end of the dining room and held me aloft, proudly. I was so happy to hang there, able to witness their children, Daniel and Elise, grow up and prosper. I would have been proud to spend generations on their wall at Avenue Foch."

"Would have?" Giovanni said. "What happened?"

"German soldiers came to Paris," the Count replied.

"The Nazis. World War II."

"War indeed. There were countless soldiers and many noisy vehicles. I shall never forget the sight of Monsieur and Madame Meyerstein as they stood by the window, tears in their eyes, as troops marched through the streets. A few days later, four soldiers, dressed in black uniforms and boots, burst into the apartment. They dragged off poor Monsieur and Madame Meyerstein and their children, Elise and Daniel. The soldiers also took Madame's sister and brother-in-law, who lived in an apartment one floor up, and their daughter Clara as well."

"Took them where?"

"I did not accompany them," the Count said, "so I cannot say with certainty."

"They were Jewish," Giovanni realized.

"Yes."

"I know where they went," Giovanni said. "Probably Auschwitz."

"The Meyersteins loved me as much as I loved them. After they were taken away, I never saw them again. Please, tell me their fate."

"It's complicated," Giovanni said. "I'll explain later. What happened after that?"

"I remained in the apartment in the days that followed. German soldiers came in and out, taking things away, it seemed at their whim. They were quite an odd group. When greeting others, the soldiers would snap their heels, stiffen their posture, and extend one arm as if pointing to the sky. I found their excessive theatrics rather absurd. They completed the ritual by hailing their leader, Hitler. I did not know of the man other than the soldier's overzealous loyalty to him, as if he were a god to them."

"His reign over Germany is a dark note in history," Giovanni said. "I'll explain later. Tell me what happened to your portrait."

"The soldiers took many items but were instructed not to touch any of the artwork, of which the Meyersteins had a considerable collection, my portrait included, of course. Some days passed and then two men visited, one clothed in an extravagant military uniform. He appeared intent to let the world know of his importance. The other man was not so pretentious, clothed in a typical jacket and trousers. They spent some time in the apartment inspecting the artwork. As they examined items and spoke to one another, I learned more about the two men. The civilian appeared to be an art historian, acting as an advisor to the man in uniform, whose name was Bruno Lothar. He was definitely in charge, and their task appeared to be the gathering of artwork throughout Paris, which as spoils of war, had become the property of Germany."

"It wasn't theirs to take," Giovanni said. "But that's another story. However, now I wonder about your portrait. Did you realize the danger you were in?"

"Their visit was by no means pleasant, though I had not sensed danger. What danger do you speak of?"

"You're unsigned," Giovanni said. "Knowing the Nazis, you'd probably have made good fuel for a bonfire."

The Count gasped. "Heavens, I had no idea the soldiers did such things."

"That and plenty more, far worse. What happened when the men saw your portrait?"

"As they strolled through the apartment, the historian gave his opinion of the various items, primarily their value. Then they both stopped in front of me. They stood there for a couple of minutes appraising my portrait. When Lothar asked the historian if it seemed like a valuable work, the historian replied that it would have been, if it had been signed by a major artist.

"*Herr Lothar,*" the historian said. "*As I doubt the Fuhrer or Reichsmarschall Goering would want this painting, would it be all right if I took this one for myself?*"

Lothar replied, "*Who in the Reich would want an unsigned faux renaissance painting? By all means, Kreitel, it is yours.*"

"Kreitel?" Giovanni became perplexed. "I've seen that somewhere before. Recently." He was certain that he had but struggled to remember where. He went to the strong room and found the crate in which the Count had been shipped, picked it up, and twisted it around to view all sides. There it was, in black spray-painted stencil lettering on the side of the crate, the name Kreitel.

"The historian's name was Kreitel?" Giovanni stepped out of the strong room.

"That is how Lothar addressed him."

"Any first name?" Giovanni asked.

"Lothar and other soldiers only referred to him as Kreitel."

"How is it spelled?" Giovanni glanced past the open door to the strong room, beyond which he could see the stencil lettering on the crate.

"I do not know," the Count said. "I have only their spoken words."

Giovanni realized somewhere else he had seen the name, and it was before he ever saw the crate. Long before. He approached the portrait. "Lothar called him Kreitel. Are you absolutely positive?"

"Of course I am," the Count said. "They were standing directly before me, as you are now. How could I be mistaken? Then Lothar instructed other soldiers to take my portrait from the wall and put me in a crate."

Giovanni seized the painting from the easel.

"What are you doing?" the Count asked.

"Putting you away." Giovanni entered the strong room.

"But why?"

"I have a hunch. I'll explain later."

"When will you return?" the Count asked. "Are you going to honor your promise to have me tested?"

"Later." Giovanni reached for the crate in which the painting had been shipped. He held up the panel and stared at the painted face of the Count. "Are you certain his name was Kreitel? Could it have been another name that sounds similar?"

"Signor Fabrizzi. His name was indeed Kreitel. I would not lie. I am a man of honor."

"You are not a man. You are a painting. And if you are wrong, I will reduce you to ashes, whether you were painted by Botticelli or not."

Giovanni slid the painting back into its wooden prison.

9

Many years earlier, Giovanni had seen the name Kreitel but had long since forgotten the incident. After all, he was only a child, and he had made an innocent assumption, which remained plausible into his adult years. His father never explained otherwise, so Giovanni clung to his youthful conclusion and never probed further.

It was shortly after Giovanni's tenth birthday when his father took him to the family studio, the first of many visits during which Federico would pass on the craft of art restoration to his son. As a young boy, Giovanni had much to learn and his curiosity was boundless. To him it was only a wooden box, but years later he would realize that it was a humidor, likely containing fine cigars. However, whether it contained cigars or other secrets, he would never learn. It all began when he came across the wooden box and noticed the brass plaque affixed to the lid, engraved with the name *Kreitel*.

When Giovanni asked what was in the box, his father became secretive and hid the box in a cabinet. "I'll explain it to you when you're older," he had said. Giovanni thought little of the event until he became a teenager and realized the reason for his father's odd reaction—he was simply shielding a child from a parent's addiction to tobacco. Or so Giovanni had thought.

It was nothing of the sort, Giovanni realized after the Count's story of Paris. There was more. There was something his father didn't want Giovanni to know. He had to find out who *Kreitel* was, and he had to know if it were true—the individual had helped the Nazis steal Jewish art.

~

Giovanni went home and logged on to his computer. He opened an Internet browser and prepared to search. For a moment he stared at the screen, uncertain of the words he wanted to enter. After his conversation with the Count, he was disturbed and couldn't think straight.

He entered *stolen Jewish art Nazis* and came upon a number of websites that looked official, in England, the United States, Germany, France, and elsewhere. Several sites had information about European looting during World War II. After studying countless pages, Giovanni learned that twenty percent of all European art had been seized by the Nazis, and over 100,000 works of art had never been recovered.

Giovanni focused his research on Paris, where the Meyersteins had lived when their art was taken. The Nazi unit responsible for confiscating artwork had a description that sounded innocent enough, the *Special Staff for Pictorial Art*. The group had been established in October of 1940 in Paris and was overseen by an organization known as the *Einsatzstab Reichsleiter Rosenberg*, the ERR. The Jewish possessions, taken from galleries, warehouses, and private homes, were stored and cataloged at an art museum in the Tuileries Gardens, called the Jeu de Paume, which oddly had once been an indoor tennis court.

The more Giovanni read, the more it astounded him. The appropriated artwork went from the Jeu de Paume to the Louvre, where it was stored, if not shipped to the personal collections of Adolf Hitler or Reichsmarschall Hermann Göring, or sold to raise cash for the Reich.

But the Count had said the Meyersteins' art was also sold via Bruno Lothar. Next Giovanni searched for *Kreitel* but could not find anything linking the name with any individual connected to the Reich.

Giovanni discovered there was a major research center at the National Archives in America, in College Park, Maryland, containing twenty million pages of materials. He found another center in Washington, D.C., operated by the National Holocaust Museum. Closer to him was the Bundesarchiv, the German Federal Archives, as well as the French Diplomatie, the Diplomatic Archive Center of the Ministry of Foreign and European Affairs.

Giovanni had obviously known of Nazi looting during World War II, but prior to that moment, he had no specific knowledge of it, nor any idea of how far-reaching their activities had been. Countless works of art were involved. It was nearly impossible to imagine anyone discovering more details about the Meyersteins, Kreitel, or the Count. If the painting had been by a specific artist, with a specific title, and within a certain time period, it might have been easier.

Giovanni leaned back from the computer screen and stretched his arms. He had spent three solid hours researching without rest. He wasn't tired, though, nor hungry. He was strangely energized, on a mission to learn the truth. If only he had similar zeal for restoring the Brueghel in his studio, which he hadn't touched in over a week.

He went to the kitchen and made a pot of tea. He poured a cup and sipped it, but the tea was too hot to drink, so he took it with him back to the computer and set his cup on the desk. As the tea cooled, he resumed his search, this time entering *stolen Jewish art largest research center.*

A website appeared for the International Tracing Service, or ITS, in Bad Arolsen, Germany. The facility housed fifty million pages in thousands of cabinets of information spread across six buildings, contributed by eleven countries. When the Allies entered the concentration camps during the final days of the war, they found meticulous details about the transportation and extermination of Jews as well as gypsies, homosexuals, mentally ill, and political radicals. The materials were taken by US forces and stored in Bad Arolsen prior to the International Red Cross forming the ITS. Giovanni concluded the ITS was his best chance to learn more.

But he also felt an urge to visit the Jeu de Paume in Paris. Also, his father had lived in Paris before moving to London, and he had spoken of friends and clients there. Giovanni could not remember their names, but he knew where to find them.

The tea had cooled enough and Giovanni took a sip. In a drawer of his desk, he had stored some of his father's belongings. There were letters he had sent to Giovanni, some pen and ink sketches from his father's art school days, and most importantly, a battered red leather address book.

Giovanni flipped through the pages, each in his father's hand-writing. Some of the names were recognizable but most were not. He scanned the pages for addresses in Paris.

He jotted down two entries from Paris although they were unfamiliar to him. He had nearly reached the last pages when he found the Paris address and phone number for *Jean and Mathilde Touissant*. He could not recall their faces, but Giovanni had the faintest memory of his father mentioning Jean before. He had been a client who had paintings restored from time to time by the Fabrizzis.

Giovanni wondered if, after so much time had passed, the Touissants could still be at the address and phone number listed. More than likely they were dead. If not, they would have to be in their late eighties, at least.

He reached for the telephone and dialed the number, fully expecting to get a disconnected message or a person who had never heard of the Touissants.

On the fourth ring, a man with a gravelly voice answered. Giovanni responded in his serviceable, although English-accented French, and politely asked if the person who answered was Jean Touissant. When the person confirmed that he was, Giovanni was truly surprised, but also thrilled.

"Monsieur Touissant," Giovanni said, "I am calling from London. My name is Giovanni Fabrizzi. My father, Federico, was an art restorer in Paris for a short time before he moved to London. I believe you knew him. I found your name in his address book."

"Fabrizzi?" Jean asked. There was a long pause, then a gasp. "*Mon dieu!* Federico. Yes, yes. How is he?"

"I'm sorry to say that he is no longer with us. But I am planning to visit Paris in the near future, and I was hoping to meet you and perhaps share some pictures I have of my father with you. It would mean a lot to me."

"Of course," Jean said. "I am sorry about your father. We are not so young ourselves, Mathilde and I."

Giovanni confirmed the Touissants' address and promised to call them the following week when he would be in Paris. He hung up the phone, exhilarated by the good fortune of actually finding one of his father's past contacts. He had not told Jean the true intent of his visit.

~

Energized by his new quest, Giovanni's hands trembled as he unlocked the door to his studio. He stepped back and chided himself, "Take it easy. What are you so excited about?"

He opened the door, deactivated the alarms, and went directly to the second strong room. Not only the portrait, he also brought out the crate in which it was shipped, then pulled out the portrait and set it on the easel. It was a bright day, not warm but sunny outside, and plenty of light streamed in through the windows. Nevertheless, Giovanni turned on every light in his work area.

The Count groaned. "Is there a reason for the excessive light? It is so bright."

Giovanni opened a drawer of his desk and pulled out his trusty Nikon 35 millimeter SLR, which had served him for decades. The new-fangled digital camera that Arabella had bought him a few months earlier was perhaps handy at social events, as it would fit in his shirt pocket, but the task at hand required the utmost quality. He pulled up the winding knob to open the Nikon and dropped in a canister of color film. Once lining up the sprockets and feeding the end into the spool, he shut the camera back and advanced the roll to the first frame.

"May I ask what you are doing?" The Count was becoming concerned.

Giovanni stepped back and adjusted his stance until the Count's portrait filled the viewfinder nicely and appeared square. Then he took shots from various angles.

"I consider it rude that you are ignoring me," the Count said. Then with a chord of fear, he asked, "You are hearing me, yes?"

"I'm taking photographs of you," Giovanni said. "Like the image you saw on my desk, of Serafina and Mau." He continued to snap the shutter.

After modeling for a few more shots, the Count sighed. "Spare me the details of your world's glorious progress. It is all so complicated and only bores me."

"Good." Giovanni knelt down and captured images of the crate as well, up close. "Saves me the trouble of having to explain it all."

The Count remained silent as more pictures were taken, then he proposed, "You are planning to show these images to people who will prove I am painted by Botticelli, yes?"

"No. I will take you to a laboratory as I promised, where they will make an analysis, and then, if necessary, others will examine you to confirm your creator's identity."

"Then what is the reason for the images, these photographs as you call them, if you would be good enough to explain?"

Giovanni smiled secretively. "I'm going to show them to some friends of my father's. I want to see if they recognize you."

"Why not simply invite them here?"

"Because they live in Paris," Giovanni replied. "To tell you the truth, Count, I am going to do some research about you. In France and in Germany."

"What about my laboratory authentication as a work of Botticelli?"

"I'll get to that after I come back," Giovanni said. "I told you—I am a man of my word. I most certainly will be in this case."

"I should very much hope so."

Giovanni finished rewinding the film and opened the camera. "One last thing before I go, Count. Have you told me everything you know about Bruno Lothar and the other man, Kreitel?"

"Of course."

"You haven't left out any details?" Giovanni waited for an answer but the Count did not reply. "I mean," Giovanni continued, "any little detail that will be helpful in tracing your background."

"I don't understand," the Count said. "You should send me to the laboratory this instant. Furthermore, I am perplexed by your reaction to my last story. You became very upset, and I have no idea why."

Giovanni wasn't ready to tell the Count, or anyone else, the reason for his upset. First he had to confirm a few details. "Let's just say the behavior of the Nazis, in general, and specifically toward the Meyersteins, angered me greatly. In any event, I must get going." He lifted the painting off the easel.

"Just a moment," the Count said. "When are you coming back?"

"It won't be more than a week, I imagine." Giovanni slipped the painting into the crate. "But I must dash. I'm leaving tomorrow and I still have to pack."

"Wait." From inside the crate, the Count's voice was muffled. "Why are you so eager to know about the Meyersteins and Lothar?"

"Sorry." Giovanni smirked. "Can't hear you, Count. See you in a week!"

Giovanni returned the crate to the second strong room, set the alarms, and locked his studio. With the roll of film in hand, he headed for the nearest one-hour photo developer.

～

While the photographs were being developed, Giovanni sat in a coffee shop and went over a checklist of things to pack. When he collected the prints and looked them over, he was pleased with the resolution of his camera and the crispness of the colors. The address on the crate was clearly readable. Next he needed someone who could analyze the handwriting, and to know if they could do it from a photograph. By his own visual inspection, he was fairly confident the handwriting would match, but to prove his hunch, he had to be absolutely certain.

Back at his flat, Giovanni searched the Internet and found a forensic services agency in London that could do the handwriting analysis. Upon calling them, he was pleased to learn that comparing a photograph to a Xerox copy was not a problem. He would not have to surrender the original letter, although doing so, they explained, would greatly improve the accuracy of their results. He assured them it would be good enough for his purpose and agreed to drop off the samples later that afternoon. Next he sorted through a box of family photos and picked out a few of his father and one blurry shot of his uncle Max. He added them to the envelope containing the prints of the Count and the crate in which he was shipped.

Then Giovanni dialed his son in Florence.

Flavio answered. He was apologetic, saying that he was working as fast as possible with Maurizio and that he would return to London soon.

Giovanni told him not to rush, and that he had called because he had some information to share with Maurizio.

"I'm looking forward to helping you when I get back," Flavio said.

"I'm sure, Flavio."

"How is it going with the Brueghel?"

The subject of the Brueghel was quickly becoming Giovanni's least favorite. "It's coming along fine," he replied. "But I really need to speak with Mau. Can you get him for me?"

"Hold on."

As Giovanni waited, he looked at his watch, then reviewed

his checklist again.

"Papa, how are you?" Maurizio said. "I was going to call you later this evening. Really. You just beat me to it."

"That's all right, Mau. I have some good news. I'm taking a little time off. I'm going on a trip to Paris and also to Germany."

"What about the Brueghel?"

"I'll get to that," Giovanni said. "Don't worry."

"But, Papa," Maurizio said. "Do you really think traveling is a good idea right now?"

Giovanni knew what his son really wanted to say. He questioned his father's sanity, and it was the only reason travel might not be a good idea. He needed to convince Maurizio so he would not doubt his father, not hound him, and not tell him he was in no condition to travel. And he didn't need everyone nagging him about the Brueghel, either.

"It's just for one week," Giovanni said. "Maybe less. I'm sure you'd agree, I need some time to relax."

"Of course," Maurizio said. "But... well, I guess I'm curious why you've chosen Paris and Germany."

Giovanni had already mentally rehearsed his excuses. "I want to see some exhibitions. I also contacted an art dealer in Paris who knew your grandpa. Did I ever mention Jean Touissant to you?"

"No, I've never heard you mention the name."

"The separation from Arabella has led me to think a lot about the past," Giovanni said. He felt good to say that because it was true. "I need to get away, see some great art, and visit some people from my past. Then I'll come back and finish the Brueghel. It will be a fresh start."

"Maybe some time away would help," Maurizio said. "But I should join you, don't you think?"

"Mau, enough. I'm a grown man. I don't need you to babysit me." For Giovanni, it wasn't a matter of getting his way. It was a matter of convincing Maurizio not to fight him. His son's resistance only made Giovanni feel worse about what he had to do, as if he were misbehaving. "I will come to Firenze as soon as I can, Mau. How about that?"

"That would be good," Maurizio said. "The sooner the better."

Maurizio made his father promise to call while traveling, to let him know that he was all right. He agreed and they said their good-byes.

Giovanni had done it. He was going on a trip to determine whether his worst suspicions were true. If they were, he didn't know how he would live with knowing it. But at the same time, he couldn't live with the question forever unanswered. No matter how it might affect him, he had to uncover the truth.

10

If he were still living with Arabella, Giovanni would have taken the opportunity to buy her a gift on Avenue Montaigne. Since the 1980s, the graceful Parisian street was home to high fashion stores like Dior, Chanel, Valentino, and the like. But instead, he wandered past the shop windows, killing time in the eighth arrondissement, prior to his appointment with Jean and Mathilde Touissant. The Golden Triangle of streets between Avenue Montaigne, the Champs Elysées, and Avenue George V provided him a breath of cleansing air after too many cloistered months back in London.

From his room at the Plaza Athénée Hotel, he called to confirm the time he would meet with the Touissants. It was an expensive hotel, but he had not traveled in so long that he felt the need to indulge himself. Exhausted, he wanted to be close to the Touissants. And why not pamper himself a little, he thought. His trip could wind up being very unpleasant, so he might as well enjoy himself before things possibly turned sour.

Giovanni was impressed by the opulence of Avenue Montaigne. He stopped in front of an expensive jewelry store. The display of glittering diamonds seemed ironic considering that, decades earlier, the Nazis exerted their evil influence over the whole area, which then boasted mostly art galleries.

Giovanni checked his watch and saw that it was exactly two o'clock. He took out the map he had printed from the Internet and followed the thick blue line he had drawn, off Avenue Montaigne and around one corner, to the building where the Touissants lived.

He climbed their stairs and pressed the bell. He was greeted by a round-faced, white-haired woman well into her eighties, who introduced herself as Mathilde. She welcomed Giovanni into their home and Jean appeared immediately, wearing a black velvet smoking jacket as if the occasion were a formal dinner.

Mathilde offered Giovanni coffee and pastries as he sat with Jean at the dining room table. The three of them enjoyed the tasty éclairs and sipped from their fine bone china cups. Giovanni talked of his father and how Fabrizzi & Sons had prospered in London. Jean and Mathilde asked about some of their clients and the artists whose work had been entrusted to the Fabrizzis.

As the pleasantries subsided, Giovanni took the opportunity to pull out a small black and white photograph of his parents, taken in Paris just before they moved to London. He handed it to Jean, who held it up so Mathilde could also view it. He sweetly put his arm around her as their failing eyes strained to examine the snapshot.

"It's a photograph of the time when you knew him." Giovanni gave them a moment to absorb the image and whatever memories it might bring to them.

"Your father was a wonderful man," Jean said. "Such a gusto for life. Whenever I saw him on the street, he would excitedly tell me what he was restoring and tell me of this gallery opening or that artist whose work had sold recently. Mathilde and I met many of his friends through events he invited us to attend." Jean's mood darkened. "I was very sad to see your father go," he said. "But it was for the best. His decision to flee was a wise choice. Life became very difficult after the Germans invaded."

Aiming to be polite, Giovanni decided they had spoken enough about his family. "And how have you been since my parents left Paris?"

"We have been fortunate," Jean said. "We lived through the Occupation and the strange and unpredictable world of fine art. And here we are, at the end of our lives, with some pains here and there, but little else to complain about."

Mathilde smiled and patted Jean on the shoulder, then she got up from the table and shuffled toward the kitchen.

Giovanni asked permission to look at some of the paintings on their walls, and Jean urged him to do so without getting up to join him. When Giovanni was done, he returned to the table, where Jean still held the photograph of his parents.

"Jean, I know it was very long ago," Giovanni said, "and you met hundreds of people in the art world, but I need to ask you about someone in particular."

"I'll try my best." His eyes twinkled with mischief. "But don't count on me for too much."

Giovanni smiled, then proceeded to the reason for his visit. "I have a painting that I think belonged to a Parisian family, the

Meyersteins. It was taken from them after the Germans invaded France."

Jean shook his head. "I don't recognize the name."

"No, it's someone else I want to know about. I have in London, well, let's call him a researcher. He insists, because he knew the Meyersteins, that after they were taken away by the Nazis, a man named Bruno Lothar who worked—"

"Lothar!" Jean blurted out. "That bastard helped the Nazis choose which art was most valuable. Helped them steal it! Well, whatever he didn't steal for himself. He was very close to Goering, you know. Provided most of his personal collection."

"Yes, I've read about Lothar. But it's someone else I am interested in. Jean, did you ever deal with anyone named Kreitel?"

"Kreitel?" He thought for a moment, but the name didn't appear to strike a memory. "What was his first name?"

"I don't know," Giovanni replied. "He was an advisor, or an art dealer, I think. He worked with Lothar, who supposedly allowed him to take the painting I now have, when artwork was confiscated from the Meyerstein home."

Jean closed his eyes and rubbed his temples, as if trying to make the memory return by magic.

Giovanni felt terrible, making this kind, old man recall a period of his life that was surely the worst, for him and his country. And the prospect of an answer from Jean was no comfort either. If Jean didn't remember, the mystery would still eat at Giovanni. And if Jean did remember, it would tear Giovanni apart.

Jean stopped rubbing his temples and opened his eyes. "I am sorry." He shrugged and one end of his mouth turned up, an odd but endearing expression of helplessness. "This is what you wanted to know most, and I cannot help you."

"It's all right," Giovanni said, though he had hoped for more.

Mathilde returned to the dining room with a fresh pot of coffee.

"Please," Jean insisted, "let me pour you more coffee." Jean did so before Giovanni could politely decline, sated as he was already. It was clear that Jean wanted him to stay longer, and Giovanni had no immediate plans to leave for Bad Arolsen. He enjoyed the idea of spending more time in Paris.

"Mathilde, darling," Jean said as he poured her another cup. "Do you remember, during the Occupation, whether we ever met someone named Kreitel?"

"Kreitel?" She sat down at the table.

"He was an art historian," Giovanni said. "Or perhaps a dealer."

"Was he a Nazi?" Mathilde asked.

"I'm not sure, but I don't think so," Giovanni said. "I think he might have been an advisor to Bruno Lothar."

Mathilde shook her head.

Giovanni nodded though the lack of solid answers was frustrating. "Would you mind if I used your..." He searched for the right word. "Uh, bathroom?"

They both looked at him blankly.

He stood up. "Perhaps my French is not the best." He smiled. "The toilet?"

Jean nodded and pointed to a hallway. "The second door on the right."

"Thank you." Giovanni started toward their bathroom, *loo*, water closet, or whatever one called it in polite company.

"Wait," Mathilde called out.

Giovanni halted.

"What is it?" Jean asked.

"Kreitel," she said.

Giovanni hurried back to the table. "Yes?"

"I think I remember." She looked at Jean. "It was maybe 1940, or 41. Do you remember the art dealer who came to our door and tried to sell us work? Wasn't his name Kreitel?"

"I vaguely remember a man," Jean said, "and we refused to buy, but I don't recall his name. I don't even recall why we didn't buy." He chuckled. "Your memory, my darling, has survived far better than mine."

Mathilde reminded him, "We thought the art was taken from Jewish homes."

"Really?" Giovanni asked. "Why did you think that?"

"It was suspicious," she said. "He did not have a gallery. He went to people's homes with canvasses."

"That was not unusual," Jean said. "The art market was absurdly inflated when the Nazis came in. Whether people sold stolen art or legitimate art, the prices went up two to three hundred percent during the Occupation."

"But this Kreitel," Giovanni said. "Mathilde, this is so important to me. Do you remember what he looked like?"

"Would it matter?" she asked. "He would look much different today, if he is even still alive."

Giovanni reached into his jacket and brought out the envelope of photographs. He quickly sifted through, selected one of the Count's portrait, and handed it to Mathilde.

"Is there any possibility," Giovanni asked, "the man you think might be Kreitel tried to sell you this painting?"

She studied the photograph in silence, during which the only sound was the ticking of a clock on the mantle.

"I do not know this painting." She passed the photo to Jean. "We didn't buy anything from the man, as we feared the art was taken from Jewish families. If he was the man you are seeking, you are right to suspect that he was not a Nazi. I am sure his name began with K, and it was a German name, but he was not from Germany."

"Why would you say that?" Giovanni asked.

She smiled. "When an Italian man attempts to speak French..."

Jean added, "No offense." He formed a wry grin. "Signor Fabrizzi."

Giovanni knew his French was imperfect but assumed his years of speaking English was to blame. He was surprised they could detect his Italian heritage from his accent. However, his brief moment of embarrassment was quickly pushed aside by the implications of the new information.

"No, none taken," Giovanni said. "This is important. It's very good."

Giovanni was swept away by his thoughts. This detail was the first solid clue that could lead to Kreitel. But he had to ask himself— would doing so prove to be a wise choice?

"Monsieur Fabrizzi," Mathilde said. "Tell us, what does this man Kreitel mean to you?"

Giovanni took a moment to consider his response, which he was not ready to share. "I'd rather not say, actually. That is, before I've confirmed my hunch. I hope you understand."

Together they nodded, then Mathilde said, "I'm so glad if I have helped."

"You have, greatly," Giovanni said.

Jean asked, "Will you be in Paris for a time?"

"Yes. I'm interested in doing more research about Kreitel and the painting. In fact, I think I will go to the Jeu de Paume."

"Then you must speak with our friend, Adele St. Martin," Jean said. "She was well acquainted with Rose Valland, the heroine of the Jeu de Paume."

"Really?" Giovanni was surprised. "Do you have her number?"

"Don't be silly," Jean said. "She is one of our closest friends." He got up from the table and started out of the room.

Giovanni wondered if he had made some cultural error, or if he had been too presumptuous. Before Giovanni could ask Mathilde if he had done something wrong, he heard Jean's voice in the kitchen. His voice became clearer when he returned to the dining room with a cordless phone into which he was speaking.

"Yes, Adele, he is a researcher and restorer, and I knew his father," Jean explained. "Do you think you might give him a tour of the Jeu de Paume? Wonderful. Hold on a moment."

The twinkle had returned to Jean's eyes. "This is Adele St. Martin," he whispered while covering the mouthpiece. "She is the perfect person for you to see."

Giovanni's heart was filled with appreciation.

Jean Toussaint handed the phone to an excited, though inexperienced, and elderly but newly energized, researcher in the field of stolen Jewish art.

~

An hour early for his appointment with Madame St. Martin, Giovanni sat on a bench outside the Jeu de Paume, content to watch the comings and goings of those enjoying the surroundings of the Tuileries Gardens. To the south was the Musée de l'Orangerie, the museum that had once housed Monet's *Water Lilies*. During his research, Giovanni learned that the building and exhibition had been slightly damaged during the Nazi incursion.

At the appointed time, Giovanni noticed an older woman who, despite her stocky physique and short legs, strode resolutely toward the Jeu de Paume, swiveling her head to and fro, looking for someone. Most likely searching for a man who fit Giovanni's self-description that he provided over the phone the day before.

Giovanni waved and she rapidly approached. He had guessed right and Madame St. Martin introduced herself. She was younger than the Touissants, in her early seventies, Giovanni estimated. Despite her age, she moved with a determined stride, and they entered the museum together. Giovanni prepared to pay for their tickets but Madame St. Martin tapped his wrist and motioned to the woman behind the ticket counter, who evidently knew her and waved for them to continue inside.

Madame St. Martin expressed her pleasure to make Giovanni's acquaintance, and rather than ask him probing questions about his research, she rattled on, quietly but without taking a breath.

"And the Jeu de Paume housed much Impressionist art until it was transferred to the Musée D´Orsay. You have been there?"

"Yes, I have been there with my..." He paused. "With my wife. A lovely museum. Like this one."

A dark cloud came over Giovanni as he thought about Arabella. Madame St. Martin noticed and they walked in silence for a while, viewing the art and avoiding conversation.

The silence was broken when they both spoke at the same time, then they shared in light laughter. Giovanni prompted her to speak first.

"No," she said. "I have been talking too long. Please, Monsieur Fabrizzi, tell me about your research and how I can help."

Giovanni told her some of what he had come to believe regarding the Count's story of the Meyersteins. Of course, he did not mention that he had learned the information through a series of discussions with the painting itself. She certainly would have excused herself and virtually galloped away on her short, sturdy legs if he had done so.

"If my source is correct," Giovanni said, "Kreitel was either an employee of the Nazis, or at the very least, a friend of Bruno Lothar."

"I am very sorry to have to say this, as a French woman," Madame St. Martin quietly admitted, "but your man Kreitel could have been a Parisian who had knowledge about art, and the Nazis found him useful. Or he could have been a gallery owner who wanted the painting. There were also French black market dealers of stolen Jewish art who would resell works and make a living that way. Or he could have been a German who came here at Lothar's urging. Or a German who had settled in Paris and had known Lothar previously."

"I have reason to believe he wasn't German," Giovanni said. "Not French, either."

"I see," Madame St. Martin said as they paced the halls of the museum. "Well, that is not unusual, as great works of art, and those who treasure them, come from all corners of the world. However, and I regret to say it, but this fact only makes your search more difficult."

Giovanni nodded, and then he brought out a photograph of the Count's portrait. "And this?" He handed it to her.

She stopped and studied the image. Shaking her head, she handed it back. "I am sorry I could not be of more assistance to your research."

They continued to wander the museum in silence.

After a time, Giovanni asked, "You knew Rose Valland?"

"Yes. Before the Occupation, my parents took me here and they were friendly with Rose. She was the only staff member the Nazis retained when they took over, but they didn't know that she understood German, which is how she compiled details of where paintings were being transported. The information she provided to the Resistance kept countless works from harm and helped in their recovery later. If the Nazis had ever known, she would have been executed for sure."

"We have her to thank for the precious works that were saved." His sentiment was genuine, himself a lifelong conservator of fine art, though no match for the heroic efforts of Rose Valland. As

Giovanni understood it, she and others had catalogued all of the stolen art. So the records should include the Count's portrait, which according to his story, was in Paris at the time. But Giovanni found no reference to the painting in all of his hours spent searching the Internet. It didn't make sense—which could be the one clue to prove the Count was wrong. At the very least, prove that details of his story were inaccurate.

"There is one thing I need to understand," Giovanni said. "All stolen art came here for cataloging. Is it possible that a painting didn't come here? I guess the question is, did all paintings go through this museum, or are there others that I should investigate as well?"

"The Nazis made all kinds of deals with all kinds of people," Madame St. Martin explained. "Some ERR staff gave lesser known works away as gifts before they had any chance to arrive here. And someone like Lothar knew many people. He would dine at Maxim's regularly and was introduced to all sorts of people who would offer him information, trying to get close to him." She cleared her throat, suggesting her own moral universe, and continued, "Lothar was a womanizer as well. He had so much control that many wanted to benefit from his power. The truth, Monsieur Fabrizzi, is that any painting could easily have slipped through a multitude of cracks and ended up anywhere."

Giovanni felt ill.

"May we go outside?" he asked. "I could use some fresh air."

Madame St. Martin became concerned. She escorted Giovanni outside to find a bench and they sat down.

"Are you feeling better, Monsieur Fabrizzi?"

"I'm getting there," he replied, patting his sweaty forehead with a handkerchief. "Madame St. Martin. My research depends on eliminating all possibilities until only one remains. From what you've told me, it appears entirely possible that Kreitel took the painting before it was cataloged. And it's entirely possible that he was an art historian, or an art dealer, and he could have known Lothar, and perhaps he was even an advisor to him."

"Oh, yes," she said. "All are very possible."

Giovanni looked away, then gazed into the blank sky. "Or an art restorer." He did not direct the comment toward her nor did he expect a reply. Everything he had learned so far matched the Count's story, which only fueled the nausea welling up inside of him. His research was leading to the one possibility that he dreaded most.

11

Giovanni gladly would have spent more time in Paris, with not only his newfound friends, but with others whose names he had written down after finding them in his father's old address book.

But the Touissants had been surprisingly helpful, and more to the point, before leaving for his trip he had made an appointment with the International Tracing Service in Bad Arolsen, Germany. The ITS had agreed to allow him access to files with regard to his research on the Meyerstein family.

He transferred between several trains during his travel from Paris to Bad Arolsen, a spa town near Munich of less than 20,000 people. After a restless night's sleep in a small hotel, Giovanni rose early, had a light breakfast, and went out for a stroll in the chilly morning air.

There was time before his appointment at the ITS, so Giovanni took in some of the sights. He had read about the *Grosse Allee*, the Grand Avenue, and wanted to see it for himself. It was about a mile long, a wide, stately street that had been built in 1676. Comprised of 880 oak trees, laid out in lines of six, the Grand Avenue's leafy beauty was calming. Despite uncertainties about his life in London, and his current journey of discovery, Giovanni needed to savor the present moment. Walking the *Grosse Allee* was a great way to set his worries aside for a time.

After walking for over an hour, Giovanni checked his watch. It was time. He got out his mobile phone and called a taxi.

He arrived at the ITS complex, an unremarkable series of buildings that housed fifty million pages describing the fate of more than seventeen million people. Giovanni paid the driver and asked for his card, as he would need a ride back to his hotel. Then Giovanni walked the long path bordered by hedges that seemed to force visitors to focus on the doors of the main entrance directly ahead. As he drew closer, Giovanni wondered if coming to Bad Arolsen would lead to further clues, or turn out to be a dead end.

Past the entrance, Giovanni approached the front desk and his appointment was confirmed. He provided a security officer with his passport and then again answered the same question he was asked on the form that he had e-mailed to them from London. Namely, to describe the purpose of his research.

He could not tell the employees at the front desk, especially in his limited German, of all that had happened to him since opening the Count's crate. Even if he could, they would never believe him and might deny him access to their files, suspecting both his motives and his sanity.

In his initial contact with them, Giovanni realized that the Service was primarily for victims of the Nazi era, or family members of victims. He could not honestly tell them he was researching the death of a relative in the Holocaust. So he repeated what he had written to them—he was in possession of a work of art that, he believed, had belonged to a family that very likely perished in the camps. After all, it was the truth, at least, as far as he could trust the Count.

Having provided by e-mail the names of Henri Meyerstein, his wife Carmella, and their children Daniel and Elise, Giovanni had received a surprisingly rapid reply from Bad Arolsen, stating they did indeed have records on Meyerstein and his family. They offered to send copies of the files for a fee but Giovanni knew he had to research more than just the Meyersteins, so instead he made the appointment to appear in person.

Giovanni had been further motivated because the ITS documentation regarding the Meyerstein family meant two other important things to him. For one, whatever the explanation for his conversations with the Count, it was certain that Giovanni was not losing his mind. He had no previous knowledge of the family, their names, or if they even existed. To imagine such a thing defied all odds, leaving the most probable conclusion. However incredible, it was true—the long-dead subject of a painting had told him.

Also significant was that the Count, despite his mercurial temperament, had been historically accurate, at least about the Meyersteins. At first, Giovanni was unsure of how to process the Count's accusation of Arabella's infidelity. But as events progressed, between her admission of guilt and the ITS acknowledgment that the Meyersteins were in fact victims of the Nazi occupation of France, Giovanni had no reason to doubt anything else the Count asserted. Which meant, for the first time, Giovanni also had to consider the possibility, however ridiculous it may have seemed—perhaps the Count was telling the truth and Botticelli really had painted his portrait.

At the front desk of the ITS, Giovanni tried to explain in his rather uninspired German that he needed to find out if the entire Meyerstein family had perished in a concentration camp, but he didn't know how to say *concentration camp* in German.

"Do you wish to have help in English?" The woman at the desk had a German accent so thick, the phrase was likely all she had ever learned to say in English.

Giovanni thanked her and sat down on a black leather sofa in the waiting area. Minutes later, a gentleman came to greet him. Giovanni was surprised by the young man's tender age, which he gauged to be no more than late twenties. He had fine dark hair cut in a straight, solid curtain that concealed his forehead, and combined with the round spectacles that he wore, it gave him an owlish, intellectual look.

"I am Johannes Roedelius," the young lad said. "I have been assigned as your records liaison, to assist with your research."

Giovanni shook hands with Johannes and was grateful that he would no longer have to mangle the German language.

Johannes led the way to a room lined with lockers for clients to store their coats and other personal belongings, as nothing was allowed in the Reading Room except for a pen and paper. Giovanni hung up his coat and stowed his briefcase in the bottom of the locker.

Before proceeding, Johannes began a client orientation. He explained that more than ninety percent of their data was digitally referenced. The procedure entailed searching for information using one of the computer terminals in the Reading Room, and then the corresponding materials, housed elsewhere in the complex, would be retrieved.

Giovanni listened but he felt guilty for not telling Johannes the full scope of his mission. Of course he would be looking for information regarding the Meyersteins, the very reason they had granted him access, but he also wanted to learn more about Bruno Lothar and the mystery man, Kreitel.

Johannes continued the orientation. "Our database contains seventeen and a half million names, and it is important to realize that within that collection, many phonetic variations exist, due to different European countries and even slight surname variations within local regions. Entering the last name of a person for whom information is sought may not produce the expected result. In your case, however, it is fortunate that the name Meyerstein has no variations listed." He smiled. "I believe your search will prove successful. Our records are organized into three major sections: Incarceration, Forced Labor, and Displaced Persons. After study-ing your application, I would say the information you seek will be found in the Incarceration section."

Giovanni liked the young lad. He was well-mannered and eager to help, which only made Giovanni feel worse about his desire to search for other information.

"You can request up to three files at a time," Johannes explained, referring to groups of documents to be brought to the individual researcher. "You will see the checkbox on the screen, in the docu-ment list. On the right. Select the documents you wish to view, submit, and I will bring you the files."

An actual demonstration would have been better. Giovanni was not even at the computer yet and already he was struggling to keep up. Next Johannes directed Giovanni to the Reading Room, where a computer was reserved in his name. Nine other people were working at different terminals. He sat down in front of his and stared at the confusing screen. It didn't look like a normal browser. On the table was a sign to indicate that talking was not allowed in the room. That ruled out asking someone for help with the unintuitive screen. Giovanni glanced at the other people engrossed in their research. No one returned any glances, then Giovanni wondered if the others were searching for family who had perished in the Holocaust, and he felt bad for even glancing at them.

After a few minutes of studying the options, Giovanni began to understand how their system worked, which wasn't too difficult after all, just that it was unusual. He determined how to perform a search and entered Henri Meyerstein. Eight references to the name appeared on the screen. They were the initial matches that led the ITS to invite Giovanni to conduct his research at their site. He narrowed his choices down to the three that looked the most interesting. Then he had to find the checkbox that Johannes had described, which wasn't difficult, but he still didn't understand what the young man had meant by *submit*. Oh, Giovanni then realized, as it was right there on the screen—the big blue button with the word right in the center. He felt a bit foolish but also pleased that he could figure it out on his own. In minutes Johannes delivered the requested files.

It was uncomfortable for Giovanni to read about one of the most despicable periods in human history. He knew nothing about these people. As in really knowing about them. Among the Jewish friends he had known over the years, he had never asked any of them about the Holocaust. What was one supposed to say? How many in your family died? It was a topic of pain, and a topic to be avoided. Giovanni's knowledge of the Holocaust came, like so many, from documentaries with horrific images shown so many times that the danger of unemotional acceptance was present. He had seen movies about the Third Reich, and he had felt the revulsion of knowing that genocide occurred and could be rationalized. Giovanni thought about the Fascism that arose in his native country of Italy, led by Benito Mussolini, which only showed that no country, no people, were immune from mass insanity.

Giovanni knew, as people around the world knew, that the Nazis had tortured and killed millions. It had passed into the category of general knowledge. But handling the files on the Meyerstein family made it uncomfortably vivid. It was one thing to see the worn, black and white footage on a television program, showing the bodies of dead Jewish concentration camp prisoners being pushed into mass graves. But touching the paper, confirming the Meyerstein's transfer to Auschwitz, and knowing the gruesome manner in which the good people had perished, Giovanni could only imagine their terror, and it put an echo of that terror into his heart and mind that would not leave him, ever, from that day forward.

During his orientation, Giovanni had been given instructions on how to handle the documents brought to him in the Reading Room. He was not to hold them in his hands but to place them flat on the table. And he had to keep them in the order that he found them in the file. Giovanni stole glances at others. One elderly man wore white cotton gloves as he carefully handled fragile, onionskin typed pages.

Giovanni lost track of time as he studied the transport forms. The Meyersteins' initial incarceration was in Drancy, a transit camp just outside of Paris. Then they were taken to Auschwitz and separated. Their deaths—father, mother, sister, brother—were systematically noted, as if they were nothing more than shipments of a product, delivered to a warehouse. Each was recorded as merely a statistic.

Giovanni needed to pause. He had to question his motivations versus the purpose of the ITS. He thought about the victims and their families who came there from all over the world, hoping to gain some kind of closure, if they could even find that.

But it was his one opportunity to learn the truth—of more than just the Meyersteins. He wouldn't be coming back for a second visit, or ever again. It was time for him to discover the rest.

He entered Bruno Lothar and the screen began to scroll pages of information, far more than it had for Henri Meyerstein. Giovanni sifted through the text and selected three files dated 1940, then requested the files be brought to the Reading Room.

The room was silent except for the intermittent pecking at keyboards. Giovanni noticed that new researchers had replaced some of those who were busy at their terminals when he had first arrived. He wondered if they had found what they were looking for, and if they had, just how heartbreaking the resolution must have been. He thought about the Count and how he described his time in the Meyerstein's home on Avenue Foch. Of all his stories, theirs he expressed with great joy. And great sadness, when retelling of how they were hauled away by the Nazis.

Johannes delivered the requested files and departed without saying a word. Giovanni opened the first. Lothar was one of Goering's top advisors on the value of artwork, which Giovanni had already learned from the Internet. In fact, few details of his biography differed from the sites that Giovanni had already visited. However, the file contained far more images of the man, most of them newspaper clippings, along with many official documents. Giovanni turned page after page. One newspaper clipping featured Lothar holding court at Maxim's, posing with members of the Reich, several attractive women, and others unknown. In his youth, Lothar could have been a movie star. His slicked-back hair, sharp jawline, and piercing eyes made him appear cruelly seductive.

Some pages into the file, Giovanni found a document dated November 23, 1940. It was a listing of art taken from two residences on Avenue Foch. For an instant Giovanni lost his breath—one of the residences was the Meyerstein's. It was the very document he had hoped to find. Carefully, as if more precious than anything he had ever restored, he took it from the file and laid it flat on the table so that he could study it in detail. The document listed the names of the artists and titles of their work. He went down the long list, searching through the names, but nothing was identified as the work of Botticelli. And there was nothing listed as an unsigned painting. The proof he was searching for—that the Count's portrait was once a possession of the Meyerstein family—simply did not exist. But that lack of evidence, it could also be argued, supported the Count's claim that he was given away, the very reason the portrait was never cataloged at the time of acquisition nor its arrival at the Jeu de Paume.

At the bottom of the document, after all the paintings were listed, the name *B. Lothar* appeared as the officer in charge of the Meyerstein art appropriation. And listed as advisor, *W. Kreitel.*

Giovanni flopped back in his chair and stared up at the ceiling. It was all too incredible. The Count's story was true. And it was another discovery to support Giovanni's hunch, which gave him no satisfaction, rather it made him ill. He would need a photocopy of the document and found an option to request one. As he waited for Johannes to return, Giovanni realized that he was exhausted from hours of work without food, drink, or any break. His stomach was growling and the room was warm, the air stuffy. When he stood after sitting too long, he felt that he might faint. He left the open file on the table in the Reading Room and went back to the lockers where his coat and briefcase were stored. At the main desk, he asked the receptionist to let Johannes know that he would be waiting in the lobby. Giovanni sat on the black leather sofa, his head in his hands, wondering if he should have stayed in London and never embarked on this crazy stolen art investigation.

"Mr. Fabrizzi?" Johannes nudged him on the arm. "Are you feeling all right?"

Giovanni looked up at him. "Just a little tired."

Johannes sat down, then handed Giovanni the photocopy he had requested.

"Actually, I'm going to need three copies," Giovanni said, having failed to find an option to request multiple copies. "And please, would it be possible to have it on a compact disc?"

"Certainly," Johannes replied. "Did you find what you were looking for, Mr. Fabrizzi?"

"Yes." The word came out more as a breath than as an actual word.

"Then this is good."

"It doesn't feel good," Giovanni said.

"I understand. But you must remember, many come here and never find what they were looking for."

"I realize that." Giovanni looked at the photocopy. "It's one step closer, but the document doesn't prove my painting belonged to the Meyersteins. I now have to find this Kreitel. W. Kreitel," he corrected himself.

Johannes rose from the sofa.

"Herr Roedelius," Giovanni said. "Would you mind if I asked you a personal question?"

He sat back down. "You may ask. And you may call me Johannes."

Giovanni nodded. "All right, Johannes. Tell me, are you Jewish?"

"No, I'm a Lutheran."

"You are a young man, not Jewish, and you were not even alive when World War II occurred. I think it's wonderful that you care enough to do this work, but I'm curious as to why you chose to be here at the ITS."

"We who did not live during the Holocaust want to understand how it could happen. I, myself, feel it is a mystery how people can become so destructive toward their fellow humans. Working here is my chance to gain a better understanding of that. I may never fully understand what happened, but this is my personal effort to try."

"I too am trying to understand, in some small way." Giovanni straightened his posture as he caught himself slumping from exhaustion.

"You look very pale, Mr. Fabrizzi. Have you eaten lunch?"

Giovanni shook his head.

"You should go and have something to eat, and then come back. You still have three hours left, if you wish to research more."

"Danke, Johannes." Somewhat ashamed of his abrupt departure from the Reading Room, Giovanni said, "I'm sorry, but I left the files on the table."

"It's all right," Johannes said. "We will keep them aside for you."

Giovanni struggled to get up and Johannes helped him rise.

"Thank you," Giovanni said.

"Now find yourself a meal." Johannes smiled and escorted Giovanni toward the exit. "Then when you return, you may ask for me." He held the door open for Giovanni.

"You are a fine young man." Giovanni gently patted Johannes on the cheek.

"I will see you soon," he replied.

Giovanni walked out into the cool afternoon, struggling to dig out the taxi driver's card in his wallet, and then from his coat, he brought out his mobile phone.

12

Giovanni finished picking at his meal, a meaty stew with a sprinkling of carrots and potatoes. He sipped his coffee and reached the bottom of the cup, his clarity renewed by the surge of caffeine. Giovanni set the cup down and was taken by a new idea. He opened his briefcase and sorted through the notes he had brought from London.

Within his notes were the names the Count had mentioned while telling his story of the Meyerstein family in Paris. There was, of course, Henri and Carmella Meyerstein. And their children, Daniel and Elise. But another, which Giovanni had jotted down but not given more thought, was Henri and Carmella's niece, Clara, who lived upstairs in the same building. He had not searched the ITS database for Clara's name.

Giovanni looked at his watch and realized he had less than two hours before the ITS would close for the day. He called the taxi driver but did not get an answer. Giovanni paid his bill and asked the waitress if another taxi could take him back to the ITS. As Giovanni struggled with his shaky German and became more panicked, a man waiting to pay his bill overheard the situation and generously offered to give Giovanni a ride to the ITS.

When they arrived at the entrance, Giovanni thanked the man and walked the long pathway flanked by hedges. He entered the building and asked to see Johannes, explaining that he wanted to use the remainder of his research time.

Johannes greeted him. "I have your photocopies and your disc."

"Thank you," Giovanni said, "but could you hold onto them for now? I forgot about Clara Meyerstein, the niece. May I continue searching the records?"

"Of course, but you need to be back here fifteen minutes before we close." Johannes looked at a clock on the wall. "You have just over an hour."

"Then I must hurry."

Johannes nodded and escorted Giovanni to the room with lockers where he could store his coat and briefcase. Giovanni then returned to the same computer that he had used earlier. He entered the name *Clara Meyerstein* and waited for the result. He closed his eyes and said a silent prayer that at least one member of the family had survived the Holocaust.

Various Meyerstein names began to appear on the screen. Then the specific target of his search—Clara. He requested the file and waited for Johannes to return. As it was late in the day, only one other terminal was still in use. The middle-aged woman looked up from her research and aimed a disapproving glare as Giovanni drummed his fingers on the desktop. He realized his nervous behavior and ceased immediately.

Minutes later, Johannes returned with the file and then left.

Giovanni opened the file and carefully turned the pages, placing each face down on the table as he studied the next.

"Oh my God," he blurted out, drawing the attention of the remaining researcher, who followed the rules and kept her mouth shut but the stern look on her face spoke volumes. Giovanni smiled sheepishly and held up one hand in a gesture of apology.

He selected the option for a photocopy of the document and submitted his request. Then he left the Reading Room and waited in the hallway, fearing his excitement might cause further disruption to the lady doing research.

A short while later, Johannes approached with the photocopy.

"Johannes," Giovanni called out. "Clara Meyerstein was released from Auschwitz. She survived the War. I want to find her. How do I do that?"

Johannes handed him the photocopy. "You realize, of course, this does not necessarily mean she is alive today."

"I realize that, but it is a possibility, however remote. I have to know, because if she is alive, the painting belongs to her."

Johannes nodded. "I will bring you the name and contact information of an investigator who specializes in this type of work. It will be up to you if you wish to retain her services."

"Yes, please," Giovanni urged.

"Will that complete your research?" Johannes asked.

Giovanni indicated the photocopy. "Yes, but I need extra copies of this one as well. And I don't mean to trouble you further, but a copy on disc, too."

"No trouble at all." Johannes smiled. "I will return shortly with your materials and a receipt."

In the lobby, Giovanni sat on the leather sofa and waited. No longer tired and hungry, he was like a child unable to sit still. Johannes returned and Giovanni signed the credit card slip. He was given the disc and his additional photocopies, as well as a business card for the researcher that Johannes recommended he contact. Her name was Jana Vogler, and she was based in Berlin.

Giovanni tucked everything into his briefcase.

"Mr. Fabrizzi," Johannes said. "One last thing."

"Please, call me Gio."

"Yes, Gio. Jana Vogler is very good at what she does. I won't pretend that success is guaranteed, but I do hope that you will use her to find Clara Meyerstein."

"I will. I'm committed."

"Do you mind if Jana Vogler contacts me with any news of your success?"

"No, of course not."

Johannes pursed his lips and rubbed his smooth chin. "Please don't interpret this the wrong way," he said. "I won't make excuses for the acts of my countrymen. As I explained, I hope to understand this history. But it would be wonderful for all concerned, I believe, if you were to find Clara still alive, and you returned the art stolen from her family."

"I completely agree," Giovanni said. "Thank you so much for all your excellent help. I will do my very best to find her."

They shook hands and Johannes excused himself. Outside the entrance, Giovanni called the taxi driver and the car arrived within minutes.

"To your hotel?" the driver asked.

Giovanni hopped in the backseat and closed the door. "Not yet. First, take me to the nicest restaurant in town. In fact, if you're available, I would be happy to invite you to join me. I have great news to celebrate."

~

Giovanni was so excited about his mission to find Clara Meyerstein, he talked almost nonstop during the meal with the driver, Helmut. Giovanni did not divulge details about the Count, other than to say that he had a historian friend in London who had known the Meyerstein family during the Occupation of Paris.

As they enjoyed dinner, Helmut would nod and ask a question occasionally, when given the chance each time Giovanni paused to eat his food. After Giovanni had exhausted his words and realized he was repeating himself, he also realized that he knew nothing about Helmut. Giovanni thought to have better manners and shifted the conversation to Helmut and his life, details of which he was happy to share. He lived with his mother, he explained, had a girlfriend, and enjoyed meeting people from all over the world who came to Bad Arolsen, either to partake in the baths or to search the ITS archives.

Giovanni offered to buy a second bottle of wine but Helmut politely declined, insisting that he needed to get home to check on his aged mother. Giovanni paid the bill, left a generous tip, and when they arrived back at the hotel, Helmut thanked him heartily for the meal and conversation.

When Giovanni asked what he owed, Helmut was adamant

about not taking any more money from him. After all, the fine dinner easily exceeded the cost of a short taxi ride. Giovanni insisted but Helmut stood his ground. Giovanni conceded, they shook hands, and Helmut wished him luck in finding Clara.

Giovanni took out his key and entered his hotel room. He was tired but in the best possible way. He sat at the small desk and looked longingly at the queen-sized bed that beckoned him. He was truly ready for sleep. The day's excitement had caught up with him in the solitary moment of reflection. It reminded Giovanni of the last time he and Arabella had gone out to dinner and the theater with friends in London. He thought of her and how them traveling together would have made him happy, no matter what he accomplished on the trip.

He opened one of the outer pockets of his rolling suitcase where he stored notes on the developing investigation. The notion struck him as odd, that he had become an investigator. He was a detective asking difficult questions, which a month earlier, he could not have imagined he would be asking.

Giovanni took out the notebook in which he had been recording his discoveries. The latter pages contained abundant notes he had taken while searching the ITS archives. He turned to the first pages and studied the names, phone numbers, and addresses that he had written down from his father's address book.

He pulled out his mobile phone and stepped onto the small balcony that overlooked a bright patch of cornflowers and the hotel's parking lot. He had already noted the country code for Switzerland, checked his watch, and saw that it was close to nine o'clock.

The call he was determined to make would change the course

of his investigation, and knowing that it would made him nervous. Once he started down the next path, there would be no turning back. He gathered his courage and placed the call to Zurich.

A man answered in German. Giovanni was more surprised that anyone picked up the phone. He struggled to speak German the best he could on the spot.

"Hello. Is that Max?" Giovanni asked.

"Who is this?" The man did not sound pleased.

"Is this Max?"

"Who is calling?"

Giovanni forged ahead even though he might soon regret doing so.

"I'm sorry to call so late," he said. "This is Giovanni, Federico's son."

The only sound was the hiss of the phone line.

"Max, are you there? It's Giovanni Fabrizzi, your nephew."

"Giovanni?" There was a long pause. "My God. I never expected to hear from you."

"I know," Giovanni said. "I'm sorry to call you so suddenly. I have to tell you, Federico died a couple of years ago and things became very difficult for me. I just separated from my wife. I don't want to burden you with these things, it's just that, well, I decided to take a trip, and now I really want to see you, more than anything. Would that be possible?"

"Where are you, Giovanni?"

"I'm in Germany, near Munich. I could visit you in Zurich. I would be happy to meet you anywhere for lunch or dinner. Whatever you like."

Again there was a long pause. Giovanni pondered what would come next.

"Tell me," Max said, less abrasive. "You say your father died?"

"Yes. I'm sorry to be telling you now, but recently I found his old address book and your name was in there."

"Did your father say anything about me before he passed away?"

"No," Giovanni replied. "But I'm so glad to have found you."

"Yes, of course. It's just such a surprise."

"Would it be all right if I call you tomorrow evening? I'd like to set up a time for us to meet."

"I suppose." Max seemed to express little enthusiasm for the idea.

"Wonderful," Giovanni said. "I will speak with you tomorrow, and thank you so much, Max. Auf wiedersehen."

The line went dead without Max even saying good-bye. Still, Giovanni thought his luck had been excellent. He had found both the Touissants and his Uncle Max still alive. And there was a reasonable chance that Clara Meyerstein would also be alive, somewhere in the world.

It was just too bad, he thought, that he was alone and could not tell his amazing news to anyone else. If only his communication with the Count were telepathic, he could share all that he had discovered. Well, perhaps their connection was telepathic. He would never know for sure, but up to that point anyway, it had only occurred in close proximity. When he called out to the Count and received no response, he considered the absurdity of the idea and had to chuckle out loud. But while no one in the physical world would believe the painting could speak to Giovanni, it certainly was real to him. It was as actual and verifiable as the records in the ITS archives. Giovanni yearned to tell his son Maurizio what had happened.

Though unsure of what he would say, Giovanni dialed Maurizio at this home in Florence. He was pleased that his call was answered by the second ring.

"Papa," Maurizio said. "I've been so worried. Why haven't you called?"

"Everything is fine, don't worry. I'm in a small town near Munich, and I've been having a great time. How are you?"

"I'm fine, but what are you doing there?"

Giovanni bent the truth some. "Catching up with friends. You know, looking up the past, the good old days. It's been fascinating really, all I've learned. And next, I am off to Zurich."

"Zurich?" Maurizio was alarmed. "Papa, don't you think this vacation of yours, I mean, don't you think you've been away long enough?"

"Don't be silly, Mau. I've had a wonderful time. In fact, I'm rather excited to tell you about it, but I'm not quite sure where to start."

"You should come to Florence," Maurizio said. "Then you can tell me all about your trip. Really, Papa, I think that would be best. We have plenty of room for you. And you know so many people here. Why not get a flight tomorrow?"

"Oh my, I would love to, Mau, but I must not stay away from the Brueghel too long. You know how it is. But as I promised, when we are both done with our current projects, I will be glad to visit."

"Sure, sure," Maurizio said. "Papa, I want you to be honest with me."

"Honest?" Giovanni wanted to be, particularly about the Count and how his latest story had turned out to be true. But Giovanni was still apprehensive after the last time he was completely honest with his son.

"Yes," Maurizio said. "Are you sad about Arabella? Or is it a kind of... I don't know." Maurizio struggled for the right words. "Is it a manageable sadness?"

His son's sincere concern touched Giovanni, and he choked up slightly. He held the phone away and cleared his throat, then continued, "Well said, Mau. It is manageable. And hearing your voice is a big help."

"When are you going home?"

"Oh, maybe in a day or two."

"You don't know?" Maurizio asked.

"I don't have my return ticket to London yet. Tomorrow, I'll take a train to Zurich."

"This is not like you."

"Well, son, I don't feel like who I used to be. But anyway, I'm sure to be back in London in two or three days. We'll talk then."

After their good-byes, Giovanni plugged his mobile phone into its charger and went into the bathroom to wash and get ready for bed. As warm water filled the basin, he said a quiet prayer. He wished that when his journey was over, he could tell his son everything and have him accept it. And while he was at it, Giovanni made another prayer. He visualized telling Maurizio and Arabella both of what had transpired and then having them nod in understanding and wrap their arms around him.

13

As Giovanni stepped off the train in Zurich, his mobile phone began to ring. Caught in the flow of arriving passengers and struggling with his rolling suitcase, he could not get to the ringing phone deep in his coat pocket. He searched the platform for an opening where he could get out of the crowd and answer the call.

The phone continued ringing. Giovanni feared he might miss the call, and worse, the caller would not leave a message. He darted out of the crowd, his rolling suitcase flailing at his heels, and found a scrap of space that was standing room only. He parked his suitcase and dug into his coat for the phone.

Just as he had hoped, it was Jana Vogler, returning the call he had made to her while in Munich, before boarding his train to Zurich.

"I spoke with Johannes at the ITS," Jana explained. "So I already know something about your search."

Giovanni asked about her fees and availability. When she began to answer, a train departure was announced over a loudspeaker and he couldn't make out her reply.

"I'm sorry," Giovanni said. "I'm in the train station. Could you repeat that?"

She explained her fees, and that she was available. She wasn't cheap, but it was not beyond Giovanni's means. Considering what was at stake, he concluded the expense was worthwhile and he agreed to her terms.

He asked, "What do you think the chances are that we can find Clara?"

"There is always a chance," she replied, "but I don't want to give you false hope. In the majority of cases, we can find the individual at some point, but more often than not, they have passed away. But at the same time, I don't want to crush your hopes, either. I have found a rare few who are still living. It is one of my greatest joys when we do."

"I understand," Giovanni said. "Whatever the resolution, it will be worth the effort. It is something I have to know."

"I can check a number of sources both in Europe and the United States."

"America? But she was French."

"Mr. Fabrizzi, you might be surprised to learn where survivors emigrated to after the war. Many fled to America, Israel, Australia, even Brazil. You never know. After their experience, I think it is understandable that, though not a complete comfort, distance was the preference. To find them across the ocean, for example, is not unusual."

"I see your point," Giovanni said, considering that if he were in their shoes, he wouldn't return to Europe, ever. "I have some further research to pursue," he explained, "related to the art world.

After Zurich, I'll be back in London in a few days. You'll be able to reach me at my studio." He relayed the phone number.

"Give me three to four weeks," she said, "and I should have something to report. Unless there is big news, in which case you'll hear from me sooner." After a pause, she added, "And by the way, I want you to know, I personally appreciate the work you are trying to do, regarding the return of the stolen artwork."

"Thanks," Giovanni said. "I don't think it's a great act of generosity. I see it as a necessity. Something that would bother me if I didn't do it."

"I still insist on complimenting you," she said.

Giovanni liked the compliment and smiled.

She continued, "If I may ask you another question, Mr. Fabrizzi. Your research at the ITS showed that none of the other Meyersteins survived. Is that correct?"

"It is."

"Then, if it is not too personal a question..." She paused, as if unable to continue without permission.

"Go ahead," Giovanni said.

"If you find Clara Meyerstein is no longer alive, will you keep the painting? Or would you consider donating it?"

Giovanni rubbed his forehead. He didn't have an answer, as he was not yet prepared to consider that possibility.

"I don't know," he admitted. "I might donate it to a museum."

"Perhaps in Paris," Jana suggested. "Since that is where the painting was last owned before it came to your family."

Giovanni immediately understood that Jana was dedicated to dealing with the loss and anger of others, and trying to make up for what had happened to millions, decades earlier. He could not blame her for asking.

He explained, "I'm trying to do two things here, Jana. One, find out how the painting came into my family. And two, learn who the artist is. It's unsigned, you know."

"Yes, Johannes told me."

"This will all become more complicated if the work turns out to have been painted by the artist I think painted it."

"And who is that?"

"Botticelli."

There was a long pause before she spoke. "Well, Mr. Fabrizzi, I'm no expert, but even I know how important he is. But stolen Jewish art, created by famous or even unknown artists, nevertheless is still stolen and deserves a special home."

It was the last thing Giovanni wanted to think about, but he had to admit, the potential quandary had crossed his mind. If his investigation somehow revealed the painting was by Botticelli, he had that entire can of worms to deal with—everybody who was privy to his discovery and their endless suggestions of what Giovanni should do with the portrait.

He wanted to a find quiet, dark place and enjoy a soothing drink. He thanked Jana Vogler for taking the case and asked her to call when she had any information.

~

As his taxi rolled through the streets of Zurich, Giovanni was too consumed by his latest dilemma to notice much of the passing cityscape. He had not expected to find a member of the Meyerstein family alive, and even though he had not yet confirmed that possibility, the new developments were leading to difficult choices. He was certain the Count's story was true and the painting had once belonged to the Meyersteins. That alone burdened him with a moral responsibility that he could not ignore. Added to that, if Clara Meyerstein were still alive, he could not in good conscience do anything other than return the painting to her, its rightful owner, even if a work of Botticelli.

It wasn't until he arrived at the Baur au Lac Hotel, paid the driver, and wheeled his suitcase toward the entrance that Giovanni took a moment to absorb the surroundings. He and Arabella had stayed at the Baur au Lac before, where they walked around the lake, strolled the Bahnhofstrasse, and took in local shopping and dining.

Giovanni checked his watch. He still had a few hours before his dinner plans, but he couldn't relax. He considered taking a walk, as the hotel was located in a splendid area of Zurich, but he was too preoccupied by the uncertain outcome that his meeting might produce. Instead he stayed in his room, unpacked some of his clothes, and collected the photographs and documents that he would bring with him to dinner. He needed to mentally prepare, knowing the meeting could well be his only chance to learn the truth about the Meyersteins and the Count.

He scheduled a taxi to arrive in two hours and take him to the restaurant Max had suggested, the Kronenhalle on Rämistrasse. Then he went over the questions he had for Max. He went so far as to write the questions on a sheet of hotel stationery, then changed his mind, scratched out some and wrote others. He did not want Max to feel as though he was being interviewed, if Giovanni could avoid it, but he needed direct answers. Then he tried to imagine responses Max might offer and formulated follow-up questions, but the myriad directions their conversation might take only frustrated Giovanni. He crumpled up the sheet of stationery and pitched it into the trash. He would simply focus on the most important questions, and if Max balked, Giovanni would have to improvise on the spot.

After a shower and once dressed, Giovanni took the elevator to the lobby and waited for his taxi. He had scheduled the taxi to come early, as the restaurant was some distance from the hotel and he wanted to arrive well before Max.

After his taxi ride to the Kronenhalle, Giovanni paid the driver and went into the restaurant. He paused to admire the setting, just as he had the last time he dined there with Arabella. If not for the tables and fine linen, one might imagine they had walked into a museum. The room itself was a work of art, the warm walls covered in wood and intricate molding, the tall ceiling as well. Among the handsome woodwork, priceless art in elaborate gilded frames hung throughout the restaurant. The works of Chagall, Kandinsky, Matisse, Picasso, and others. Any one of the paintings would have fetched an enormous sum on the international art market.

Giovanni told the maître d´ his name and was shown to a table. As he settled in his seat, still admiring the fine art, it reminded him of his dilemma. What if the Count's portrait really was a Botticelli? It would bring much comfort to an aged Clara

Meyerstein. Or perhaps she would sell it and live her remaining years in luxury. There was nothing wrong with that. But he had a disturbing thought. What if he found Clara still alive, but she was unable, due to age, to remember her past during the Occupation? Ironically, Giovanni considered, it might be a mixed blessing to have an impaired memory. It might be preferable if the incomprehensible brutality her family had endured, and millions of others, was a vague flicker of a memory, if that. It would be a gift to be forgetful, after what she had been through.

Sitting, waiting, and doing nothing only fueled Giovanni's growing anxiety about the meeting he would have shortly. He sipped his mineral water and nibbled on a slice of bread. Giovanni checked his watch, saw that Max was ten minutes late, and wondered if his uncle had intended to keep their dinner appointment in the first place, or if he was just leading Giovanni astray.

Then Giovanni spotted a frail man with white hair, speaking to the maître d´. They both looked at Giovanni and the old man nodded, then started toward the table. He used a walking stick that looked expensive, adorned by hammered silver. As he drew near, Giovanni gauged that more than his walking stick came at great expense, though the sight was somewhat of a contradiction. The man was ancient, but hanging from his ailing frame, he wore a suit tailored from the finest cloth.

Giovanni stood and extended his hand. "Hello. I'm Giovanni."

"Well, well. Giovanni. I am your Uncle Max. At last we meet."

He reached out to Giovanni's hand but rather than shake it, his gesture was more of a quick slap. Giovanni did not judge it as disrespectful, rather a matter of Max's advanced age and vulnerability.

"Didn't we ever?" Giovanni asked. "Not even when I was an infant?"

Max didn't respond and Giovanni felt awkward, worried that his response might have been taken as an insult. He was no youngster himself, so his words might suggest that he and Max were from different centuries. Max had survived to a remarkable age, which was difficult to ignore, but Giovanni didn't want to make it a topic of conversation.

They sat down at the table and spent a moment studying each other, neither of them sure of where to begin the conversation. Max chose a safe route.

"You have been here before, at the Kronenhalle."

"Yes, with my wife, although I'm sorry to say we're separated right now. It's been very hard." Giovanni hadn't intended to make his marital problems a topic but it just came out that way.

"I know how it is," Max said. "My wife has been gone many years."

"It's hard to be alone."

"I have a butler and a beautiful home. I don't travel much any-more, but I think I am more fortunate than most."

A waiter came and Giovanni was surprised when Max ordered a vodka on the rocks with three olives. No less than three, he insisted, as if he had been cheated in the past. Giovanni wanted to remain clear-headed, so he kept to his mineral water.

"I'm truly sorry I didn't find my father's address book sooner," Giovanni said, "and tell you he was gone."

Max nodded. "We were out of touch for a very long time."

An uncomfortable silence passed, then Max's drink arrived. Before he could take the first sip, Giovanni clinked his glass against his uncle's.

"A toast to making up for long absences," Giovanni said.

Max raised an eyebrow and sipped his glass, perhaps annoyed that his drinking was delayed, Giovanni pondered. Or maybe because Giovanni's glass of mineral water somehow made the toast invalid.

The waiter was ready for their order, further postponing the conversation that Giovanni wanted to get started, but he couldn't seem to light the fuse. He resolved to get down to the matter after they had ordered their meals. Giovanni chose a house specialty, the *bollito misto,* a stew of boiled beef, chicken, sausage, and tongue. Max ordered veal. As the waiter moved off, Giovanni eased into the conversation with casual questions about Max's life in Zurich, the art world, and other relatively safe topics.

"I never really understood," Giovanni said, "why you didn't visit when I was a child. My father never told me much about you." Giovanni reached into his pocket and brought out an old black and white photograph of Max and Federico, standing together in a garden. He put it on the table, facing Max.

Max sipped from his glass and then set it down. He reached for the photograph, slid it closer to him, and raised it up so he could study it. Giovanni watched carefully. Max did not make a show of emotion, although he did appear in concentration, as if unwinding a puzzle.

"Oh, Federico." Max sighed. "I am sad we missed out on all

those years. And I didn't even know of his funeral."

"Why was it that way between you two?" Giovanni asked.

Max put down the photograph and looked at his nephew. "Your father was an excellent restorer. I am sure you are one as well. The House of Fabrizzi. I tried hard to live up to that name. Your father believed I was trying to avoid work, that I was more interested in Parisian girls than working. He had a wife, your mother, and his great talent. I had nothing."

"He told me that you stopped working with him in Paris," Giovanni said. "Was that because he placed a lot of expectations on you as a restorer?"

The waiter arrived with their meals and interrupted the conversation. They both unfolded their napkins and began poking at dinner while Giovanni waited for an answer. Max did not appear in any hurry to provide one, rather he indulged in his veal. As they continued eating, Giovanni did not push for a reply, though his repeated glances at Max seemed enough to prompt a response.

Max set down his fork and knife. "I'm sorry to say this, and possibly I shouldn't say it at all. That is, to you, his son."

"No," Giovanni said. "Please, say what you have to. I need to understand."

"Very well. Your father and I parted ways. My abilities as a conservator could never satisfy him. There was, of course, also that I enjoyed the nightlife. Montmartre. Montparnasse. Music. Theater. Art openings. Women. But most of all, I believe Federico was cross with me because I deserted our family heritage of art restoration."

"How was that?" Giovanni asked.

"I had to make living, and it wasn't going to be restoring art as your father did, and as you do. I never had that talent. So I became an art dealer. And I became very successful. It took a good long while, believe me, but by the time your father left Paris, I was making far more money than him. I do not think that made him feel any better about matters between us."

"I suppose not," Giovanni said, but he was distracted to learn that Max, by his own admission, had become an art dealer. "When you were in Paris," Giovanni asked, "did you ever sell any work by well-known artists?"

Max took a long sip from his glass and finished it. "There were some, eventually." He laid his napkin over the unfinished plate of veal and signaled for the waiter to bring the check.

Giovanni stiffened. His question had touched a nerve, as he had feared it might, once probing Max's history as an art dealer. Giovanni had to do something. His one opportunity to learn the truth was slipping away.

"Can I get you some coffee or dessert?" he asked.

Max seemed to ignore him, more interested in the waiter.

When the check came, Giovanni reached for it.

Max slapped Giovanni's hand. "You are the visitor," he said. "Not the host." He placed a credit card in the tray and the waiter took it away before Giovanni could protest. Soon the waiter returned and Max signed the receipt. "Now," he said, "you will have to forgive me, but my stamina is not what it used to be. I will have to pass on dessert." He struggled to rise from his seat.

Giovanni moved around the table to help.

"Stop that," Max said, and he got up by himself. "You make a man feel older than he already is."

He didn't care to have his hand slapped again, so Giovanni backed off. But all of his plans were crumbling. He had no way to hold his uncle there, to ask him the questions he wanted answered the most, and to find the truth.

"Uncle Max, there's so much more we haven't talked about. Is there any way we could meet tomorrow? It would mean a great deal to me."

Max looked at him for a long while. "I will have to think about that."

"All right. May I call you in the morning? Is ten too early?"

"Eleven. Then I will tell you if I'm feeling up to another visit."

He turned around and hobbled away on his walking stick.

14

After breakfast, Giovanni sat in the hotel courtyard enjoying his morning coffee, as he considered the results of his meeting the evening before. He was still unsure if he had somehow offended his uncle, beyond touching a subject that he would rather not discuss. Max didn't have the most agreeable disposition, but there could be plenty of reasons for that, the most likely of which was his advanced age. It was not uncommon for men in their golden years to be abrasive. After all, the daily aches and pains must be enough to ruin anyone's good cheer, and Giovanni had to keep that in mind. It was enough of a miracle that his uncle could still get around. Most anyone Giovanni knew near Max's age were bedridden and being spoon-fed in a nursing home. At the very least, Giovanni had expected his uncle would have been confined to a wheelchair. In one respect, he had to admire Max for his perseverance if nothing else.

But Giovanni was still obsessed by his hunch and that it might be true. Max had been an art dealer, the most important revelation during dinner, and all the other clues were fitting into place.

Giovanni had not yet stumbled across even one fact that proved his hunch was wrong.

However, it was only fair to give his uncle the benefit of the doubt, and Max's reasons for friction between him and Federico were all plausible explanations. It remained completely possible that their falling out had occurred for no other reason beyond those Max had expressed.

The time approached when Giovanni would call his uncle, and again he felt nervous, as he had the night before, about confronting Max. Partly because he feared, after their first encounter, that he had made some mistake, possibly said the wrong thing, which alone could be the reason Max excused himself from dinner so abruptly. As a precaution, Giovanni concluded that he should offer an apology, just in case it was all a misunderstanding due to an error on his part.

He pulled out his mobile phone and made the call.

Apparently Max had caller ID, as he skipped past the entire ritual of hello and who is calling.

"Gio," he said firmly. "I want to apologize for last night."

Surprised, Giovanni didn't know what to think. So he chuckled. "Well, I accept. In fact, I was going to offer the same."

"There is no need," Max said. "I was a complete ass, and I am truly sorry. Please understand..."

"I totally understand, Uncle Max. Say no more, please."

Giovanni was more interested in speaking to him face to face, as they had the night before, and continuing the conversation they had started. He expressed the desire and his uncle agreed, further suggesting they have dinner that evening, at Max's home no less.

Giovanni juggled the phone on his shoulder and jotted down the address.

After their call ended, Giovanni was mildly astonished. Some turnabout that was, he thought. Perhaps the Ghost of Christmas Past had paid Max a visit in the dark hours of the night. Not bad, considering it took two more ghosts before Scrooge changed his ways.

~

As Giovanni looked out of the window of his taxi, winding through the streets of Zurichberg that evening, he understood that Max had not just done well. He had excelled. He must have made a significant fortune selling art, as the exclusive area in which he lived was populated by homes the status of opulent mansions, situated on hills or hugging the lake, all caked with expensive veneer.

The sun was tucked away but in the dwindling light, Giovanni could see the grandeur of Max's home, its white, two-story, Palladian columns standing out prominently. Giovanni paid the driver and retained his business card for the ride back to the Baur au Lac. As he approached, he peeked around the side of the house to catch a glimpse of the lake below. At the front door, he pressed the bell.

The door was answered by a butler dressed in black. Giovanni introduced himself and the butler led him through the entryway, then into a marbled hallway. Giovanni was struck by the abundant art decorating his uncle's home. Sculptures, paintings, and tapestries adorned the walls overlooking a gently rising and wide, curving stairway to the upper level.

The butler escorted Giovanni to a balcony overlooking the lake. The view was stupendous. In minutes, Max approached with drinks in hand, one for each of them. As they strolled through the house, Giovanni remained fascinated by the old master paintings his uncle had come to own. His compliments were unceasing, that Max could acquire such treasures. Giovanni was truly in awe of the collection.

Max thanked him for the kind words, here and there mentioning the percentage of profit he had made on the works displayed and others he had not kept, but never specifying their exact cost, where he had found them, or to whom he had sold them.

Their tour ended at a formal dining room, the long table with room enough to feed thirty people. Spread across the fine linen tablecloth, places were set, cut crystal, gleaming silver, and polished china. Dinner awaited them, two choices of wine and succulent game hens on wild rice that Giovanni had no qualms about devouring. Beyond the fact that he was enjoying the meal immensely, Giovanni concluded it was best to postpone conversation with Max about his past until after they had finished eating.

As they enjoyed after-dinner coffee and the butler cleared away their plates, Giovanni wanted to resume his pointed questions but the setting still didn't feel right.

"Uncle Max," he asked, "would it be all right if we spoke in private? I'd feel more comfortable."

When the butler returned, Max spoke to him in German. Giovanni could make out enough to understand the request that he bring brandy to the library. Then Max beckoned Giovanni to follow and they proceeded there. Along the way, Giovanni continued to admire the fine art decorating every wall.

The dark wood paneling of the library provided a softly-lit, comfortable space, and they sat in overstuffed armchairs that flanked the crackling fireplace. Giovanni sipped at his brandy, its smooth bite warming his insides and calming some of his edginess.

Max dismissed his butler. At last, Giovanni and Max were alone.

Giovanni was about to plunge into his rehearsed line of questioning, but Max raised his hand in a gesture to pause.

"First," Max said, "I want to explain last night."

"There's really no—"

"I insist." His eyes flared. "Now be quiet and let me continue." He took a breath to refresh himself. "It's no secret I am no longer a young man, so stop trying to console me with your attempts to ignore that fact, which by the way, you're lousy at. But that's neither here nor there. Reaching this age has its downsides, as you can imagine, and it doesn't make anyone chipper."

"Uncle Max, please. You don't have to say any of it. I understand. Really."

"You'll understand when you get to my age, if you do. Most people expected me to be dead by now. I certainly did. Yes, some days it seems best if life would just end. I've had my time. But after the life I've lived, all the struggles to survive, of trying to stay alive just another day, it all comes back to haunt you in the end. You still can't give up. It's conditioning, pattern, habit. A wretched curse is what it is. I am forced to stay alive."

Sipping his brandy, Giovanni considered his uncle's immaculate estate. Particularly the art it housed.

"The wealth you've amassed can't hurt," he said.

"Plenty else hurts." Max looked perturbed. "But you're right and I won't deny it. I started with nothing, and I got to all of this." Arm outstretched, he swept across the works of art in the library. "Yes, I am going to miss my treasures when I go."

Giovanni seized the opportunity. "That's what I wanted to discuss with you. A former treasure of yours. You see, there is a painting I received after my father died. As it turns out, you had sent it to him some years earlier, I'm not sure how many, but I am sure that you did because I found a letter, from you to him, inside the crate."

Max took a sip of his brandy. "I am sorry, Gio, but I don't remember. It must have been ages ago."

"Perhaps I could refresh your memory." Giovanni reached in his pocket and produced the actual letter, which he had brought with him. He handed it to Max and let him read it.

As Max absorbed the letter, Giovanni continued, "Sadly, it seems the two of you had not been communicating for some time. I suppose you were trying to get him to talk with you again. But the thing is, after finding the letter, I studied the crate. It was sent to my father in Florence, from Zurich, and it had a name stenciled on the outside. *Kreitel.*"

Max put the letter down and took a long, hard look at Giovanni.

"The artist, surely," Max suggested.

"I don't think so," Giovanni said, but he wasn't ready to tell

Max the work was unsigned. Nor was he going to let Max keep the letter, which Giovanni deftly retrieved and slipped back into his pocket.

"Then it must have been a gallery along the way," Max claimed, "before I used the crate. I shipped works constantly and often reused crates." Max dismissed further implications with a wave of his hand.

"There's more." Giovanni brought out a photograph he had taken of the crate, back at his studio in London, with the shipping label in full detail. But then he reconsidered. He should hold back that evidence for now, until he could establish more of his uncle's recollection. Instead, Giovanni would lay the next seed. "Or maybe it was an associate," he said. "Another dealer you had worked with. In Paris, perhaps."

"Kreitel, you say." Max pondered for a moment. "It's a name I have not thought about for many years. I may have known someone by that name in Paris."

"During the Occupation?" Giovanni asked.

Max sighed. He took a long sip of his brandy, savored it, and then set it down. "This may be hard for you to understand, Gio, as you were not yet born. When the Nazis took over Paris in 1940, some people suffered and others prospered. I'm speaking of the art world, of course. Your father, as I've already explained, was not happy that I was not a better restorer. He simply had that talent and I didn't. But there was something else that he resented even more." Max was hesitant to continue, perhaps ashamed. "There was a Nazi organization called the ERR. They took Jewish art and furniture and appropriated it for Hitler, for Goering, for the Reich."

"Is that so?" Giovanni nodded understandingly and didn't reveal the research he had already done on the subject.

"And the terrible truth is," Max explained, "I may have been an inadequate restorer and of little use to your father, but I did know a great deal about art, its history, and the value of paintings on the international market. Whatever you may think of the Nazis now, at that time they were in control, and they offered opportunities to people with experience in the world of art. The gallery owners, the collectors, the dealers, even restorers like your father, we all knew what was going on. There was nothing we could do to change it. But at the same time, the Nazis wanted to know the value of art."

"You appraised art for the ERR?" Giovanni asked.

Max did not answer.

Giovanni realized the accusatory tone of his question. He didn't want to push Max too far and risk him walking out like the night before, even though walking out of his own home was hardly likely. Still, pushing too hard could make him balk, and he might dismiss further discussion for the evening.

"I'm just curious, Uncle Max. That's all."

Still delaying his response, Max poured more brandy for them both. Max swirled the liquor around in his glass, studied it, then took a sip.

Giovanni raised his glass to his lips but did not let the liquor pass, as he did not want to become too relaxed. His investigation, approaching the pinnacle of discovery, required his utmost focus.

Max explained, "Federico had the luxury of making a living on his own. I believe he did not want to speak with me again because he misinterpreted my new opportunity, which to him appeared as supporting the Nazis. When the ERR asked for my opinion on works, they paid me. Federico had every right to loathe the Nazis, as I did, as we all did, but I survived by being a consultant. There is a world of difference between being a Nazi supporter and someone who consults on artwork they have appropriated."

"Of course," Giovanni agreed, though the Nazi appropriation of any art, Jewish or otherwise, was theft plain and simple, and it was the last thing he would ever agree with. To keep their conversation on an even keel, he added, "You would have starved to death if you did not make that money." Perhaps an exaggeration, but it did the trick.

"Exactly," Max said. "I'm glad you can appreciate the position I was in. Many non-Jews were in the same position at that time." Max sighed and seemed to relax. He poured more brandy for himself and then took the neck of the bottle and reached toward Giovanni's glass.

"Just a little, please, Uncle," Giovanni said.

Max obliged with an additional finger's worth and Giovanni thanked him. Again he raised the glass to his lips but did not let the liquor pass.

"This is excellent brandy," Giovanni said. "It's such a terrible shame that Papa didn't better understand the complexities of what was going on in Paris at that time. If he had, you and I would have had a relationship over the years."

"Yes, I wish the same," Max said.

"I read a little about Paris back then," Giovanni said. "I guess

Goering was in charge of the artwork they took."

"Yes. Works of art were catalogued and stored at the Jeu de Paume and the Louvre. Some of it was taken by leaders of the Reich, Goering and Hitler, mostly."

"Goering actually asked for your opinion on the value of art?" Giovanni pretended to be impressed.

"Oh, no, certainly not." Max shook his head and waved his hand to dismiss the idea immediately. "He did not deal with people like me. It was the ERR. There was an officer who was my contact. I was introduced to him at Maxim's, I think. The Nazis had taken over all the finest restaurants in Paris, you know. Someone introduced me as an art historian, and later I was asked to give my opinion on certain works of art they had in their possession."

"Do you remember his name?"

"Oh, no," Max replied. "It was so very long ago. It was just some underling."

Giovanni nodded and did not contest his uncle's reply, though it was almost certainly a lie. Instead he lightened the mood, but only for a moment.

"I read the Nazis liked the Old Masters and Renaissance painters but considered Impressionism and other modern art as degenerate."

"Madness, isn't it?" Max chuckled. "I consider my Picasso, Matisse, and Monet among my favorites in my collection."

Giovanni reached inside his jacket for the envelope of photographs he had brought. "I'd like to talk more about the crate you sent to my father. Actually, about the painting that was inside of it, along with your letter." He found the image of the Count's portrait.

"I brought a photo of it." He handed it to Max.

He studied it. "I sent this?"

Giovanni nodded. "And now I have it. I'm quite fond of it, actually. It looks Renaissance, doesn't it?"

"It certainly does. Who is the artist?"

"That's the remarkable thing, Uncle. It is unsigned. Even though it's been many years, I was hoping you might know the artist's name."

Max took another look at the photograph, shook his head, and handed it back to Giovanni.

"Do you remember where you got it, Max?"

"It's hard to say," he replied. "The passage of time, of course. And I don't remember if I got it in France or Switzerland, frankly."

"It was France," Giovanni said with forceful certainty.

Max became confused, but also suspicious. "Are you asking me, or telling me?"

"It was France." Giovanni fabricated an excuse for his certainty. "The letter to my father you included in the crate, which I showed you." Giovanni patted his jacket, inside of which was the letter safely tucked away, beyond the reach of further inspection that would expose his outright lie. "Perhaps you didn't have a chance to read it entirely. In closing, you mentioned the collector from whom you acquired the piece. Meyerstein, I think it was. Does that ring any bells?"

"Meyerstein?" Max took a sip of his brandy. "I don't recall anyone by that name."

"Surely you remember," Giovanni prodded. "He lived on Avenue Foch. He had a major collection. But his collection was confiscated by the Nazis. So forgive me, but I'm just a little curious as to how it came into your possession."

Max became concerned, and it was written all over his face—he was getting the hint of where this line of questioning was leading.

"I don't know what you're talking about," he said. "I don't know any Meyersteins, and in fact, I don't even know if the painting ever belonged to me."

"Max, we've already been through all that. You sent the painting to my father. I have the crate."

"That doesn't mean anything."

"That's ridiculous, Max. It means everything, and we haven't even got to it all yet." The moment had come for Giovanni to produce the photograph he had held in reserve. "Here's a photo of an older shipping label on the crate. Which, by the way, matches the handwriting on the letter that was inside the crate, written by you. I had it checked. The only difference is that you signed the letter *Your loving brother, Max*, but the sender on the label was *W. Kreitel* and your former Zurich address, which I found in my father's address book. And furthermore..." Giovanni brought out yet another photo, this one of the crate in full, showing all of its markings. "See here, the spray-painted stencil on the side. *Kreitel*, right there on the crate. It's your crate. You are Kreitel."

For Giovanni, it was no longer a hunch.

Max set down his brandy and crossed his arms. "And what if I am? So I used the name to send a painting to your father. I've done nothing wrong."

"We'll see about that." Giovanni pulled out a photocopy he had made at the ITS in Bad Arolsen. "The International Tracing Service in Germany lists W. Kreitel as accompanying Bruno Lothar when the Meyersteins, sent off to die, had their art confiscated. Stolen is what I call it. Look, there is your signature, right next to Lothar. I suppose you're going to tell me you don't know him, either. Seems to me the two of you were buddies back in 1940."

Max did not respond.

"It's all clear now, Max. My father saw the war coming and got out of Paris, but not you. It was your big opportunity. Before coming here, I visited with some of my father's old friends who live in Paris. They had some interesting things to say. Seems that during the Occupation, an art dealer named Kreitel came around peddling works they suspected were stolen from Jewish homes. Apparently it was all the rage at the time. Plunder their art and make a buck. Only glitch for you is the fake German name and your lousy French couldn't hide the fact you're Italian."

Max stood up, his eyes flared, and his face flushed. "How dare you come into my home and make these accusations. Is that the reason you traveled all this way? Not because I am family but because I volunteered to advise on the value of art in order to survive?"

"Volunteered?" Giovanni shot back. "To make a profit, maybe."

"They took the art," Max said. "I merely suggested its worth. That doesn't make me a Nazi. I had to live."

"*Live?*" Up from his chair, Giovanni turned with arms out, indicating the opulent room. "This is not living? And what about the Meyersteins? Did they get to live?"

"I did nothing to harm them."

"You stole from them!" Giovanni grabbed his uncle's arms and drove him backward, into a bookcase. Books fell and Giovanni realized, though furious, he had gone too far. He relaxed his grip and stepped back.

Max brushed himself off. "I think you should leave now."

Giovanni asked, "What other paintings in this house belong to the Meyersteins?"

"I have nothing of theirs."

"Of course, because you've already sold it for a profit, when it wasn't yours to sell."

"You have no right to judge me," Max said.

"No? I think I do. They should have shoved you in the oven."

His eyes grew wide and Max hollered, "I want you out!"

"I'll be happy to leave," Giovanni said, "but let me say this before I go. It's clear now why my father wouldn't forgive you, and neither will I, ever." Giovanni couldn't resist the urge to leave Max with one last revelation to stew over for the rest of his days. "And you know what? That painting you sent my father, the unsigned, apparently worthless portrait of the Count. It's that very painting that led me to discovering what you did, Max. That painting belongs to a survivor of the Meyerstein family, Clara. I'm going to find her and return the painting. And here's the best part, Max. That painting is by Botticelli. You sent a painting to my father that is worth millions."

Max was dumbfounded, staring at Giovanni, who couldn't tell if Max had understood the words, did not believe them, or simply did not want to believe them.

Giovanni found his own way to the front door, which he flung open and didn't bother to close, letting the cool night air chill his uncle's hell.

15

Giovanni arrived in London, exhausted from his trip. During his taxi ride home, the gray skies encouraged him to sleep, which he was very much looking forward to doing. The driver, on the other hand, had apparently just polished off his hourly jumbo latte and wanted to talk ceaselessly, asking where his passenger was returning from, a question which Giovanni made the mistake of answering. The driver launched into a tirade about Germany, the war, and how none of his relatives would ever visit that despicable country.

Giovanni really didn't care.

"Sir," he said abruptly, "I don't want to insult you, but I've had a particularly disturbing trip. Could we please complete this ride in silence?"

The driver studied Giovanni in the rear view mirror.

"Right, Mate. You're the boss."

The taxi wended its way through early evening traffic. When they arrived at Giovanni's flat, he paid the driver and wheeled his suitcase to the front door of his lonely home. By the time his clothes were hung and he had whipped together a snack, it was 7:30 in the evening. He turned on light background music, stretched out on the sofa, and tried to relax, but his mind could not stop replaying events from his trip.

In recalling the night before, Giovanni's emotions bounced between anger and shame over what his uncle had done and his harsh reactions to it. Shoving the old man into a bookcase, of all things, he thought. What if he had injured him? Would he have taken him to the hospital, despite his fury? There was no way of knowing, and it was worthless to think about anyway. In the end, there was no excuse for that kind of childish behavior. But then Giovanni's mind turned back to the spite he had for Max, and the cycle of unresolvable thoughts started again.

If only his father were still alive, Giovanni would've had someone to talk to. Someone to help clear his troubled mind. How absurd, he thought, even cruel, that he could talk to the subject of a sixteenth century portrait, yet he could not talk to the one person he wanted to most. He longed to sit with his father and discuss what Max had done. He wanted to know what his father knew, which must have been so much more than the scarce evidence that Giovanni had discovered.

The longing for those closest to Giovanni overwhelmed him. He wanted his father and mother alive again. He wanted to see his son for more than a quick weekend twice a year, to see his old friends, and yes, to be with Arabella again, despite her infidelity. He wanted his life back. It had been upturned for one reason, which was safely stored in a strong room of his studio.

~

As he unlocked his studio, Giovanni realized that he should have had dinner. Snacks only go so far. But he was determined to confront the Count, despite the late hour. He opened the second strong room and turned on the light. In his haste to grab the crate, he almost dropped it, but he recovered and brought it to his work area, where he set the portrait on the usual easel.

He sat on his stool and stared at the Count, who was silent.

"I hate you," Giovanni said.

"Signor Fabrizzi," the Count said. "One should carefully consider their words, particularly when choosing any so harsh that one might later regret."

"You've ruined my life."

"Pray tell, just what have I done to ruin your life?"

"You've made me doubt my sanity, then waste my time listening to your endless, self-involved stories. Add to that, you spied on my wife and then told me about her affair. You have utterly destroyed me, but you don't stop there. You had to go and tell me about Paris, which led to a rather unfriendly reunion with my Uncle Max."

The Count was silent for a moment, then said, "First, I must remind you that I did not care to tell you about Paris. As I warned you, it was a disturbing period, but you implored me to tell the story of Sergei."

"I don't care about Sergei and his boyfriend. Whatever they did is nothing compared to the disturbing facts I learned about my Uncle Max."

"That would be my second concern, this uncle of yours. I am

afraid it is difficult to relate when the topic of conversation is a person I know nothing about nor have ever met. I am already kept in the dark, as they say, more than enough."

"You've met him," Giovanni said. "He's *Kreitel*."

The Count hesitated. "I see."

"Right, now you see. So you should see how you've ruined my life."

"Is this perhaps your hunch, the details of which you refused to share with me?"

"Yes," Giovanni said. "But it's not a hunch anymore. It's true, I'm afraid. He stole artwork from Jewish families and sold it for a profit. And he did rather nicely for himself, I must say."

"It is evident that this revelation has upset you."

Giovanni vaulted upright. "*Yes!*" he screamed. "I'm furious. My own uncle, how could he?" He began to wobble, then clutched his chest and dropped to one knee.

"Fabrizzi!" the Count called out.

Giovanni steadied himself and took a few deep breaths. Slowly, he got up and retook his seat on the stool.

"Are you all right?" the Count asked.

"If you're so concerned, why didn't you help me up?" Giovanni joked about it but didn't laugh. "Can't you see? You're a spirit locked inside a painting. You yearn for action, for company, to see, to travel. I'm not a young man anymore. All that's happened since you came into my life, it's just too much. I can't bear it. I'm not strong enough." Giovanni's voice cracked and he held back his tears.

The Count waited a moment. "Signor Fabrizzi. You must realize that I did not know Kreitel was your relative. The odds are incalculable."

"Maybe so, but it's true. And while I can't prove it, I know it in my bones, my father knew about Max and hid it from me. A lot more makes sense now. The cigar box, when I was young, with the name Kreitel engraved on the lid. Like your portrait, it was another useless gift from Max, trying to appease my father. He must have hated Max for selling stolen art, but he didn't send your portrait back to Zurich. He kept it, knowing when he was gone, it would come to me. As if he were leaving me a chance to find out on my own."

"Perhaps your father had hoped that you would do what he could not."

"And what would that be?" Giovanni asked.

"Forgive Max. After all, he is family."

"That is going to be difficult," Giovanni said. "Maybe one day, but not now. Certainly not for some time."

"I am truly sorry to have brought you this pain," the Count said. "It was never my intention that you would learn of your uncle's deeds, nor that any action on my part would lead to you losing your wife."

"Don't say *losing*," Giovanni said. "We say that when a loved one has died."

"You are still very much in love with her," the Count said.

Giovanni hung his head. "I am."

"Then forgive her. And forgive me. And begin your life anew. Cautiously, but anew. Trust me, I know better than anyone. It is dreadful to be alone. But you have a choice. You don't have to be alone."

Giovanni rose from the stool. "I'll consider your advice, Count." He reached for the crate, preparing to put the portrait away.

"Please," the Count said. "Leave me here. I have been in the dark too long. If you would, turn me toward the window. I want to see the street life of London. At least, as much as I can."

Giovanni turned the easel around and moved it closer to the window.

"How is that?" he asked.

"Perfect."

Giovanni turned off the lights, set the alarms, and left the painting alone to stare out into the night.

~

Giovanni returned home just before eleven o'clock. It was late, but he had to eat something after skipping dinner. He made a quick sandwich, then brushed his teeth and got into his pajamas.

As he pulled the covers back to get into bed, he noticed on the nightstand, a blinking light on the phone that indicated a message. Whoever it was, they could wait, he concluded. He adjusted his pillow, stretched out flat, and pulled the comforter up to his neck. It was good to be home, he thought, even if he was alone.

The phone rang.

He growled. How rude for anyone to call so late. But then it occurred to him—any call coming so late might be an emergency. As his outgoing message played, he dragged himself across the bed, toward the phone machine, and turned up the volume.

"Leave your message after the tone..." came from the speaker, and he waited to hear if the caller had bothered to record a voice mail.

"Mr. Fabrizzi. This is Jana Vogler, calling from Germany. I left a message earlier. I'm sorry to call so late but it's very important that I talk with you right away. I've found Clara Meyerstein."

Giovanni reached for the phone, but in the dark, he knocked it off the nightstand. He scrambled out of bed and picked up the receiver.

"Hello?" he said. "I'm sorry. Hello?"

"Mr. Fabrizzi?" Jana said.

"Yes, I heard your message." Seated on the edge of the bed, Giovanni reached for the lamp and clicked it on. "Please tell me everything." Giovanni wasn't going to get much sleep after receiving this important news. He scrounged through a drawer in the nightstand and found a pen and pad.

"There was no listing with the archives in Germany or France," she explained, "and the U.S. Holocaust Museum in Washington D.C. could not find her either. And then, just to see if we might have some luck elsewhere, I checked *Aufbau*, a German-language newspaper that maintained a list of European refugees arriving in New York between 1944 and 1946. And there she was. Clara Meyerstein. She arrived August 1, 1946."

Giovanni asked, "Is there any way to find out what happened to her?"

"Mr. Fabrizzi," Jana said with great satisfaction, "it is my pleasure to tell you that Clara Meyerstein is presently living in Manhattan, in an area I believe New Yorkers call Hell's Kitchen."

"She's alive?" Giovanni was stunned.

"Yes. I went through the records of the borough of Manhattan. She is living in an apartment on Ninth Avenue. I left a phone message for you earlier tonight. And I have already e-mailed her address to you."

"I'm not at my computer right now," Giovanni said.

"When you are, the message should be there." With a thrill in her voice, she continued, "This is very special. So many times I cannot find a missing person. And most times when I do, the end of my investigation is only to learn of their death. But this—this is what I live for, Mr. Fabrizzi. She is alive."

"I will visit her," he said. "And tell her about the painting."

"This is wonderful," Jana said. "Is there anything else I can do for you regarding Clara?"

"Do you have a phone number for her?"

"I could not find one listed. But I have confirmed her address on Ninth Avenue. Check your e-mail."

"I will," Giovanni said. "This is remarkable. How much do I owe you?"

"I've already received your check," Jana said. "I'm pleased to say the retainer covered your costs in full. All you owe me is a full account of your meeting with Clara Meyerstein."

"Thank you so much, Jana."

"Thank you. Please let me know how it goes."

They said their good-byes and Giovanni hung up the phone, then he switched the lamp off and slipped back under the covers. But sleeping was next to impossible, as his mind went round and round, imagining the trip he would soon take to America.

~

The next morning, Giovanni went to his studio and told the Count the great news. But there was even greater news. Finding Clara alive also meant that it was time to have the painting analyzed by a laboratory to confirm its authenticity. The Count was more excited by that news, and sincerely thanked Giovanni for keeping his promise.

As Giovanni prepared to pack the portrait back into the crate, he paused to ask for the Count's cooperation. Giovanni wanted his promise that he would not speak when Giovanni showed him to the director of the laboratory. Giovanni explained that he wanted to be focused and professional when he told the laboratory staff that the painting might possibly be the work of one of history's greatest painters. The Count assured Giovanni that he understood and agreed to remain silent during his entire visit to the laboratory.

Nevertheless, Giovanni remained apprehensive about his meeting with Vincent Drysdale, the director of L & D Laboratories, whose expertise in the authentication of significant works of art was renowned.

When Giovanni entered Drysdale's office, the director rose from his seat. He was exceedingly proper and ramrod stiff, outfitted in an impeccable suit. He greeted Giovanni with a strong handshake and offered him a seat, then asked if Giovanni wanted a coffee, which he politely declined.

Drysdale lowered to his seat behind the desk. "Well, I must say, I am most anxious to see this sixteenth century panel of yours."

Giovanni took the cue and opened the crate. As he brought out and unwrapped the Count, Drysdale kept up the conversation.

"We haven't seen much of you of late, old chap. I did hear about you and Arabella from someone, I don't recall whom."

Giovanni did not look up.

"I'm terribly sorry, Gio. Really, I am. And how is the work going on the Brueghel?"

"I took a little time off." Giovanni prepared to unveil the painting to Drysdale. "A European trip."

"Of course. Keep yourself busy."

Giovanni pulled out the panel with a flourish and held it up.

"May I?" Drysdale rose from his seat and came around the desk. Giovanni handed the panel to him. As he held it with great care, the director studied the painting for some time, shifting the angle so the light would strike it differently.

Giovanni was relieved that the Count had remained silent.

"It appears from the right period," Drysdale said. He carefully set the painting on an easel next to his enormous, mahogany desk. "Botticelli, you are thinking."

"I suspect it is possible, yes."

As he gazed at the painting, Drysdale nodded a few times, then he moved around his desk and returned to his chair behind it. He hesitated a moment before proceeding.

"Gio, we've known each other a long time, and I've always admired your skills with restoration and your eye for fine art. So please, don't take this the wrong way and let it be an insult, but you have to realize the implications of your suggestion. Remember, your reputation is at stake here."

208

"I fully realize that, Vincent. I am prepared, whatever the outcome may be."

Drysdale nodded though he still appeared concerned. "If I may ask, what has led you to believe it might be the work of Botticelli?"

"The trip I just went on," Giovanni explained. "I did some research in France and Germany, and ultimately in Switzerland. The painting had belonged to a Jewish family who lived in Paris. The Nazis confiscated their collection in 1940."

"Then you have documentation," Drysdale said.

"Sadly, not any to verify this particular work, only others. You see, the item was taken by a hired appraiser, an art dealer, before it could be cataloged."

"Then it went to a private collection," Drysdale said. "So you've been in contact with the collector. Care to give any names?"

"I can't say. And it doesn't matter anyway. The collector doesn't have any documentation either."

Drysdale's eyes grew wide. "Heaven's sake, Gio. You have this notion and no documentation whatsoever?"

"I'm afraid so."

"You're operating on a hunch," Drysdale said. "This isn't like you, Gio."

"I realize that, but you have to trust me, Vincent. I have to know one way or another."

Staring at Giovanni with a look of disbelief, Drysdale was silent, then he began to nod slowly. "Anyone else I'd say they were crazy. But the years we've worked together are something I can't ignore. If you're that confident, so be it. But, Gio, what if we test and discover the work is a knock-off created early last century?"

"I'm confident that won't be the case," Giovanni said. "I'm certain of that much."

Still disbelieving, Drysdale nodded. "All right, but the tests come at considerable cost. That's a lot of money to throw away if you're wrong, and it's not a Botticelli."

"The expense is peanuts if I'm right."

16

Shortly after she left their home, Arabella Fabrizzi had sent an e-mail to her husband, informing him in straight-forward, businesslike terms that she could be reached on her mobile phone and that she would be staying with a girlfriend in Islington.

Giovanni had received the e-mail with no great surprise, but as it reminded him of her affair and the failure of their marriage, he had transferred the message to a separate folder in his e-mail program so that he would not have to see it over and over again.

But after his meeting with Vincent Drysdale, although still fatigued from his trip, Giovanni felt that his life had changed for the better. He had positive expectations for the first time since he and Arabella had split. And so, after staring at pictures of her and Maurizio, and re-reading her simple, informative e-mail many times, he gathered his nerve and called her.

He reached her voice mail, but just to hear her speaking, even though only a recording, both excited and saddened him. The tone, indicating a message should be left, came so quickly that he was unprepared and immediately hung up. He stared at a photograph of her on the beach at St. Tropez, the sun acting as a backlight separating her from the crowd, as if she were on a sandy stage with scores of actors milling about.

Giovanni studied her face. Her smile was subtle, like the Mona Lisa, and she held her sun hat, straw with a purple and gold band. She was standing carefree, unaware of anyone or anything, except for her husband as he captured the image. Giovanni studied the photograph, and in that moment he resolved to do whatever it took to be with her again. If she were still carrying on her affair, he would ask her to break it off. He would not beg her, nor would he command her. He would ask politely, lovingly. He picked up the phone and prepared to leave a message for her to call him.

He was startled when she answered after one ring. Not her voice mail, but her.

"Gio? Is that you?"

"Yes," he replied, and then he was silent.

"Did you call me a few minutes ago?" she asked.

"I had some trouble with my phone." He thought about his white lie and that he was being a coward. "No, it's not true," he said. "I got through to your voice mail and... well, I didn't know what to say."

"And now?" she asked.

"I don't mean to bother you. I'm sorry. It's just that so much has happened." He felt awkward. He hadn't talked with her in weeks.

"Are you calling about us?" she asked. "Or is it something else?"

"Both, I suppose. A lot has happened since..."

"Since you asked me to leave?" she said. "If you're calling to invite me back..."

"No, I mean... I didn't mean to say no, I just wasn't... it's just, it's all been so difficult."

"Gio, whatever you have to say, please, just be certain it's what you want."

He hesitated. Then it hit him like a slap in the face. "You don't want to come back."

She quickly replied, "I didn't say that. I just want you to be sure, and if this is really something you want to talk about, I don't think we should do it over the phone."

"I completely agree," he said. "We should meet somewhere."

"All right," she said. "When?"

"As soon as possible. Are you available today?" he asked, but then he wanted to rephrase his words, fearing that he was being too aggressive.

"I could be," she said cautiously. "Where would we meet?"

His heart beat stronger. She had not rejected him.

"How about the wine bar down the street from our flat?" Without thinking, he had said *our* flat. "Or if that's not convenient..."

"That's fine," she said in a level voice, neither cold nor warm. "How about four?"

"Yes, great. See you then."

"Bye."

He stayed on the line until he was sure that she had hung up.

~

Giovanni arrived at the wine bar well before Arabella, hoping to find a table in the corner as far away from other customers as possible. When she entered the wine bar, Giovanni spent a breathless moment staring at her. She looked professional in a blazer and matching skirt, a woman's version of a business suit. Her upswept hair revealed the contours of her neck, and for Giovanni, it was like viewing her for the first time, all over again.

She spotted him, and with no recognizable expression on her face, she approached the table, her high heels clicking on the smooth tile floor. He stood and waited for her, wondering if he should kiss her on the cheek or dispatch all pretense and pull her into his arms.

Arabella arrived at the table and stopped, similarly unsure of how to proceed. She shifted her stance, waiting for Giovanni to make the first move.

"It's good to see you again," he said, in a daze as he took in her beauty. It was so true what they say about what you have and once it's gone.

"Are you going to invite me to sit?" she asked.

He snapped out of his trance. "Oh. Yes, of course." He moved to pull out a chair for her.

She set her purse down and sat at the table.

He returned to his chair. "Arabella, so much has happened, I don't know where to begin."

A waitress arrived and Giovanni ordered a bottle of wine. He and Arabella made small talk for a time, inquiring into each other's well-being since their separation. Once the bottle arrived and Giovanni downed his first glass, he launched into his story of the painting and hearing the voice, not giving her a chance to speak for fear she would call him crazy and leave. He continued in a rush of words and described all that had happened in Paris, Germany, and Zurich. He told her every detail, and then the news of submitting the painting to the laboratory for analysis.

He caught his breath after speaking without pause, then reached for his glass and drank more wine.

"Well," she said, "I don't know where to start. You actually hear a voice from the painting?"

"I know it sounds incredible, but really, we talk."

"Do you have many other imaginary friends?" she asked sarcastically.

"You don't believe me."

"It's difficult, and I have to wonder about your mental well-being. People generally don't hear paintings talk to them."

"Obviously not. But you have to understand. If not for the Count telling me, I would never have known any of it. Consider that, Arabella, please. I can show you all of the documents I've collected. There is no way I could have imagined all of these facts about the painting, the Meyersteins, the Nazis, my Uncle Max. It's just not possible."

"And a talking painting is?" she asked.

"I can't explain it. You just have to believe me. Max confessed in so many words, and that alone confirms what the painting told me. And what if it's true, and the painting really is by Botticelli? Then will you believe me?"

She thought about it. "How much would it be worth?"

"Millions," he said.

Her eyes grew wide. "Really? That much? We would have, I mean, you would have such prestige for discovering it. Imagine what that could do for business."

"It would be grand, I imagine, but honestly, I hadn't given it much thought." Giovanni wasn't ready to tell her that he intended to return the portrait to Clara. "There are other matters I must resolve first. To start, the subject of us. I don't mean to pry, but I think I have right to know. After all, we are still married." Giovanni waited until she looked him in the eye, then he aimed his question point blank. "Are you still with him?"

"I was a fool." Arabella opened her purse. She took out tissue and dabbed the corner of her eye. "I know it's taken you a long time to get over her. I should have been stronger. But I needed you, Gio, and you were so cold. And then, I had this young man constantly flirting, flattering me, clearly wanting me. I laughed off his advances but eventually, I believed you wouldn't ever touch me that way again. And I was weak. I gave in to him. It was wrong. I was wrong. But that's why it happened, Gio. I'm being as honest as I can."

"You didn't answer the question."

"No, I am not still with him. I haven't been since you asked me to leave. I called him that night and told him we could not see each other anymore."

"And...?" Giovanni probed.

"All right, it's true." Tears streamed down her cheeks. "He did call again, more than once, but I never went back to him. I never will. I swear it, Gio."

"Then come back home." He reached out to take her hand in his. "All that's happened since we parted, it's been unbelievable. I feel I could do anything, but not without you." The Count's advice came to mind. "I forgive you, Arabella. And I need your forgiveness as well. This wasn't all your fault, I realize that now. I was cold, distant, and I only drove you away. Please forgive me."

"Of course I'll forgive you, Gio."

"Come back home," he said. "Come back now. Right now."

She wiped at her tears. "But my things, they're still at my girlfriend's."

"We'll get them later," he said. "Together."

Through her teary, mascara-smeared eyes, she stared at Giovanni for a long, hard moment. She began to slowly nod her head, yes.

Few words were exchanged as they walked home together, Arabella hanging on his arm and her head against his shoulder. When they entered the flat, she looked around as if seeing the place anew. He watched her fondly as she wandered about, touching things and viewing photographs of them together, still arranged just as she had left them.

"I want to start over with you," he said. "I promise to never ignore you again, my beautiful one."

Giovanni took her in his arms and they kissed passionately. He began to move back, bringing her along as their embrace continued, into the hallway and he opened the bedroom door. They fell on the bed and kicked off their shoes, then he unbuttoned her blouse as she unbuttoned his shirt.

"One thing," he said. "I won't ask you to believe I can hear the

Count's voice. Just don't treat me like I'm crazy. I couldn't bear that."

She softly caressed one side of his face. "I believe you can hear a voice," she said. "I respect that. Just don't ask me to hear it too."

They made love into the night, as if it were the first time.

~

The next morning, Giovanni basked in the warmth of Arabella's embrace, their bodies entwined beneath the comforter. He had no urge to get up and attend to anything in particular. She was equally content to curl into his body and keep him near. The morning was unlike any other, as normally they would have been up and had breakfast long before the lazy hour of half past eight.

The phone rang.

Giovanni didn't budge, too inclined to indulge in the rare instance of sleeping in late, best of all while cuddling Arabella.

She was more obliged to answer the call, or simply wanted the ringing to stop. She slid across his chest and reached for the phone.

"Don't," he said. "It can't be anything important."

She smiled and returned to the warm pocket of his embrace. "Fine with me. I'm exhausted. In the best possible way." She kissed his cheek and pulled him closer.

"Leave your message after the tone..."

"Gio, are you there?" the caller said. "It's Vincent Drysdale."

Giovanni sat up in bed and let Arabella fall out of his arms.

"Listen," Drysdale said, "normally I wouldn't bother you so

early, and I did call your studio first. Here's the thing, dear boy. I have some very good news, and I wanted to speak with you about it as soon as possible. Ring me back at—"

Giovanni grabbed the handset. He covered the mouthpiece and whispered to Arabella, "Sorry." Then into the phone he said, "Vincent, I'm here. Forgive me. I'm having a late start today. What is the good news?"

"You may be on to something, old chap. The tests of the panel and tempera place your painting in the right period. To be honest, I was surprised, but now there are some other things to discuss. How about lunch?"

"When?"

"Today. I'm buying, and I promise you'll leave the restaurant with a big smile on your face."

~

Giovanni thought to invite Arabella along, but she declined before he could even ask. Though excited, perhaps even more than he was, she insisted that his lunch meeting was an important business matter rather than a social call, and it was not a wife's place. Besides, she wanted to get her things back to their flat that morning rather than wait a moment longer. Giovanni kissed her and held her tightly, then expressed how he would miss her during their few hours apart, determined to never again let her feel neglected.

At the appointed hour, Giovanni entered the bistro where Drysdale had suggested they meet. Giovanni spotted him immediately and joined him at the table.

Vincent Drysdale reached into his pocket and pulled out an envelope with the logo of L & D Laboratories on it. Somewhat ceremoniously, he handed the envelope to Giovanni.

"With sincere congratulations," Drysdale said.

"Thank you." Giovanni took the envelope, then pulled out the lab results and glanced at them. "Although, we are not quite home yet."

"The newer technology these days is quite fantastic," Drysdale explained. "We've been able to pinpoint dates with ever increasing accuracy and within remarkably narrow ranges. If you'd care to take a closer look at those lab results, I think you will be pleasantly surprised. Not only does the panel date to the right period, and the wood is from Italy, but the estimate falls within the years most likely Botticelli might have produced such a work, according to the historian with whom I've already consulted. This notion of yours is turning out to be a pretty strong case."

"You've already consulted with others?" Giovanni was surprised. "Aren't you moving a bit fast, Vincent?"

"Just the one," Drysdale said. "Just to see how the dates aligned."

Giovanni studied the pages and returned them to the envelope, which he then offered back to Drysdale.

"You keep it," he said.

Giovanni tucked the envelope into his jacket.

A waiter arrived and they ordered lunch. After the waiter moved along, Drysdale glanced to one side and seemed to recognize an old friend. "Well, good afternoon, Teddy."

A portly gentleman moving past their table noticed Drysdale

and stopped. "Very nice to see you, old boy."

Drysdale stood and shook hands with the fellow, then said, "Theodore Schierholz, allow me to introduce Giovanni Fabrizzi. The Fabrizzi family has been in art restoration since time immemorial."

"Well, not quite that long." Giovanni rose and shook the gentleman's hand.

"Teddy's on the board at the Tate," Drysdale said, then turned to him. "You know, Teddy, Gio and I are celebrating. His lab results came back positive for an undiscovered Botticelli he's had in the family, stored away. Can you imagine that?"

"Now hold on." Giovanni was shocked that Drysdale would be so bold. "The dates are favorable, so it *could* be a Botticelli. Let's wait until it's verified."

Schierholz seemed to ignore Giovanni and said to Drysdale, "I say, that is cause for celebration. I'm sure you two know all the best experts." Smoothly, Schierholz pulled out a business card and placed it next to Giovanni's plate. "I wish you well with your painting." He turned to Drysdale and said, "Vincent, you and I are overdue for lunch."

"I quite agree. I'll ring you, my good man."

Drysdale shook hands with Schierholz, who then continued on his way, though he did glance back with an eager smile and nod aimed at Giovanni.

"Vincent," Giovanni said once Schierholz was out of earshot. "I'm hoping it's a Botticelli, but really, we should wait until—"

Drysdale called out to another fellow who conveniently happened to be walking past their table, and he went through the entire routine again. Giovanni remained gracious, then after the curator to whom he had been introduced moved along, Giovanni eyed Drysdale warily.

"Vincent, if I didn't know better, I'd say you invited me specifically to this restaurant because you knew friends of yours would be lunching here, and you could mention the lab results."

Before Drysdale could explain himself, the waiter arrived with their meals.

As they proceeded with lunch, Drysdale paused to reach for his napkin and wipe his mouth. "Gio, I'm truly excited for you. I haven't told you the other news."

"What? That you've already sold it?"

"I've already arranged for the examination," Drysdale said. "When the results came back, I got on the phone. I've talked with the Courtauld, the Warburg, and the National Gallery. They have all agreed to examine the portrait to determine if it's a Botticelli. They want to have a look as soon as possible. Do I have your permission?"

"Of course," Giovanni said. "Vincent, I don't want to seem unappreciative, but at the risk of being presumptuous, you said you had other news. The lab results are favorable so the examination is a given. I assume that's not your other news."

Drysdale leaned closer to Giovanni as if preparing to tell a secret. "Gio, this is not official, and you didn't hear it from me, if anyone asks."

"Fine. What is it?"

"My contact at the National Gallery, whose name I cannot divulge, told me that if the work is authenticated as a Botticelli, he wishes to have the opportunity of making the first bid. And, unofficially, he said that if you did not donate the work, he expected the market value of a Botticelli today to be somewhere around twenty million pounds."

"Twenty?" Giovanni's eyebrows rose to the sky.

"Yes," Drysdale said. "Pounds, not dollars."

"That's a lot of money." Giovanni was still in shock.

"If you don't mind my asking," Drysdale said, "do you think you might sell versus donate? Or I suppose it's a little early for such questions."

"Why?" Giovanni asked. "Because of your friend at the National?"

"Actually, news of the lab results have been disseminated to others, outside of Britain."

"Hard to imagine that," Giovanni said sarcastically. "Unless of course, you had lunch in another country this morning." He glanced about the bistro and imagined the entire crowd approaching their table, armed with business cards and plastic smiles.

Drysdale chuckled. "No, that's ridiculous. You see, when I heard the National unofficially bid on the Botticelli even before its authentication, I thought, well, others are going to find out about it. And I have spoken with Pino Vitarelli at the Uffizi."

"I happen to know Pino," Giovanni said.

"Yes, he mentioned it. And he told me he wants to talk to you about sending one of his experts. He said the Uffizi may bid on the work for inclusion in the Botticelli Room."

"I must say, Vincent, you certainly don't waste any time."

Drysdale's enthusiasm dampened. "Gio, is there a problem?

You don't seem very happy about this. You realize, you may be considerably richer in the near future. And every major museum and collector in the world is going to know your name, if they don't already."

"*May* know my name. What if the authenticators do not agree?"

Drysdale looked confused. "Are you telling me you doubt it's a Botticelli?"

"No," Giovanni said. "I'm saying I believe it is, and you believe it is, but what if the experts don't agree? There will be doubt, and doubt is not good."

The waiter brought the bill and asked if they wanted anything else. Drysdale waited for Gio, who shook his head. Drysdale then handed his credit card to the waiter.

"Before I go," Giovanni said, "There is something I should tell you."

"Absolutely." Drysdale appeared distracted, watching for the waiter to return with his credit card.

"Vincent, I told you the painting belonged to a family in Paris."

"Yes, I recall. And the Nazis confiscated their collection. Very sad indeed, and a most unfortunate end for the poor folks."

"A member of the family is still alive."

Drysdale became concerned. "So we may have a legal battle to contend with. I see. Not good, Gio. This could complicate matters."

"I don't think you understand, Vincent. If the painting is a Botticelli, I am obligated to fly to New York and give it to her. It's the proper thing to do."

Drysdale's jaw dropped. "Are you serious? You're joking." When Giovanni didn't respond, Drysdale grew louder. "Tell me you are joking!"

His reaction didn't surprise Giovanni. It was tame even, compared to the reaction he expected later, once he could find enough courage to tell Arabella of his plan to return the painting.

17

Giovanni had difficulty telling his son all that had happened. On the phone with him, he gave a partial explanation, describing how the Count's portrait had come from Max via Federico and that if it was authenticated, it could be worth upwards of twenty million pounds.

Maurizio had expressed delight at the splendid news, and he was also pleased that his father and Arabella were back together again. Maurizio insisted on flying to London to celebrate.

There was no way Giovanni would have told his son not to come, but he dreaded informing him and Arabella of his plans that would not only suggest his business judgment was cloudy, but also that his state of mind was unstable.

As Giovanni drove with Arabella to the airport to pick up Maurizio, using the excuse of listening to a CD of Chopin etudes for his lack of conversation, Giovanni wondered if Arabella could help him convince his son that hearing a voice from a painting was in the realm of possibility, and that it should not be looked upon as encroaching senility. After all, Arabella had accepted his communication with the Count. But she also assumed they would be receiving millions for the sale of the painting. When she and Maurizio learned of his other intentions, their reactions could be harsh.

As they waited in the passenger arrival area, Arabella again expressed her excitement about the Count's portrait. Earlier that morning, she had shown Giovanni newspaper clippings from the British press about the possible discovery of a Botticelli painting. She had collected them in a photo album for safe keeping and excitedly pointed out where Giovanni's name appeared in each article.

He had done his best to smile, chuckle even, and encourage her, though he dreaded the revelation that he would soon have to share. Drysdale certainly had taken it badly during their lunch date, even suggesting that Giovanni was being self-destructive and possibly hurting Drysdale's own credibility in the art world. Giovanni had pointed out his moral obligation to Clara Meyerstein and insisted that obligation was bigger than any benefit to Giovanni, Drysdale, or any collector or museum in the world. Lunch ended with a tight-jawed Drysdale politely urging Giovanni to reconsider. Give Clara a portion of the proceeds, he suggested, rather than the entire painting. Giovanni had walked away, noncommittal.

"Here he comes." Arabella waved as Maurizio appeared among the river of airline passengers flowing into the arrival area.

Maurizio, striding energetically with an overnight bag slung over his shoulder, finally caught sight of his father and waved. He hurried out of the crowd and threw his arms around Giovanni, then Arabella.

"I have to show you," Maurizio said. "I have newspapers from Italy. Your name is in them."

Arabella took over, telling Maurizio of the meeting with Drysdale, of the scrapbook she assembled, of all the new developments she could think of, as they walked through the busy terminal, navigating the crowd.

"Let's get you something to eat." Giovanni entered an airport cafe. "We'll let the traffic die down and then head home." He found a table and then waited for Maurizio and Arabella to catch up.

Maurizio sat down and unzipped an outer pouch of his overnight bag, from which he took out the Italian newspapers he had brought. He had already folded each to the pages of specific interest.

"Here, Papa, see? *Renowned restorer Giovanni Fabrizzi may be sitting on the greatest discovery in a generation of an Old Master's artwork.* And look, here's another."

Giovanni took the papers, not wanting his son to continue reading them aloud. He glanced at them to be polite, patted Maurizio's face affectionately, and then pushed the papers toward the empty side of the table.

A server arrived and Maurizio asked for a bottle of champagne before Giovanni or Arabella could order.

"Fine with me," Arabella said. "We are celebrating, after all."

Arabella and Maurizio began talking at the same time, then they laughed.

"You go first," Maurizio said.

"I was just going to ask how work is going."

"Yes," Giovanni chimed in, "how is it?"

"Fine, fine," Maurizio replied. "But I have so many questions, Papa. It felt like you weren't telling me everything when we talked on the phone."

Giovanni held up his hand to interject. He looked at them both. The thrill of the possible future they imagined made their eyes shine. It was going to make what he had to say all the more disappointing. Nevertheless, the time had come to say it.

Before he could begin, the server returned with the champagne and three glasses.

"Celebrating, are we?" she asked, then popped the bottle and poured.

"Too early to say," Giovanni grumbled.

Arabella offered the first toast. "To my dear husband, who has shown me great love and patience. May your dreams come true regarding the Botticelli."

The three of them clinked glasses and drank.

"And may I add," Maurizio said, "a toast to my dearest papa, who has imbued in me both the love and the preservation of fine art. It is my greatest wish that your art repay you with all the money and acclaim you so richly deserve."

"Here, here!" Arabella said, and again their three glasses met. She asked Giovanni, "And what do you have to say?"

He studied the bubbles in his glass, as he wondered how he had arrived at such a strange place in life. He lifted his glass, and his wife and son did the same.

"My dear ones," he said. "I love you both and cannot adequately express how important you are to me. The last thing I would ever want is to hurt or disappoint you. So here is a toast, a toast to my love for you and a prayer that if we should ever disagree, it will not change the love we shall have for one another, forever."

Arabella and Maurizio exchanged puzzled glances. Then they

shrugged it off and continued the celebration, clinking their glasses into Giovanni's.

"Now that we agree," Giovanni continued, "allow me to tell you something very important. The Count's portrait belonged to a family named the Meyersteins. It was taken from them by the Nazis in 1940. I employed an investigator in Germany who has found one survivor of the family, Clara, who is living in New York City. If the authenticators determine the Count is a Botticelli, I am obligated to visit Clara and return the painting."

In chorus, Arabella and Maurizio cried, "*What?*"

"Listen to me," Giovanni said. "I would be happy to sell this work and make millions, but it doesn't belong to me. And furthermore, the way it came to me is shameful."

He drained his glass. His son and wife were too astonished to move a muscle. Giovanni explained his confrontation with Max and how the painting had been acquired, which amounted to theft, pure and simple.

The server returned and asked if they wanted anything to eat. Neither Arabella nor Maurizio responded, and Giovanni had lost his appetite. He told the server they were fine. But they were far from fine.

"This is incomprehensible," Arabella said. "Hearing a voice is one thing. I agreed not to fight you on that. But giving away a portrait worth millions…"

"I'm not giving it away," Giovanni argued. "I'm *returning* it, to its rightful owner."

"But, Papa," Maurizio said. "That's crazy. If not for you, she'd never have known. You've discovered something that was lost."

"We're not talking about someone's misplaced pocket change. And stop saying I'm crazy. I won't hear any more of that from either of you. The Count is real, and I'm returning the painting, and no, it's not because I'm under some kind of mental strain you're convinced is afflicting me. Enough!"

Silent, Arabella and Maurizio glanced at each other. Then she said to him, "Mau, this is your father's decision. After all, he has to honor his conscience, and we have to respect that." She glanced at Giovanni. "I'm thankful we're back together again."

Maurizio thought about it. "I understand. You don't want to risk another upset." He shifted to Giovanni. "But, Papa, please, at least keep your options open. Maybe you can convince Clara to place the work in a museum where it belongs."

"And why might I do that?" Giovanni asked. "To secure a handsome fee from the museum?"

"And protect your reputation," Maurizio said. "Remember, you also have an obligation to the world of fine art. Think hard about this choice. If the work simply goes from one private collection to another, there could be resentment toward you. For crying out loud, it could be a Botticelli. It deserves to be on public display."

"I won't convince her of anything. The decision is hers, and hers alone."

~

Later that evening, Giovanni lounged in the living room while Arabella and Maurizio were busy in the kitchen preparing fettuccine with carbonara sauce, one of Giovanni's favorite dishes from his youth. He had made it for Maurizio when he was a boy, as had Maurizio's mother, and it came to be accepted as comfort food by them all, and now, Arabella too.

As Giovanni waited for dinner, he stretched out on the sofa in the living room, talking on the telephone with Vincent Drysdale.

"I know you did me a great favor," Giovanni said, "and I appreciate it, Vincent. Whatever the outcome, I'll ensure you're recouped for any extra expense."

"No, no, dear boy," Drysdale said, then emphatically assured Giovanni, "That is not what this is about. I understand your concerns about properly compensating Clara Meyerstein, and I am sure you will figure that out. It's just that the Uffizi and the National Gallery and, well, frankly others have asked me why you aren't returning their calls."

Giovanni sighed. Exasperated, he had trouble forming a good response. He looked toward the kitchen and saw his wife and son busy preparing dinner.

Arabella called, "It's just about ready, Gio."

He sought to wrap up his phone conversation. "Vincent, let me call you tomorrow. I'm about to sit down for dinner. My son is visiting as well."

"I understand," Drysdale said. "Please, Gio, just talk to them. Even if you don't have a definite answer yet. They all want to make bids."

"I told you." Giovanni sat up. "First I have to talk with Clara."

"Gio, you've put me in an awkward position here. Unofficially, you have three museums willing to buy the painting. The National Gallery's offer is somewhere in the neighborhood of twenty-five million pounds."

"I didn't ask anyone to make an offer." Giovanni stood and approached the dining room table. "I only wanted to have it authenticated."

"You work in the art world," Drysdale said. "You know very well a discovery of this magnitude is going to cause a lot of attention. Can you please just communicate with them so they don't turn on me? It will impact my business if they resent me. They already think I've deceived them into believing it was for sale."

"That's your own fault for assuming it was."

"Fine." Drysdale was frustrated. "Just tell them something. Anything."

"All right. I really must go."

"Thank you, Gio. Let me know how it goes."

Gio hung up the phone just as Arabella and Maurizio emerged from the kitchen with dinner, which they brought to the dining room table.

"What did Vincent have to say?" Arabella asked as they sat down to eat.

"The National Gallery is up to twenty-five million," Giovanni said glumly.

"Twenty-five?" Maurizio was excited. "That's fantastic, Papa." He looked at Arabella, who pursed her lips and gave the slightest shake of her head. Maurizio began to sprinkle peppers on his pasta and toned down his enthusiasm. "I mean, if you decide to sell it, that's a great price."

"Yes," Giovanni tiredly agreed. "It's a large sum of money. Even for selling one's soul."

"Oh, pooh," Arabella said. "Let's see what happens after you visit Clara."

"Can we not talk about it?" Giovanni asked. "I'd really like to enjoy this meal."

The phone rang.

"Don't answer it," Giovanni said. "We're eating dinner."

"It might be for me, you know," Arabella said.

"It's about that damned painting."

Arabella went to the phone and looked at the display. "Gio. It's Pino calling from the Uffizi."

"I'll call him back."

"Nonsense." She picked up the phone and exchanged pleasantries with the museum director in Florence.

Giovanni shook his head and continued eating. Maurizio did the same and kept quiet as he shifted glances between his father and Arabella on the phone.

"Darling," Arabella said, "come say hello to Pino."

"I'm eating," Giovanni replied.

Arabella covered the mouthpiece and became stern. "Giovanni. This is not how you treat friends you've known for over twenty-five years."

"Good friends don't interrupt one's dinner." He threw down his napkin, got up, and took the phone from her. "Pino, we're just sitting down to dinner with Maurizio who is visiting. Can I call you back tomorrow?"

"Gio, sorry to disturb you," Pino Vitarelli said in his thick Italian accent. "Yes, call me tomorrow. We don't have to talk now. I am just a little confused because Drysdale tells me you are planning to give the painting to Clara Meyerstein in New York. If you were to sell to us, we would be happy to discuss some generous compensation to her as well."

"That's kind of you, Pino, but the offer is premature. Let me visit her first. All right? She has a say in what happens, too." Giovanni shook his head, frustrated that others could not fathom the simple logic of letting someone decide the fate of their own personal property.

"Okay, Gio," Pino said. "Let's talk tomorrow. Give my best to Mau."

Giovanni hung up the phone and returned to the table. He stared at his bowl of fettuccine noodles and noted the lack of steam rising from them. The cold dinner had lost its appeal thanks to the unpleasant interruption. He pushed the bowl away.

Maurizio was concerned. "You're not eating, Papa. Are you feeling all right?"

"Physically, I'm fine. I just feel heartsick. I feel like whatever I do with this bloody painting, it will be the wrong thing."

The phone rang.

"For Christ's sake!" Giovanni hollered.

"I'll get it." Maurizio got up from the table.

"I don't want to talk to anyone," Giovanni said forcefully.

"Hello?" Maurizio listened. "Just a moment, please," he told the caller and then said to his father, "It's Hugo Coates, art critic from the Guardian."

"I don't care if it's the Pope calling."

Maurizio looked at Arabella who shrugged. Maurizio told the caller, "Mr. Coates, we're having dinner now. Would it be possible for Giovanni to call you tomorrow?"

"I'm not calling anyone!" Giovanni shouted.

"Gio!" Arabella scolded. "Don't be rude."

Maurizio wrote down a phone number and promised the reporter that someone would get back to him.

Giovanni flew out of his chair and went to the hall closet. He grabbed an overcoat and then his keys.

"Where are you going?" Arabella asked.

"The one place where I can be left alone." Giovanni moved rapidly toward the door. "I'll be at my studio. Don't bother calling, I won't answer."

Maurizio rose from his chair.

Giovanni halted and pointed his finger. "Not another word from you."

Sheepishly, Maurizio said, "I was just going to offer to drive you."

Giovanni stepped out and slammed the door shut.

～

Having the Count gone for days, at the lab being analyzed, had made Giovanni nervous. The Count had promised to remain silent, so it wasn't that, but Giovanni was constantly worried about just where the portrait might be floating about, in this person's office or another, or possibly even being transported offsite for a different test. Once the authentication was complete, his concern only grew as news of the work's value spread quickly. When it came time for the painting to be returned, it was not a simple matter of

Giovanni dropping by to pick it up. The event required armed guards who accompanied the painting into the strong room and stood by to ensure that Giovanni locked the door before their departure. Of course, the additional people around had prevented Giovanni from speaking with the Count. Even so, Giovanni was sleeping better knowing that the Count was back where he belonged—for the time being.

Upon arriving at his studio, Giovanni opened the strong room and brought out the Count's portrait, then set it on the usual easel.

"Did they treat you well?" Giovanni asked.

"It was uncomfortable, though tolerable," the Count said. "I am pleased the ordeal has passed. The lighting was very harsh."

"And the x-rays?"

"I felt nothing, though from what I understand, the excessive exposure should kill me, eventually. Were I not already dead. Why have you come here tonight?"

"I have a difficult decision to make."

Giovanni poured a glass of wine, turned off a bank of overhead lights, and lowered to his stool. He stared into the shadow of the painting.

"Thank you for having my portrait authenticated," the Count said. "I appreciate that. You know by now that I am honest, not an idle boaster, a passer of rumors. I am a work of great art that belongs only in a great museum."

Giovanni remained silent.

The Count asked, "Are you here to tell me when I am going to the Uffizi?"

"I'm here because I'm sick and tired of my wife and my son and everyone in the fucking art world telling me what to do with you."

"Surely you have told them of my wish to return to my homeland."

"Do you have the slightest understanding of the position I'm in?" Giovanni asked. "My wife and son already think I'm nuts for talking to a painting. Oh, but let's make it even better. The painting wants to hang in the Uffizi. Sure, that will change everything."

"The sarcasm in your tone indicates you are irritated."

"Very," Giovanni said. "No one understands that Clara Meyerstein, the only survivor of the family, has a right to the painting. All everyone cares about is how much money your portrait will fetch. Does anyone have a moral code anymore?"

"I have a moral code," the Count said.

"Glad to hear it," Giovanni. "It does neither of us any good, though."

"Out of curiosity," the Count asked, "how much are the offers?"

"Twenty-five million pounds for the National Gallery."

"My Lord, that sounds like a lot."

"It is."

"And how much will the Uffizi pay?"

"Less than that, at this point."

"But still, you have to remember," the Count said, "the only true place for a Botticelli is in the Uffizi. Anything less is unacceptable."

"You're no better than the rest of them. Everybody has an agenda."

Giovanni reached for the panel and lifted it from the easel.

"What are you doing?" the Count asked.

"Putting you away. Then I'm going home to buy a ticket for New York. I'm sorry, but your portrait belongs to Clara Meyerstein, not me, not the Uffizi, not anyone else."

"You can't," the Count said.

"I can and I will." Giovanni said. "The poor woman lost her entire family. The Nazis sent them to die and stole their entire art collection, except of course, your portrait, swiped by my shameless uncle who has the audacity to offer you as some kind of pathetic olive branch to mend his feud with my father. By God, I will return you to her, and nothing you or anyone else can say will stop me."

Giovanni slid the Count into the crate and locked the strong room door.

18

Giovanni walked out of the New York subway station and headed up Ninth Avenue, marveling at the variety of ethnic restaurants along the way. He studied the address he had written down for Clara Meyerstein and determined that she was only three blocks away. Hell's Kitchen looked safe enough at that time of day. The area didn't seem as marginal as when he and Serafina had visited New York almost two decades earlier. Their exploration of the city after seeing a Broadway play had only urged them to race back to the safer environs of the Plaza Hotel.

Giovanni was relieved to be in another country—on another continent—far away from everyone and their opinions of the painting's best outcome, the phone calls, and the pressure to make the right choice. At last he was beyond the reach of anyone who could interfere with his decision to return the painting. Others might have called him a fool, but he wouldn't have to live out his days with a heavy conscience. The moment he had boarded the plane to America, a great weight was lifted from his shoulders, and with every step forward his mind became clearer, certain that he had made the right choice. It was going to be a good day, he thought, and all the days to follow, knowing he would no longer have the burden of decision regarding the painting.

Giovanni had brought along a copy of the *New York Times* that he purchased a few days before in London. The Arts and Leisure section had a story about Giovanni, the reclusive art restorer who would not consent to an interview, despite being officially heralded as the owner of a heretofore unknown Botticelli. Giovanni was not interested in collecting stories about himself and the painting of the Count, but it did not stop Arabella from doing so. After the authentication of the work, she checked the papers and magazines daily at their neighborhood newsstand. When Arabella had shown him that even the *New York Times* had announced his discovery, Giovanni bought an additional copy, thinking that it might have an impact on Clara when they met. After all, he had no idea what condition she might be in. She could be a victim of Alzheimer's disease, or other ailment that had stripped away her memory of events in Paris and Germany. Perhaps she was of sound mind but simply would not believe he was in possession of the most important work in her family's art collection, now of astronomical value, unless she read it in a newspaper. He had prepared the paper, folding it to the section and having outlined the article with a red marker, so that he could direct her attention to it.

The variety of Ninth Avenue restaurants was like a tour of world cuisine. Jamaican, Ukrainian, Argentine, Korean. Giovanni pondered how far he had traveled since the Count had first spoken to him. He also wondered if perhaps Jana Vogler in Germany was wrong and Clara Meyerstein was in fact dead, or if Jana had found a different Clara Meyerstein. Then the painting would go to the highest bidder, he assumed, which led to an unsettling thought. If the public learned the painting had at one time belonged to the Meyersteins, Giovanni might be seen as a profiteer, selling a piece of Jewish-owned art, made all the worse if anyone were to discover that his uncle had assisted the Nazis.

Giovanni went over and over the words he would say to Clara Meyerstein when she answered the door. Or perhaps a nurse would answer, if Clara were infirm and cared for by live-in help.

A block away from her address, Giovanni stopped in front of a small grocery store. Next to the produce, carefully piled up in little mounds, there were bundles of flowers wrapped in light green paper, in a scratched and dirty, white plastic bucket. He studied the flowers, pulled out the best two bundles, and bought them.

Giovanni found her address and climbed the stairs to the building's entry door, which of course was locked. He leaned closer to a panel of buzzers with the residents' names listed. His information from Jana indicated that Clara was in apartment 4C, but he could not verify it, unable to read the names as the lettering was old and smudged. He rang the buzzer to 4C but there was no answer. He sat down on the steps and waited.

About ten minutes had passed when the building's entry door opened. A middle-aged Hispanic woman was coming out of the building.

Giovanni leaped up. "Can you please hold the door?"

The woman stopped in the doorway. "Who you want?" she asked, suspicious and concerned.

"Clara Meyerstein," Giovanni replied. "I'm told she lives in apartment 4C."

The woman studied him thoroughly, all the way down to his shoes.

"The elderly lady," he said. "French accent?"

Again she studied him. Giovanni hoped the gray the years had given him would help convince her that he wasn't a street thug looking for easy prey.

"You from Social Services?" she asked.

Giovanni thought to say yes, but he reconsidered. "No, I'm..." He resorted to bending the truth only a little. "I'm an old friend of hers. Please, I haven't seen her in many years."

The woman hesitated, then moved aside and held the door open. "She lives here. Her name is Clara?"

"Yes."

"That's good. She don't see many people. She don't come out a lot."

Giovanni thanked the woman, slipped into the building, and the door swung shut and latched behind him. The tiny, dark lobby was dirty and paint was peeling from the walls. He found an elevator but an out-of-order sign was taped over the call button.

After climbing three flights of creaky stairs, Giovanni was winded and had broken a sweat. He didn't want to appear as though he had run the entire distance from the airport to her apartment, so he took a moment to compose himself and catch his breath.

He leaned close to the door marked 4C and could hear nothing on the other side. He brushed back his hair with his hands, mopped up the last of his sweat with a handkerchief, and knocked

244

on the door.

A long moment passed with no response. He heard no footsteps. He knocked again, louder and for a longer time. Across the hallway and a few doors down, one opened, though only enough to peek out, the gap limited by the security chain inside. In the narrow opening, the face of an older man appeared, staring curiously at Giovanni.

"I'm here to see Clara," Giovanni said. "I'm a friend."

"She's old," the man said. "You have to make a real racket to get her attention." He shut his apartment door.

Giovanni pounded again on the door to apartment 4C. He shouted, "Clara Meyerstein. Are you there? Clara?"

Still there was no response, so he pounded and shouted again. Then from beyond the door came the voice of a woman who spoke with a heavy French accent, meek though she sounded annoyed.

"Who is it?" she asked. "What do you want?"

"Clara." Giovanni cleared his throat and tried to sound warm and caring despite the fact he had been shouting. "I'm an old friend of your family. My name is Giovanni Fabrizzi."

The door remained shut.

"Who?" she asked.

"Giovanni Fabrizzi. I knew your uncle and aunt in Paris. On Avenue Foch. Your Aunt Carmella and I are both from Florence. May I come in?"

"How did you find me?"

He had reached his first hurdle. He couldn't tell her the truth, not until he was inside. But he could tell her a portion of it.

"I found you through the International Tracing Service in

Germany."

There was no sound of movement from inside the apartment. Giovanni was not going to accept being turned away after getting this close. So he resorted to guilt.

"Please, Clara. I brought you some flowers. And I'm worn out from climbing your stairs. I'm not a young man."

A deadbolt turned, then another lock, and the door opened enough to catch on the security chain. Her face appeared in the gap as she peered out to look at Giovanni.

He held out the bundle of flowers. "For you."

She studied the flowers and Giovanni carefully watched for her reaction, slight as it was, the tiniest smile for only a second, and her eyes brightened. The door closed and she unlatched the chain, then she pulled the door open.

She was short and had a head of snow-white hair, in contrast to her loose, colorful dress patterned with flowery designs that was decades out of fashion.

Giovanni handed her the flowers and then stepped into the small apartment, sparsely furnished and decorated. She carried the flowers to her tiny kitchen, large enough for just one person, and placed the bundle in a discarded milk carton that she then filled with water from the sink.

Giovanni sat on the sofa, its cushions sagging from age, and watched her put the bouquet and milk carton on a small dining table, only room for two.

"How did you know my family?" she asked, moving away from the table slowly, but without the aid of a walker or even a cane. She sat down in a straight back wooden chair that appeared uncomfortable. "You don't look any older than I do."

Giovanni didn't want to lie to this poor old woman, but without something to convince her, she might ask him to leave.

"My father was an art restorer," he said. "Henri and Carmella used his services for some of the art in their home. My father brought me along a time or two, when I was young."

Clara didn't smile or say anything. He was a little surprised that she hadn't at least offered him something to drink.

He took a chance. "It's so nice to see you again," he said, trying to win her over.

"I don't remember you," she said.

"It was a long time ago." He reached inside his jacket and pulled out a photograph of the Count's portrait. "I have a photograph of a painting your aunt and uncle owned. My father worked on it. I wondered if you might remember it."

He scooted across the sofa, closer to her, and passed the photo to her.

In her first show of aged vulnerability, her liver-spotted hand trembled as she reached out and took the photograph of the painting. She studied it intently, looking down at the photograph only inches from her face. Her arm dropped to her lap, the photo with it, and she looked up at Giovanni. The expression on her face had changed. She was disturbed, perhaps even angry.

"You know where this painting is?" Her tone was accusatory.

Giovanni smiled. "Clara, I have much to tell you about the painting. I am an art restorer, as my father was. I've researched this painting extensively. I know it was taken from your family in 1940 when you lived in Paris." He didn't want to expose his own family's dirty secrets, so he opted to smooth over the part about Max taking it from their home. "My uncle was an art dealer in Paris at the time, who came into possession of the painting. He later gave it to my father."

"You have it?" She was surprised but also seemed almost horrified, which puzzled Giovanni.

"I do," he replied. "But there is more. I've had it authenticated as a work of Botticelli. You are familiar with the artist, I assume."

She nodded slowly, confirming that she knew of the artist, but she didn't appear pleased by this news. Not pleased at all.

"You realize, of course," Giovanni continued, "as the work of Botticelli, the painting is of considerable value." From his jacket he pulled out the copy of the *New York Times* that he had brought along, folded to the article about him and the painting. He handed it to her.

She took a moment to study it. As her gaze moved down the page, her eyes began to widen. "Seventy-five million dollars?" She looked up at Giovanni.

"Yes," he replied.

"You have done nicely for yourself, Mr...."

"Fabrizzi. Please, call me Gio, but I'm afraid you don't understand, Clara. I have no desire to profit from the painting. It belonged to your family, and now, as you are the only survivor, it belongs to you. I've come here to give it back."

The newspaper fell on her lap and her gaze dropped. She brought the back of her hand to her forehand, and her round shoulders quivered as she began to weep.

Giovanni gave her a moment, then scooted across the sofa, closer to her. "You won't have to struggle anymore," he said. "You're a rich woman now, Clara."

She looked up with fire in her eyes. "I want nothing to do with that painting."

"What?" Giovanni shifted back. "I don't understand."

She looked away. "I think you should leave now."

"What?" Giovanni tried to catch her gaze. "What have I said, Clara? I didn't mean to upset you, please, but I don't understand. This should be great news to you, but..."

"You don't know what happened to me," she said.

Giovanni realized that he had opened a deep wound. He gave her some space and thought carefully of how to proceed. "I learned a lot during my research," he said. "I know about Drancy and Auschwitz. I'm truly sorry about you and your family, really. I can't imagine the horror you must have all faced, and I won't try to pretend."

Her hollow stare focused on him. "You know nothing."

"Then please," he said, hoping to comfort her rather than be a source of pain. "Tell me, Clara. I care. Really, I do."

"I don't want that painting," she said. "Daniel and Elise should have it, not me. I'm not worthy of it."

"But they're gone," Giovanni said, then he regretted using words so unfeeling. He didn't know how to talk with her about it—talk with anyone about a subject so delicate—and he had never imagined in his life that he would be put in the position of making any person relive such tremendous pain. "Nothing would please me greater, Clara, than to return the painting to Daniel and Elise. I would if I could, believe me, and I'm here to do the best I can and give it to you instead, the one member of your family to survive."

"No!" she screamed, then rose from her chair and went to the window, her back to Giovanni as she gazed out at the traffic and noise of Ninth Avenue. In a distant voice, she said, "It doesn't matter how much money the painting is worth. I don't deserve it. You may think because I survived, I should have it, but you're wrong. You don't know how I survived."

"I want to know," he said softly. "Would you tell me?"

She turned from the window and looked about the room, seeming to stare through the walls and into a dark past.

"It was frightening," she said, "when they took us away. But we had no idea then. I was so naïve. Yes it was terrible, but we thought they would hold us in a camp until the war ended, we would suffer of course, but then someday we'd get our lives back. We would try to bear it, and make it through. That hopeful thinking died when we got to Auschwitz. We were separated and very quickly I realized it was the end. No one was leaving that camp alive. Think about that, Mr. Fabrizzi. You wake up one day and you know, with absolutely certainty, that it could be your last. Maybe not that day, but the next, or another very soon."

"I am sorry." He didn't know what else to say.

"There was an awful sense of apathy," she said. "My family was gone, elsewhere in the camp or already dead, I never knew. The strangers with me became my only family. We all knew our fate. We would cry and hold one another, saying good-bye for as long as we could, as each day another was taken away, sometimes one or two or other days a whole group, herded like animals by the evil guards. But when I was taken, it was not to join the others. Despite my shaved head, sunken cheeks, and the number tattooed on my arm, a Nazi officer found me attractive. How he could find a girl of sixteen attractive in that condition, I have no idea, but he did. He took me to his office. He told me that if I did certain things, he would keep me alive, give me more food, give me medicine. If I didn't fight him, if I pleased him, if I performed the acts he desired, if I did everything right, I wouldn't die. At that time, the urge to survive was so strong, I would do anything, and I did. He was happy with me, and there were other Nazi officers as well, taking turns as I was passed around from one to another. I traded my virginity and self-respect for the chance to live."

She paused, hanging her head. Giovanni remained silent. There was nothing he could say that could possibly comfort her.

She turned back to the window and gazed out at the street below. "It was the wrong choice. Even though I survived, I have lived every day since then—and it's been a long life—thinking that I had no right to do what I did. A Jewish aid organization provides me money to live and yet I turned my back on my own people. I don't want that painting. It only reminds me of the terrible thing I did."

Giovanni rose from the sofa. "Clara."

She did not look at him.

"Please, can we sit down?" he asked. "I need to tell you more. It will be easier if we're both sitting."

She returned to the straight back chair, and he lowered to the sofa.

"First," he said, "I have to say that nothing in my experience can parallel the horror of what you've been through. But I too feel guilty about my past. Well, my family's past, and it relates to this painting. I wasn't completely honest earlier, what I told you about my uncle. It is true he was an art dealer, but I didn't tell you the rest. He had helped the Nazis appraise the collections of many Jewish families, but he did something even worse. He took some of the art for himself. The painting of the Count is one case I know of, but I'm guessing there were many more. Then he resold the stolen art, claiming it was the only way he could survive the troubled times. That was his excuse anyway, but it turns out that he became very rich as a result. Apparently, he never managed to sell the Count's portrait, and instead he gave it to my father."

"The Count?" Clara asked.

Giovanni realized his mistake of referring to the painting in such a personal manner, likely to be perceived as too casual for an inanimate object. He considered telling her of his ability to communicate with the Count, but decided against it, as it would only confuse matters.

"The subject of the painting," he explained. "Your family's painting, that is. I have taken a liking to the Italian nobleman, you could say."

She nodded. "That particular portrait was dear to Uncle Henri as well."

Giovanni nearly agreed, vocally, as the Count had told him about Henri's love for the painting. But Giovanni quickly realized how odd that might appear—for him to know such details about Mr. Meyerstein, a man he had never met.

"The painting does move some of us," Giovanni said, then he used the opportunity to steer the conversation to where it belonged. "And now it is capturing the attention of many others, which has been troubling for me. You see, many of my friends and colleagues are advising me to the sell the painting because it is worth so much. But I couldn't while knowing you had survived, and that I possessed something that belongs to you. Especially knowing how the painting had come into my family. It's shameful."

"Did your father know what your uncle had done?" she asked.

"I'm pretty sure he did, but he never told me, though I suspect he wanted to. Otherwise he would have sent the painting back. My father is gone now, so I'll never know for sure." He thought about what the Count had said. "A friend suggested that my father wanted me to know so that I might forgive my uncle, because my father couldn't."

"Can you forgive him?" she asked.

Again his thoughts turned to the Count. "Someone else asked that recently. As I told him, it won't be easy. One day maybe, but not now."

"Then you should understand my feelings," Clara said. "Your uncle can say he sold stolen art because he had no other way of surviving. And I can say that I gave my body to Nazi officers because I had no other way of surviving. Those things are true. But that does not make them right. You have every right never to forgive your uncle. And me, I have every right never to forgive myself."

"But I want to forgive."

"So do I," she said. "That does not mean it will ever happen."

There must be something else he could say, he thought, to convince her to stop berating herself for something that happened so many years ago. He could think of nothing, so he ended where he had begun. "Clara, the painting is legally yours. I'll arrange to have it sent it to you, then we'll see how you feel. All right?"

"No. You can send me papers and I will sign them, to state the painting is yours. You're a good man, Mr. Fabrizzi. I trust that you will do what is best. But please, once I have signed the papers, I do not want to see you or that painting ever again."

19

The intense Tuscany sun warmed Giovanni's face as he drove their rental car into Pisa. Arabella and Maurizio enjoyed the scenery, admiring the Leaning Tower and the Piazza del Duomo. Giovanni wanted to drive past the Medici Palace as well, considering the Count was a relative of that renowned clan. There was no smirking from Maurizio, no eye rolling. The drive through the city was filled with contemplation and reverence for their surroundings.

Arabella and Maurizio were relieved, as was Giovanni, with how everything had worked out. More than relieved, his wife and son were bubbling with hopeful expectations for the future, knowing the happiness they would all share despite the family wrangling they had endured.

A few days earlier, Giovanni had arrived in Florence to supervise the hanging of the Count in the Botticelli Room at the Uffizi. The portrait would be in the gallery well beyond Giovanni's lifetime, and he wanted to ensure that it was displayed in a manner that served the work best. Fortunately, his friend Pino Vitarelli, in charge of the museum, agreed with Giovanni's opinions on the placement and lighting of the work. By donating a painting of such incredible value to the Uffizi, Giovanni had mended all differences he and Vitarelli may have developed during the time leading up to the work's authentication.

Giovanni had promised that after he accompanied the painting to the Uffizi, he would join his wife and son for a few days of relaxation, touring the Italian countryside. Their trip along the coast ended at Pisa, from where they would complete their journey and return to Florence in time for the Count's unveiling. Then Giovanni would return to his studio and resume the work that he and his father, and his father before him, had mastered. Once the Count was displayed in the Uffizi, there would be no more distractions to further delay Giovanni's restoration of the Brueghel.

As he guided their rental car through the streets of Pisa, Giovanni asked, "Do you mind if we go to the Campo Santo? Many Medicis are buried there. I feel like I should visit, considering how important the Count has been to me."

"You're the boss, Papa," Maurizio said. "Wherever you want to take us."

"Grazie, Mau," Giovanni replied.

After a short drive, they parked near the walled cemetery and got out. The expanse of blind arches of the Camposanto Monumentale towered above them as they walked around the exterior, and then they went inside.

As a conservator, it was heartbreaking for Giovanni to walk the interior of the Compo Santo. During the war, a bombing raid had led to a fire, and much of the artwork was destroyed. The restoration of the many frescoes had begun after the war and still continued, the damage had been so devastating. If only Giovanni were born earlier, he could have enjoyed the works of art that were now gone forever.

His thoughts turned to his time in Bad Arolsen, where during his research he had learned of other treasures being lost forever. However, not as the result of an errant bomb, rather the errant thinking of men who had sought to force their beliefs on others, though only those they deemed worthy of living. Adding to the eradication of millions of lives, the Nazis had destroyed countless works of art that they similarly deemed unsuitable to exist within their flawed vision of a perfect world. Thousands of paintings were torched in raging bonfires supervised by the Berlin Fire Department. And there were other bonfires in Paris and elsewhere throughout German-occupied Europe. Paintings by Picasso, Leger, Braque, and Masson went up in flames. It just goes beyond all understanding, he thought.

As they wandered the interior of the Campo Santo, Giovanni said, "Thank you both for being so good about my decision."

"It was only right," Arabella said. "Yes, the painting is worth an amazing amount of money, but we're certainly not hurting for cash. Most important is that you're happy." She paused for a moment before continuing. "You're not having second thoughts about what you've done, I hope."

Maurizio said, "You did the right thing, Papa."

"You really think so?" Giovanni asked.

"Donating it," Arabella said, "rather than selling it, says much about your generosity."

"Maybe," Giovanni said, "but since the story hit the media, I've been contacted by almost everyone I've ever known in the art world, and some people I didn't know. I've got more work than I can handle. I won't complain about that, but the thing is, I really wanted Clara Meyerstein to take it. A big part of me is disappointed. I wanted her to be happy. I wanted to improve her life, not ruin it. I feel like I've made matters worse."

"Because she never wants to see you again?" Arabella asked.

"When she said that, it felt like I had touched an electric fence."

"You have to understand, Gio. No one wants to relive pain like that. Wait a few months, then write to her. Maybe things will be different."

"God, I hope so," he whispered.

"Papa," Maurizio said. "Look on the bright side. At least the Count is happy now that he'll be in the Uffizi."

Giovanni was shocked to hear it from his son. "Now you believe the Count is real?"

Maurizio shrugged. "I can't say I do, but I also can't say that I don't believe. I mean, before all of this, when you told me the portrait was an unsigned Botticelli, I didn't believe that, either. We all know how that turned out."

~

Before his current visit, Giovanni had not been back to Florence since the Count had first spoken to him. He had a new perspective after listening to the Count's stories, many of which included events in Florence. In the Oltrarno district close to the Pitti Palace, Giovanni thought about the Count living in that same palace centuries earlier, and it caused him to smile.

Giovanni and his family drove past many familiar and beloved spots. They passed through Santo Spirito on the way up to Piazzale Michelangelo, where they had a wonderful view of the city. They descended again, taking in a quick view of the Campanile, the Gothic bell tower designed by Giotto, then passed the Piazza della Signoria, where the Bonfire of the Vanities had taken place in 1497.

Giovanni, Arabella, and Maurizio all knew Pino Vitarelli. When they entered his second floor office at the Uffizi Gallery, there was much hand shaking and cheek kissing. Vincent Drysdale had already arrived, and soon Vitarelli's assistant brought in a tray of champagne and passed out glasses to all.

"There's quite a mob of reporters downstairs," Drysdale said. "Pino has done a remarkable job of getting the world press here for the unveiling."

Giovanni smiled. "I hope there's a back door so I can duck out." Others laughed at his joke, although he wasn't entirely kidding.

"Now, now, Gio," Vitarelli said. "You promised a few photographs in the Botticelli Room."

"A few," Giovanni said.

"And we would greatly appreciate it," Vitarelli added, "if you would say some words to the press as well. I already plan to speak but you should also."

"I didn't promise that," Giovanni said.

Arabella jabbed him in the side, gently. She said, "Gio will be happy to say a few words about the greatness of Botticelli and how fortunate he was to find the painting." She turned to Giovanni. "Right, dear?"

"Yes, dear," he replied.

Vitarelli smiled. "Now, all the rest has been taken care of. As you asked, we have made a handsome donation to the Jewish charity in New York that has been looking after Ms. Meyerstein all these years. They are very appreciative and asked me to let you know, they will put the money to good use. I've also arranged to send you the color prints of the painting, as you requested."

"Thank you," Giovanni said. "Pino, I do have one other small request before the unveiling. As you can imagine, I've grown very fond of this work. It would mean a great deal to me if I could spend a few minutes with the panel in the Botticelli Room before we get started."

"Of course," Vitarelli said.

Giovanni turned to Arabella and Maurizio. "I'd like a few minutes alone with the painting."

They both nodded. They understood.

~

Downstairs, Vitarelli escorted Giovanni into the corridor and through large double doors into a wide gallery.

"Here we are," Vitarelli said. "And there it is, as I promised, between Saint Augustine and the Old Man."

Giovanni stopped a distance away from the Count. There he was, hanging in the prestigious, famous gallery, as a carefully aimed, low-wattage light accentuated him.

"You are happy with the placement?" Vitarelli asked, despite the fact that he and Giovanni had already agreed to everything.

Giovanni's mind was elsewhere. He thought about the series of events that had brought him to that moment. All that had happened was almost too much to believe. Yet all of it was true, and most importantly, that he had honored the wishes of the long-dead subject of the painting. Giovanni waited for the Count to call out, complaining that it was too light, too dark, or that he wanted to be on a different wall. The room was silent. There was no voice of the Count to hear anymore.

Vitarelli awaited a reply to his question about the placement.

Giovanni realized that he was daydreaming. "It's excellent, Pino. I'm sorry. I'm just a little taken aback. It's very moving."

"I'm glad you're pleased, Gio." Vitarelli looked at his watch. "I'll come back in ten minutes. Is that all right?"

"Fine, fine," Giovanni said absentmindedly, his focus on the panel as he stepped closer to it.

Vitarelli silently excused himself.

Giovanni approached the Count but kept a distance, farther away than during their many conversation back in his studio.

"Well, Count, here we are. Your dream has come true. You're in the Botticelli Room at the Uffizi."

He waited for the Count to respond, but he was greeted by silence. Giovanni hung his head. In a way, he expected this possibility. Whatever the reason for his communication with the Count, it always took place in his own studio, among Giovanni's works of art, books, and bottles of wine. The studio was Giovanni's exclusive corner of the world, but the Uffizi was open to all. From then on, the Count belonged to everyone. But only Giovanni would ever know the Count's true personality.

Moving closer to the panel, he admired the subtle restoration he had completed before bringing the Count to Italy. It was in his blood, the restorer's understanding that the idea was not to make the painting look as pristine as it had on the day of its creation, but to retain a suggestion of its original appearance while at the same time not let restoration efforts erase indications of age. Giovanni studied the Count's shirt. No doubt when Botticelli had created it, the white of the garment stood out considerably. But half a millennium later, the grayish tint of the shirt was to be expected. Giovanni had very carefully and purposefully allowed the white to appear dulled.

He imagined the Count saying *Are you looking at the shirt?*

Yes, Giovanni thought. I see it for what it looks like, for our time, not for yours. "We all get gray with age," Giovanni said aloud and smirked.

"When a white shirt turns gray, I say *throw the damned thing away!*"

Giovanni could not contain a smile that stretched across his face. He was not speculating what the Count might say. The Count had actually said it.

Giovanni stepped back and looked into the eyes of the Count. As usual, the portrait's expression remained unchanged, the same elitist Florentine looking down his nose at all who dared to cast their gaze upon him.

"Count, you can hear me!" Giovanni said. "My Lord, I did it.

I got you into the Uffizi, just as you wished. And you're complaining about the color of your shirt?"

"It is no small matter," the Count said, "to be on exhibit in one of the greatest museums in the world—and painted by one of the finest artists of all time—and have people visit to admire you, only to notice your soiled attire, doubting not only the artist's use of color, but one's hygiene as well."

Giovanni laughed. "Count, you play at being tough. You're happy, I know you are. You've been authenticated and put in your rightful place, here in the Botticelli Room."

"I can see the room somewhat, but it is blurry. Describe it for me, Signor Fabrizzi."

Giovanni listed the magnificent works of art that filled the room. "And your placement is just as I requested, and I have to say, Count, it is the perfect choice. Between St. Augustine and the Old Man."

"That is wonderful," the Count said. "Tell me more."

"What else can I say? You know the Medicis created the gallery. You now hang among famous works by Michelangelo, da Vinci, Titian, and Rubens."

"I am not so impressed by Rubens."

"Count," Giovanni scolded, though playfully.

"All right, my dear Signor Fabrizzi. You have honored me in the finest place I know, in my hometown, in my country, and for that, I am eternally grateful."

"It has been my pleasure." Giovanni smiled.

The Count cleared his throat. "Signor Fabrizzi. During our many conversations, there may have been occasions when I was short-tempered and perhaps even rude to you. I hope you will forgive me. At times I must have behaved like Botticelli's little bastard."

"Of course I forgive you, Count. Likewise, there were times when I was irritable and did not afford you, as a Medici, the respect that you deserve. I hope you will forgive me too, Count."

"You have looked after me well. I know it is a difficult subject for you, and I fully recognize your strong feelings that I should have been returned to Clara Meyerstein. However, I must admit, I am thankful that she declined, allowing me to be placed in the Uffizi."

"Don't get me wrong," Giovanni said, "but it makes me sad. I'm glad you're here, too, but I just wish that Clara would have taken you back and let it be her decision to donate you. She haunts me, Count. She's like a body walking around without a soul. It hurts to see anyone like that."

The sound of footsteps approached.

Giovanni turned to see Pino Vitarelli coming closer.

"I'm sorry, Gio," Vitarelli called out, "but everyone is here and we'd like to start the press conference now."

Quietly, the Count said, "Please come back to see me, to talk to me."

Giovanni moved closer to the portrait. "Of course I will, Count."

"What's that?" Vitarelli asked.

Giovanni took one long, last look at the Count.

"Tell me," the Count said. "Is there a plaque identifying me?"

"Yes," Giovanni said aloud, not caring that Pino was aiming a quizzical stare at him. "Portrait of Count Marco Lorenzo Pietro de Medici by Sandro Botticelli. Donated by the Fabrizzi Family and an Anonymous Donor."

"Very nice," the Count said.

Vitarelli tapped Giovanni on the shoulder to gain his attention.

Giovanni ignored it and proudly gave a small salute to the Count. "Until the next time, my dear Marco."

Giovanni joined Vitarelli, who was somewhat puzzled, and they exited the room.

"Good-bye, dear Gio, and thank you," the Count whispered in the stillness of the Botticelli Room.

Ambition

2013 USA Best Book Awards Finalist, General Fiction
2013 Rebecca's Reads Choice Awards, First Place, General Fiction

Having it all will never be enough for George Tazoli, an ambitious dealer on the trading floor of a prominent California bank. He is hand-picked for a special assignment to sell off bad loans, but not because he is dating the daughter of the bank's president, rather for his skill at working the market. The promotion sends him to New York, putting a strain on his relationship, but then a scandalous discovery lures him into the gamble of a lifetime. George must gauge the risks—his direct superior is the bank's president and his potential father-in-law, who is married to an heiress worth billions, all the more reason for George to vow his fidelity. Back at the bank's headquarters, the president and his father, the chairman and grandfather of George's L.A. girlfriend, are embroiled in a long-standing feud with another family of stockholders competing for control of the bank. The boardroom tension and ultimate showdown keeps everyone busy while George makes difficult choices that will teach him a lesson learned the hard way—even wealth has a price.

Fans of the film Wall Street will recognize the basic theme, but Ambition brings it to the next level. The term "page-turner" is cliché, so let's just say that his writing sucks you into the story and holds you there throughout the entire book. As Kitty Kelley states in her testimonial, "it's un-put-downable."

ForeWord Reviews

Hardcover ISBN 978-0-9832596-5-7
Paperback ISBN 978-0-9832596-6-4
E-book ISBN 978-0-9832596-7-1

ALSO BY STEPHEN MAITLAND-LEWIS

Emeralds Never Fade

2012 Benjamin Franklin Award winner, Historical Fiction
2011 Written Arts Award winner, General Fiction

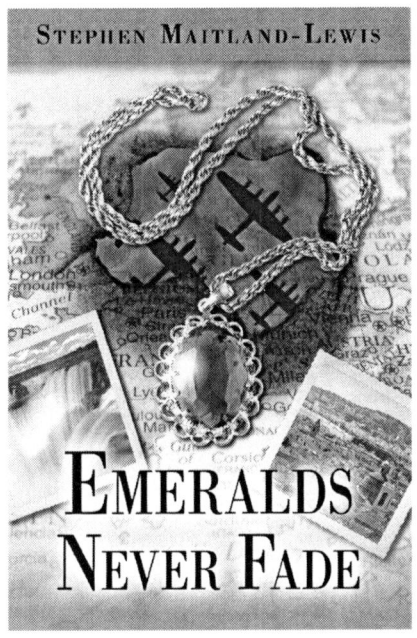

Before World War II, two German boys enjoy playing piano, and one visits each week to teach the other. When the Nazis seize power, the lessons must end—one of the boys is Jewish. Leo Bergner, the Jewish pupil, escapes Germany while his piano teacher, Bruno Franzmann, is called to serve the Fatherland. As the war ends, Bruno escapes to Buenos Aires and Leo begins a career in banking, only to uncover a conspiracy of Jewish persecution that puts him in direct opposition to his beloved Israel, while also jeopardizing his career, his marriage, and his life. In Argentina, Bruno hatches an unscrupulous plot to finance a multi-national corporation, and in time, his efforts require a business trip to London—his first visit to Europe since he escaped. After forty years, a lost family heirloom will decide their fate.

Hardcover ISBN 978-0-9832596-2-6
Paperback ISBN 978-0-9832596-3-3
E-book ISBN 978-0-9832596-4-0

Hero on Three Continents

A chronicle of the twentieth century as the protagonist, Sir Henry Brown, participates in events both cataclysmic and personal that interface with characters both famous and imaginary. From the jazz age of the twenties, to the war-torn 1940's, to the international crises of oil and terrorism in the 70's, this novel makes history intimate, the work of any epic. After Oxford, Henry Brown serves on the staff of the Viceroy in India where he meets his first wife, the youngest daughter of one of England's premier dukes. Service in Kenya follows where he is awarded the Military Cross for a heroic defusement of explosives on a strategic railway route. Maitland-Lewis demonstrates the importance of uncompromising research as well as the art of writing in a fast-flowing, enjoyable, can't put it down style.

Hardcover ISBN 978-1413414295
Paperback ISBN 978-1413414288
E-book ISBN 978-1453569832

ABOUT THE AUTHOR

Photograph by Nathan Sternfeld

Stephen Maitland-Lewis is an award-winning author, a British attorney, and a former international investment banker. He held senior positions in the City of London, Kuwait, and on Wall Street before moving to California in 1991. He owned a luxury hotel and a world-renowned restaurant and was also the Director of Marketing of a Los Angeles daily newspaper. Maitland-Lewis is a jazz aficionado and a Board Trustee of the Louis Armstrong House Museum in New York. A member of PEN and the Author's Guild, Maitland-Lewis is also on the Executive Committee of the International Mystery Writers Festival. His novel *Hero on Three Continents* received numerous accolades, and *Emeralds Never Fade* won the 2012 Benjamin Franklin Award for Historical Fiction and the 2011 Written Arts Award for Best Fiction. His novel *Ambition* was a 2013 USA Best Book Awards and 2014 International Book Awards finalist and won first place for General Fiction in the 2013 Rebecca's Reads Choice Awards. Maitland-Lewis and his wife, Joni Berry, divide their time between their homes in Beverly Hills and New Orleans.

www.maitland-lewis.com

CPSIA information can be obtained at www.ICGtesting.com
Printed in the USA
BVOW04*0652170714

359108BV00001B/1/P